PRAISE FOR *THE EMBALMED HEAD OF OLIVER CROMWELL: A MEMOIR*

2015 Cult of Weird Fall Reading List
2015 Halloween Book Festival Winner
2016 Communication Arts Illustration Annual

"*The Embalmed Head of Oliver Cromwell* is an exceptionally well-researched and thoughtful look at an influential figure in history and how he might've reacted to the many events that followed his rise and fall. The idea that Cromwell's spirit continued to observe the world through the eyes of his severed head is a fascinating one, and it provided a storytelling perspective unlike anything I'd read before. ... *Cromwell* is historical fiction done with grace, style, and ingenuity. What an unexpected treat."

— SAN FRANCISCO BOOK REVIEW

"Compulsively readable and genuinely fascinating, this is history from a perspective you've never encountered before--and may never again. A surprising delight for the morbidly curious."

— BESS LOVEJOY
Author of *Rest in Pieces: The Curious Fates of Famous Corpses*

"Hartzman's genius narrative, a three-century panoramic portrait of English society, is as unexpected as it is innovative. As if he's channeled Thackeray through the mind of Terry Gilliam. His Lord Protector, though separated from brain & body, is a fully formed man. Still curious, still ambitious, still able to learn a thing or two as he leads us through backroom and bar room accompanied by his keepers who must forever defend the provenance of their beloved Lord Cromwell's extraordinary head."

— TODD FIELD

"Brilliant! Is this horror, cult fiction, science fiction, or a half-true travelogue through time as told by a dismembered head? Whatever you call it, the story is one of the most original pieces of writing this decade."

— TIM O'BRIEN
Ambassador of Odd for Ripley's Believe It or Not!

"Delightfully wicked."

— REBECCA REGO BARRY
Editor of *Fine Books & Collections*

"Just because you're dead and buried doesn't mean your severed head can't go on an amazing, 300-year journey -- and talk about it. ... this fictionalized account recounts one of history's strangest tales in a way you'll never forget."

—BUCK WOLF
Executive Crime & Weird News Editor, *The Huffington Post*

"Marc Hartzman's latest book is far from your typical history text. But that's pretty evident by the book's title ... He's putting an unorthodox and engaging spin on English history."

— ALEX BIESE
Asbury Park Press

"In his deliciously twisted book, Hartzman tracks the unhappy fate of Cromwell's pate over the course of 300 years, and in a ghoulish turn of ventriloquism, he lets the head do the talking. From beginning to end, this startling yarn is recounted by Cromwell's long-suffering skull, and it has quite a story to share. Unsettling, yes, but also irresistible."

— BOOKPAGE

"Delightfully macabre ... If you're into weird, out of the ordinary historical episodes, this is definitely the book for you!"

— READING LARK

THE EMBALMED HEAD of OLIVER CROMWELL

A MEMOIR

BY MARC HARTZMAN

Cur*i*ous
PUBLICATIONS

NEW YORK

ISBN-13: 978-0-9862393-3-5
The Library of Congress has catalogued the hardcover edition with the
Control Number: 2015900034

Curious Publications
101 W. 23rd St. #318
New York, NY 10011

curiouspublications.com

First paperback edition.
Printed and bound in the United States.

For Mom and Dad

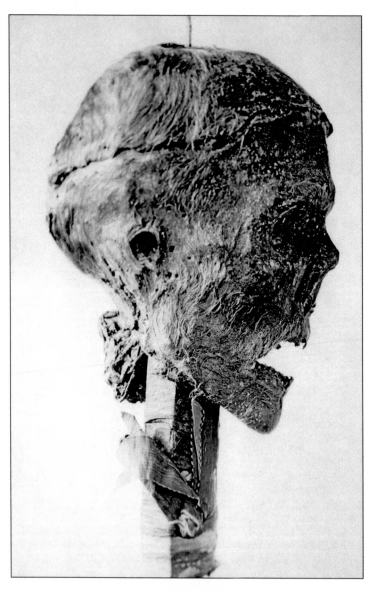

Memoirist, Oliver Cromwell's Embalmed Head (1661-1960).

THE EMBALMED HEAD

OF

Oliver Cromwell

A MEMOIR

THE COMPLETE HISTORY

OF THE HEAD OF THE

RULER OF THE COMMONWEALTH

OF

ENGLAND, SCOTLAND AND IRELAND

✳

With Accounts from Early Periods of Death and Impalement

And Subsequent Journeys Through the Centuries With

COLLECTED TALES AND GATHERED ILLUSTRATIONS

Until, That Is, A Second Burial Brought

A MOST UNFORTUNATE

END TO THIS REMARKABLE

PHASE OF AFTERLIFE

CONTENTS

9

XV

XVI

XVII

Oliver Cromwell, with head attached.

PROLOGUE

Victory swept through the cold, grey air that 30th of January in the year of Our Lord 1649, when, upon the scaffolding, my greatest military and political efforts at last proved triumphant. The trial at Westminster Hall resulted in grand success and the High Court of Justice made its unprecedented decision, sentencing King Charles I to be the last the Commonwealth would know of his tyrannical kind.

The judgment announced: "He, the said Charles Stuart, as a tyrant, traitor, murderer and public enemy to the good of this nation, shall be put to death by severing of his head from his body."

On that most delightful morning of the execution, Charles enjoyed one final walk in St. James Park through the naked trees and along the lake with his faithful dog. One last moment of companionship; one last moment to bask in the glory of the land he ruled.

At two o'clock in the afternoon, the festivities commenced. An escort led the king through the Banqueting House at the Palace of Whitehall, out a window, and onto a scaffold built on the street, draped in black cloth. There, amongst the crowd of joyous Parliamentarians and dismayed royalists, the masked executioner stood over the powerless tyrant.[1] Charles dressed warmly in thick robes over his waistcoat to avoid shivering, fearing that witnesses might see him as the weak man he truly was. He wore heels to elevate his short stature, though this deceived no one. As he awaited his fate, the realisation grew clear that Providence would not save him, for He had granted no such divine rights to the throne after all. God's will, in fact, appeared quite the contrary.

"Is my hair well?" he asked the executioner. Vanity prevailed even in his final moments. Assured his appearance was in order, including his neatly tapered Van Dyck, the pious king looked upward and uttered a prayer imperceptible to anyone but himself and the Lord above and then said these last words, for only the closest gathered to hear:

"I have delivered to my conscience; I p-p-pray God you do take those courses that are best for the g-g-good of the kingdom and your own salvation. I shall go from a corruptible to an incorruptible Crown, where no d-d-disturbance can be."

I appreciated the brevity of his words, for it spared us his awful stammer and the moment of glory would be prolonged no further. Charles informed the axe man that he would stretch his arms forward when he was ready, and implored him to make the deed quick. With tension mounting amongst those gathered in the street, he at last stooped to the scaffold and laid down upon the block, his neck without defense, and gave the signal. The executioner slowly raised the axe as the hushed crowd looked on in disbelief, awaiting a moment unparalleled in history. Seconds later the blade fell swiftly and, with one clean blow, severed both the head and the English monarchy. Blood splattered like a fountain of treason. The executioner held the pate up high and exclaimed, "Behold the head of a traitor!"

Acclamations of the soldiery mixed with the collective groans and sobs of the royalists, all of which echoed harmoniously through London. Those who still believed in the power of the king stepped up to the scaffold and, for a fee, dipped handkerchiefs in his blood to be wiped upon wounds. This, they foolishly alleged, would serve as a cure to their ailments. At the very least, it would be a fine souvenir.

After these events, I assumed control of the Rump Parliament and within a short time became the first Lord Protector of England, Scotland and Ireland.[2] Never, though, did I expect to meet a similar fate just a few short years later. Nor did I expect that my own head, severed posthumously, would experience a new life and journey through the land for the next three centuries.

Charles I prepares to part with his head.

I

No Rest in Peace

D eath is, without question, the worst part of life. A moment that strikes fear in our innermost thoughts, regardless of how strong, powerful or confident our exteriors appear. When one considers his own death, there is nothing but the certainty of leaving all behind, and the uncertainty of what, if anything, lies beyond. Worse still is the one thing that we do know awaits—burial. Eternity is six feet below the earth's surface, immobile in a small box offering but a thin, penetrable barrier from soil and the subterranean creatures that prey upon the vulnerable flesh of the dead. These are the angels that return us to the dust whence we came. Heaven or Hell we know not, but this much is assured.

This existence does, however, have its varying degrees of wretchedness. Those who achieve greatness, like

myself, avoid plots bevelled into the dirt. As Lord Protector of England, I commanded a more fitting burial, spared
from the elements in the hallowed confines of Westminster
Abbey. Within its sacred walls, the dead are never forgotten and achieve a form of immortality.

It is here that my afterlife story truly begins. I lay
buried in an east-end vault of Henry the VII's chapel, just
behind the king's gaudy tomb, where his bones resided
next to those of his wife, Elizabeth of York. Carved images
of saints and a spirited dragon covered Henry's crypt. I required nothing so fanciful, though I had oft admired this
chapel's space for its architectural magnificence, particularly its stone fan-vaulted ceiling prodigiously embellished
with carved pendants and pewter emblems. Clerestory
windows give entrance to the sun's light and feathered
mouldings and sunk panels robustly cover the side walls. It
was a fine place to rest.

The day after my death, on the 4th of September,
1658, my physician, Dr. George Bate, had sliced open my
chilled corpse to investigate the cause. Bate was a knowledgeable man of fifty years with a broad moustache, curled
locks and firm hands who had aided Charles I during his
reign.[1] Before resting my eyes forevermore, I told those attending me to go on cheerfully, and repeatedly praised God
from my deathbed, muttering, "Truly God is good, indeed
He is, He will not leave me." I was at peace, for I had been
in Grace. Dr. Bate had done all that the ancient teachings
from Galen and Hippocrates offered, yet the Lord was not
to be denied; it was my time. Now Bate sought answers as

he shifted my organs with invasive fingers. His bloodied hands finally uncovered disease in several locations, particularly my spleen. A bout of malarial fever and kidney trouble had previously been deemed the main culprits in my passing, but surely damaged innards offered little help. I also suspected my internal defences had weakened after my anguish over the death of my second daughter, Bettie, just a month prior. She had taken ill in June, partly because of the death of her youngest son, Oliver, who lived but a year. Doctors claimed she had an inward imposthume of the loins, but they lacked the knowledge to properly treat her. I fought my emotions in her presence, hoping to hide my sadness and fear and give her strength through my confident exterior. She, too, struggled to appear optimistic, so as to mitigate my worry. Yet our close relationship made such feigned dispositions entirely futile. When her life at last slipped away, the shock overwhelmed my being and I collapsed to the ground, motionless for days. Though they were not visible to Dr. Bate during his examination, my heart suffered deep wounds as well.

After the inspection, the Commonwealth's finest embalmer joined Dr. Bate to begin work on the preservation of my flesh. He was a curious fellow: short and rotund, a balding head, wearing large spectacles and a stained smock. He worked eagerly, perhaps demonstrating too much enthusiasm for his art and the morbid studies of thanatology and taphonomy. His eyes grew wide, as did his thin-lipped grin, whilst he opened my chest plate and pulled away my failed, blood-soaked organs one by one, as if unpacking a trunk of life. He carefully embalmed each piece of me individually and placed it in a barrel. As he slowly unravelled my bowels from the depths of my corpse, I felt a strange ticklish sensation conflicting with utter horror at the spectacle. Pink in colour, the intestines were a nightmarish image: elongated and twisty like an overgrown worm engorged with rations. The entire pile was discarded into a heap of waste. This was not a sight I would wish upon anyone, even Charles I. Man likes to think he is made of courage, strength, integrity. Yet in reality, what we are made of is nauseating. The embalmer revelled in the dripping guts, taking no notice of the odour that surely emanated from them. A true craftsman, he replaced my innards with an array of spices: wormwood, sage, rosemary, thyme, oregano and more. One could almost desire such a technique in life, for the scent was certainly preferable. However, I did regret seeing my bowels treated with such a lack of respect, for these were God's handiwork, and few bowels are given the opportunity to contribute to the functions of great men such as this set had. They deserved a preservation and memorial of their own.

Next, the fret saw exacerbated the entire process as it rhythmically scraped across my skullcap to remove my beloved brain. The gelatinous lump that had served me so well was placed in a brain-box, severed from my consciousness. With exceptional skill, the embalmer then kindly sewed the top of my skull back into place. My head whole again, another fellow poured wax over my face, which dripped slowly but cooled quickly to create my death mask. I ex-

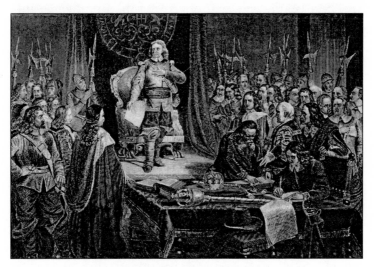

A striking portrait of me rejecting the crown.

pected they would make many plaster casts from it, right-fully, to preserve my likeness. As for the rest of me, I was swathed in a fourfold of cerecloth, then gently placed into a lead coffin with a handsomely gilded copper plate laid upon my chest bearing the coat of arms of the Commonwealth and my own on one side, and these words on the other:

OLIVARIUS PROTECTOR REPUBLICAE, ANGLIAE, SCOTIAE, ET HIBERNIAE NATUS 25 APRILIS ANNO 1599 INAUGU-RATUS 16 DECEMBRIS 1653. MORTUUS 3 SEPTEMBER ANNO 1658 hic situs est.[2]

I then was swiftly moved to the vault.

There, in the silence of eternal night, I thought I would forever reflect on my life and ponder the path the Lord had laid forth for me. Though the body no longer lived, the soul remained, and with it, thought. And with thought, memories. And with memories, ideas. And with ideas, nothing, for they could go nowhere, never to be put into action. Thought was infinite, but forever caged, with no way out.

I wondered about my lovely wife, Elizabeth, and our surviving children. Shortly before my death I named my eldest son, Richard, as my successor to carry on the Pro-tectorate, and I expected him to protect his mother and siblings as well. Had the Commonwealth accepted him as it had me? Would the royalists attempt to rise against him? Henry, who advised me to reject the office of king, became a fine Lord Deputy of Ireland.[3] Bridget had married Henry

Ireton, a most distinguished general under my command. This brought comfort, knowing she was safe under his care. Just a year previous to my death, Mary began her connubial bliss, and with good fortune Frances would soon follow with a healthier second husband.[4] My legacy would be carried forward; the Cromwells would indeed persevere.

Regarding my recently deceased daughter and grandson, it seems the Lord, blessed is He, had greater plans for them, though I knew not what. Zealous in my faith, I dutifully carried forth His will in overtaking the monarchy. What He could want with a young woman and her child was beyond my comprehension. The only knowledge I possessed on the matter was that death did not bring us together once again. The solitary confinement of our coffins assured that. Oliver, I supposed, may have still held out hope for such a reunion, for he knew nothing of his mother's parting, nor mine. This notion, to me, was an undeserved punishment fit for Hell, yet the boy had not even time in life to sin. Separated in life and forever after in death.

Although this division brought sadness, it was joined by the relief of other divisions—namely the many Englishmen who had departed this world at my hand. In particular, Charles Stuart; I do not suppose he would have been pleased to see me once again. It made me curious, though: If we were to exist as spirits in the afterlife, able to commune, at what stage would we appear to each other? If it were the point at which we departed life, Charles would be in two pieces, perhaps finding solace with Anne Boleyn and Catherine Howard.

During this subterranean sojourn, I had ample time to also consider the way in which people viewed me in life. Not in the sense of being aligned with or opposing me, but in their reactions to my personal appearance. Warts plagued my face, particularly the large one protruding from my forehead. Devil take them! Had they been a source of displeasure for those around me? Had my own power caused friends, family and my soldiers to refrain from commenting or suggesting treatment? Time never allowed for me to attempt wart removal; one keeps quite busy when overthrowing a monarchy and protecting a nation. I did, however, wear them with pride. I remain proud of my words to Sir Peter Lely, the masterly portrait artist: "Mr. Lely, I desire you would use all your skill to paint my picture truly like me, and not flatter me at all; but remark all these roughnesses, pimples, warts and everything as you see me, otherwise I will never pay a farthing for it." The monticulous pimples, and occasional carbuncles, however, brought no joy, particularly at their point of rupture.

At times I simply missed the joys of eating, particularly Elizabeth's delectable eel stew. She oft fixed it at our home in Ely and knew just the proper amount of ale, vinegar and sweet herbs to add. This delicacy led me directly to another: eel pie with oysters. Elizabeth flayed and cut the eels into long, hearty pieces, seasoned with salt, pepper, nutmeg and large mace, then added eggs, anchovies dissolved in white wine, and generous portions of butter into the pie. Our bellies were filled over a merry meal. I no longer had a need for food, yet I found myself tortured by hunger.

As I defied decay, these thoughts haunted me, racing through my head, ricocheting mercilessly. Time seemed no longer to have meaning. This was it. Life had been nothing more than a short story, and we are all doomed to relive it again and again, contemplating choices and alternative endings. There is no resting in peace.

Then, one day, three years after interment, this existence was interrupted. The lid of my coffin was disturbed with the rustle of men struggling to pry it open. The clangs of crowbars and shovels and the grunts of these tomb desecrators echoed through the vault. Their slow progress finally gave way to rays of light peeking through as they lifted the heavy top away. There, staring into my sightless eyes, was a band of royalists plucking me from my misery. For a brief moment I felt the warmth of candlelight before being transferred into a thick, prickly burlap bag.

I was exhumed.

II

Separation

R evenge is sweet, but cowardly when your enemy is long dead and helpless.

After my lengthy journey on a rickety cart at last came to a stop, the royalists carelessly pushed me off and let me drop to the ground like a lump of rubbish. The burlap unravelled and I found myself on the floor at an inn in Holborn, away from witnesses, save the ghouls who had raided my tomb. They had been industrious, for lying next to me were two other bodies. One was my own son-in-law and trusted general, Henry Ireton, who had also been embalmed and retained many of his flowing chestnut locks, but his once handsome face was sunken and hideously cracked. Though rotting and wretched, I recognised the other as John Bradshaw, President of the High Court of Justice. Bradshaw, a great ally, had laid the death sentence upon Charles I. On four separate occasions during the trial, the Serjeant-at-Arms escorted the king into the Hall, followed by six trumpeters on horseback. Each time Charles faced the charges of tyranny and treason; he defiantly challenged the bench, showing arrogance, refusing to recognise the legality of the court, even refusing to remove his hat to show respect for the attending judges. President Bradshaw would not be swayed. It saddened me to see him here so dreadfully decomposed, for I knew not that he had died.[1]

As for Ireton, after the Battle of Naseby, my daughter Bridget took kindly to him, and the two wed a year later. Despite Bridget's pleas, he continued to fight valiantly by my side, particularly as we stormed Drogheda and Wexford. So trusted was he that I made him Lord Deputy of the New Model Army and allowed him to complete the conquest of Ireland in 1650, when I had to make a return to England and prepare to invade Scotland. The next year he took a fever after the capture of Limerick and succumbed to the illness. A great sadness, for not only was it a loss to my administration, but he was to be a father; Bridget gave birth to my grandson just months after his passing. A good man Ireton was, brave at heart and noble in character.

Now, many years later, here we were, the three of us, together once again.

"What d'ya s'ppose His Majesty will do with 'em?" asked one of the ghouls.

His Majesty? So the little Stuart boy had returned. In my absence, all my efforts, all the battles, the lives lost, the trial had been undone. My final enemy, son of the beheaded king, had resumed the monarchy.[2] Long live the king once again, it seemed. Twelve years had passed, perhaps exactly, since his father's execution.

"He'll do to 'em like he did to the king's other murderers—drag 'em through the streets, a bit o' drawin' and quarterin', hang 'em," another resurrectionist answered. "Then cut their goddamn heads off."

"Like he did to Harrison, then? Nev'r seen a man look so cheerful awaiting such brutality," the first ghoul remarked.[3] "Disembowelled 'n' all. Nev'r heard such shouts of joy at the sight of a severed head and a heart torn from the chest."

Poor Harrison! He had been my Major-General and a good friend and supporter, an honest man who aimed at good things, until, that is, I assumed the position of Lord Protector. Of this he was not fond, and several times he attempted to betray me, resulting in numerous imprisonments. Clearly, he did not get along with or approve of the new king either.

"Be plenty more of that with these murderers. Though I don't reckon any o' 'em got a heart left."

"Did they ev'r have one?"

The king's retaliation was off to a brutal start. And now it was my turn.

As the heathens' rant carried on, I ascertained that it was the Lord's Day, the 30th of January 1661, and that Charles II had different plans for my exhumed companions and me. Whilst the sun rose and the cool morning woke the town, we were dragged upon a sledge to Tyburn, where

throngs of horrified Englishmen awaited the spectacle.
Charles' face radiated with excitement. The young
king glowed with triumph, as I had twelve years earlier. I
should have been more diligent in my battle against him after the death of his father. With luck on his side, he had escaped. I was informed later that this heir to the throne had
disguised himself as a peasant, journeying along the lesser-
known roads through the night and passing the days in the
most remote cottages, where he would not be recognised.
Coarse bread and milk provided limited sustenance. Once,
out of desperation, he reportedly found safety by climbing
to the top of a large oak tree, where he overheard pursu-
ers passing by, speaking of him, expressing their desire to
discover his place of concealment. Charles had been quite
fortunate, indeed. After months of pursuit, it was learned
he'd finally escaped to France. I imagine that as with the
beheading of his father, this difficult period added to his
anger. Here, now, that anger became his joy.

Our dead bodies were wrapped in chains, hoisted to
the gallows and hanged. Thence our lifeless limbs dangled,
swaying with the wintry breeze. Mine was still freshly embalmed, and shrouded in a green seare cloth like a mummy; Ireton's dehydrated body was similarly wrapped, while
Bradshaw looked like a dried rat and, to judge from by the
irritated noses surrounding us, emitted a powerful stench.
This punishment carried on for the length of the day. Some
onlookers found great jubilation in this event, cheering and
shouting, hurling stones or pieces of rubbish at our bodies
in support of their king. Many joined the festivities simply

because a hanging was always a rousing event, oft attended by entire families with children raised upon their fathers' shoulders to see over the rumbustious crowd. In this case, however, our dead bodies denied them the excitement of catching our last twitch of life. Others seemed bemused by the whole ordeal, surely wondering why such measures were needed against three dead men. Did the king not have more urgent matters to deal with concerning those who still lived?

By day's end, as the sun prepared for its descent and dusk loomed over the grounds, Charles II eagerly antici- pated the culmination of his posthumous party. He must have been nearly thirty years of age by then. Long dark hair framed his smug face, whilst a thin, feeble moustache underscored a plump proboscis. His deep red royal robe seemed to symbolise the blood that no longer flowed in our bodies.

My remains, and those of my fellow deceased regi- cides, were cut down and laid upon the executioner's block. There, the official assassin stood tall and firm with his axe, as one had twelve years earlier over Charles I, but this one wore no lily-livered mask. He severed the heads of my col- leagues without fear or remorse. They snapped off with ease. Apprentices gathered their blades and diligently cut off Bradshaw's decayed fingers and toes as small memen- tos. Next came my corpse; a grand finale. My head lay now where the king's once had, and though I had bade farewell to life once before, I found myself saying good-bye to my arms, legs and torso, all of which had served me well. Parting thoughts were quick, as the executioner, who appeared anxious to be done with these affairs, brought the blade down for a third time that evening. However, I am proud to say, my head put up a good fight. More than one blow struck my protesting neck before the separation was complete.

III

IMPALEMENT

———

Darkness followed my decapitation as I was transported in a sack to my next destination: a spiked post atop Westminster Hall. There, I was skewered with an iron point upon an oak stake, which a royal henchman gleefully thrust upward into the space once occupied by my neck, straight through the top of my embalmed head, penetrating the skull. "Old Ironsides" quite suddenly became "Old Irontop."[1] Fortunately, the sensation of pain had perished with life, but the indignity stung mightily. My new pointed tip jutted upward, which offered a gruesome resting spot for weary pigeons (and was taken advantage of far too frequently). With my head elevated high above the crowds milling about on the streets, it was as if I were ascending toward Heaven, yet forever tethered to the depths of Hell.

I was intended to be a deterrent to anyone who wished to follow in my anti-royalist footsteps and attempt to rise against Charles II. And as a deterrent, I excelled. For who would dare end up like me?

Skewered alongside me were Ireton and Bradshaw. Bradshaw sat in the middle, which admittedly aroused my anger, as I believed the Lord Protector deserved what I considered the centre stage. Still, the reunion brought comfort and a new manner of comradeship. God had blessed us with glorious times when we rose above the people with honour, and with heads still firmly attached. Now we stood once again, side by side, above others, tormenting not the king, but all his subjects who glanced our way.

According to my mates, my face remained partially intact from the excellent craftsmanship of Bate and his colleague. Despite the hard, dry, leathery appearance of my flesh, I still retained suitably distinctive features. A small hole upon my forehead marked the home of one of my larger warts, and my eyebrows still met in the middle. My chestnut-coloured hair clung to my face and head, though some had been stained yellow from the embalming fluid. Several teeth remained in my mouth, along with parts of my gums and the membrane of my tongue. My nose had been flattened a touch during the decapitation. In back, the marks of my executioner's axe were distinguished near my vertebrae. His struggle to finish the loathsome task was evident in the jagged bone.

Several posts away sat the heads of two fellow regicides, John Cooke and Thomas Harrison.[2] The former had led the prosecution against Charles I, quite successfully, fighting for those who delighted in freedom more than servitude. The decomposition process appeared to have been at work for several months now and had left them in a most unattractive, pitiful state.

All of us faced outward from the south-end tower. Erected in 1097 by the son of William the Conqueror, not only is the structure one of England's oldest, it is truly one of its most remarkable as well. Several hundred years later, Richard II renovated the roof with a magnificent wooden hammerbeam design. He was another tyrant who deserved a good beheading for his persecution of adversaries, both actual and perceived. Still, the craftsmanship he promoted was admirable. Great oak beams run horizontal along the thick stone walls, fixed as supports. Atop these, wooden arches meet, more than sixty feet high above all who pass through. Deftly carved wooden angels adorn the halls from the ends of the beams; each clutches a shield with Richard's coat of arms yet still extends a sense of God's solemn presence throughout. Tremendous stained-glass windows at the north and south ends further welcome the Lord and His light of day. Within these historic walls, coronation banquets were held for many newly crowned kings and queens, including Richard the Lionheart—a fine warrior. I was honoured to become a fixture of this exceptional architecture, a new chapter of its annals. I could imagine no finer place to be speared.

From our posts, we were spectators to the narrow streets of London below, many of which were covered with soiled water, rubbish, waste dumped from chamber pots and dirty townsfolk.

Though some passersby tried not to look up at us, curiosity forces the head to turn, and the eyes obey. Each stare spread shock, disgust and horror. I was more a monster dead than I was when alive to the enemies I conquered in battle. Bradshaw and even Ireton by now were in a most ghastly condition.

Despite the dreadfulness, being a deceased head with an aerial view had its advantages. We found ways to stay entertained and pass the long days.

"What's the count?" Ireton asked at the end of each day.

"Faintings or screams?" Bradshaw would joyfully respond.

Loud shrieks of terror, sudden weeping and moans of faintness offered a true sense of pride, particularly when emerging from grown men. On a good day, we'd cause a dozen faintings, scores of screams and innumerable tears. Women in tight corsets often lost consciousness on warm days, when heat, lack of oxygen and the sight of us created a vicious combination.

Some would gaze upon us without fear, taking pity on us instead. "Wasn't right what they did to those men," they'd mutter. "Diggin' 'em up like that and all, cutting off their noggins when they was already dead. God have mercy on their souls."

As they stared upward, we often reciprocated their pity as we watched street urchins pick their pockets.

Nights shrouded us in darkness with nary a passerby to be seen, save the poor night-soil men making valiant attempts to cleanse the day's raw sewage that accumulated in cesspools. Without sleep, we had only our wits to entertain one another, which generally proved ineffective. The occasional mocking of the monarchy, anecdotes of past victories and the day's nausea we induced brought a simple joy, but our conversations inevitably revolved around our current situation and ended in useless complaining. As Ireton and Bradshaw bickered, I let my soul seep into the moonlight and stars above. I longed for the telescopes of Galileo and Kepler to gain a better view of all that surrounded us. As an adolescent I read of how the former had used his lens to discover the four moons of Jupiter—far superior to our mere one. Was this planet so far from our own inhabited by a more intelligent, more deserving life form? Did it mirror ours, with severed heads of state populating architectural wonders, arguing amongst themselves whilst the living slept? What might these Jovian heads look like? I envisioned larger skulls to accommodate more massive brains, eyes on all sides of the head to remain cognisant of their full surroundings at all times, and more acute ears for better listening and in turn, greater wisdom. I intrigued myself, yet shuddered at the thought of such creatures existing out there. Still I believed, as Kepler did, that God in all His mastery created everything with reason. Just as our moon serves us, Jupiter's moons must serve some purpose and benefit some form of life, for surely they are not for our enrichment. My naked missing eyes were not privy to these moons, nor Jupiter, nor the other planets, and my spirit remained tethered, unable to hurl through space and satisfy my celestial wanderlust. But each flickering star, we know, holds the ability to illuminate a planet and potentially sustain life forms, be they intelligent or not. Or, as here: intelligent life forms and the men who call themselves kings. Yet if other heavenly bodies were inhabited, what did this say about the Lord? Are we His masterpiece, or merely an exercise in His quest to create the perfect being? I opted for the former, and I alone was evidence as the pinnacle of His efforts.

Come morning, an early shriek of horror routinely snapped me out of my planetary pontifications and reminded me that I had the people of earth to terrify.

I stated earlier in these pages that the king's purpose was for me to serve as a deterrent, but among the populace, anti-royalists remained. Those who once followed my lead and believed in my mission visited to pay respects. As they congregated outside, gazing upward, we heard whispers of their unshaken conviction against the king. This gave us great pleasure. I became a source of inspiration, strengthening the will of these brave pilgrims. Some spoke of assassinating Charles II by way of gunshot, and if that method should fail, through poison. One fellow, an elder Catholic, who had faced much hatred from the Protestants, knew of a capable chemist who could provide the poison, and softly communicated his plans to arrange its acquisition and a way in which to get it into possession of the king's physician. Intricate, but it had potential. Discussions of fire were also widespread amongst the misguided but angry Catholics. Or perhaps they would attempt another Gunpowder Plot and succeed where Guy Fawkes failed.[3] Of course, had any of the king's men or loyal subjects overheard these ruminations, the plotters' heads would join mine. Fortunately for them, no matter what we heard, secrets are always safe with the dead.

Regular visitors were not uncommon. One youngster, perhaps no more than fifteen years of age at his initial sojourn, came on numerous occasions over time. He bore a disfigured face encumbered with a severe cleft palette and crooked nose that appeared in worse condition than mine. Rags adorned him, ripped at the elbows and knees and covered in grime. His feet were bare and stained with muck. It looked as if he had been to battle and fared quite poorly. He'd been cast away by his family, an embarrassment to their social status, whatever it may have been.

"Why have you done this to me?" he would shout, venting his anger and startling those around him. "What am I to do? Look at me! I am a monster! I belong there with you upon the post!"

"I reckon you do!" Ireton would say in jest. "This boy needs military training. Make him into a man. Toss him into a fray and let him lose a limb, then he shall knoweth suffering."

I disagreed. I did not want this creature on a post beside me. I'd sooner look in a mirror than upon his vile countenance.

"He is a public disturbance. He'll undoubtedly be

driven to crime, then maybe he'll be happier in prison or dangling upon the scaffold." Bradshaw countered.

As for me, I had little compassion. His mother, the boy told us many times over, had seen other impaled heads such as mine in this place during her pregnancy, and doctors claimed the shock created his deformity in the womb. Maternal impression was the disease; I, the collective scapegoat. Yet in comparison I, and any of my beheaded mates, made him look quite handsome. His flesh still had colour and remained fully intact, and blood circulated through his head and his body—these last two parts, most important, remained connected to each other. I suspect deep down his true motive in visiting me was to boost his fragile self-esteem.

※

Seasons passed, and with each, the vicissitudes of weather took their toll, slowly eroding my features on a methodical quest to reduce me to a bare skull. Fortunately, patience poses no challenge to the dead, and so the years elapsed with monotony.

Over time, I grew to welcome my impalement and determined that the punishment inflicted upon Ireton, Bradshaw and me was in fact a blessing. Nay, a discovery, albeit one I could share with no one or in no way offer as a benefit to humanity. In our graves, we see nothing and hear nothing but our own circulating thoughts. Here, towering high above London, we had a window to life.

Mankind has buried its dead through all of time, with the intent of affection and respect. Yet there could be no greater disservice to those we love. The soul does not rise to the gates of Heaven or descend to the fiery pits below. Faith in the Lord leads us all to this belief, though one could never know the truth until his demise, at which point it is too late.

In life, it is said God is all around us, but we forget this at death. The soul belongs where it is best energised and stimulated, surrounded by Providence's entire domain; we are not to be trapped beneath the ground. The coffin is Hell. The Devil is darkness. Burial destroys the afterlife. Let these words serve as a warning.

I have found Heaven here at Westminster Hall. Should this knowledge be commonplace, more of the dead would join me. Heads of powerful leaders should adorn each of the iron spikes. Bodies of architects, men of science and those of exceptional character should be situated at the most scenic views, overlooking the Thames, the majesty of London, or at least at home in the company of loved ones.

This vision of Heaven, though, filled with enlightened corpses, would be anything but for the living, and so it would never be. The dead will be forever damned.

※

In my fourth year, change seized the streets as vast numbers of the slithering royalist population took ill. I began to perceive a greater degree of fear in the eyes staring upward into mine. Had I grown even more grotesque? Had I affected onlookers not only mentally, but physically as well? It seemed that more and more townspeople passing through the Westminster grounds were suffering, dying. Death by disgust.

Rats scurried about more frequently and fervently, leaving trails of filth, whilst droves of Londoners packed their things and moved out of the city. Those who remained did not fare well. The number of the sick grew rapidly, and I came to realise I was not at fault, for many of those I saw ill had never been in my presence prior. The poor wretches were covered in agitated sores and clouded in misery. Swellings the size of eggs bulged beneath armpits, and black pus-filled carbuncles spotted all areas of the flesh. Bloody coughing and frequent vomiting furthered the putridity of the air and grounds. Something else was responsible. Fires lit up the night, apparently in hopes of burning out whatever disease wafted maliciously through the air. Shutters and curtains were drawn closed as far as I could observe. Constables impounded any swine, dogs, cats or conies wandering the streets and removed swarming beggars, presumably putting an end to their agony. The quickness of the rats, however, allowed them to elude capture.

Posters and bills began to fill street corners and buildings, proffering assistance in various forms. They promised, "Precise regulations for proper conduct of the body and preventative pills proven to be an infallible remedy to the plague" and "Consummate cordials guaranteed to combat the corruption of air."

Opportunistic swindlers capitalised on the tragedy by posing as doctors. These quacks displayed notices that gave invitation to the ill for instruction and physick: "Eminent doctor having extensive knowledge of plague with universal cure to infection. Advice to poor gratis."

But whether quack or physician, they had no true cure that I could detect. The poor raved angrily in the street about the "gratis" advice, claiming trickery. Advice required no payment, but the suggested physick did. This treatment would provide no hope anyway, unless the belief in it alone would be enough to ward off the illness. I saw, however, no evidence of this. Just more lifeless bodies, thousands of them perishing each week, which included many of the supposed doctors who I had seen peddling elixirs and "fail-proof" services.

This sickness created a regrettable new line of employment: collectors of the dead. These men pushed a wooden cart through the roads and alleys below, fetching the recently deceased from homes and the streets and piling the breathless lumps one atop another. It was a task that had to be done, though it seemed those who elected to do it also accepted a greater risk of infection. My disfigured visitor became one of these collectors. He who had cursed me for his appearance now found himself busy at work, surrounded by men, women and children who could whisper no comments, give no stares and offer no pity.

"Room for the dead! Bring out your bodies!" he would bark through the streets. "Hurry now, toss 'em over!

Heave-ho! Heave-ho!"

The harelipped lad seemed, at last, content. I imagined he would soon join those whom he dragged along on his cart. I could not see where the heap of carcasses was to be disposed of, and found good fortune in this ignorance.

As I observed this plight around me, hope revealed itself. Not in a glimmer of truth in one of the corner posters, but rather that at last, my faith was being rewarded. For this plague was the Lord's way of punishing the royalists. It would be but a matter of time until the king himself was stricken with the Distemper, and the monarchy would once again come to an end. He Above works in mysterious ways, though admittedly, this one seemed extreme, and I couldn't help wondering if He might have been more efficient in delivering regicide.

The increasing scent of bodies surely led to even more illness. I had but a trace of a nose left and was thankful that it no longer functioned, for even at my high post, the horror below was inescapable.

And so I waited, eager for news of the king. But would anyone have the health to organise a celebration upon his passing? More important, who would drag him to Tyburn to be dangled from the gallows?

I had shown mercy and respect after the beheading of Charles I, allowing the head to be sewn back onto his body for the sake of his grieving family. I made him a promise that no hair on his head should be injured, which I would not violate, even when Bridget requested a lock after the decapitation. If I could be reunited with my body, the four humours in perfect balance, and return to life for even just a day, I would exhume Charles II's head from wherever it would lie and deliver it to his father's crypt in St. George's Chapel so the two could face each other in darkness, staring into empty eyes for eternity and basking in their hatred of me together. Afterward, I would welcome a return to Westminster Abbey, exposed as I am now, propped above Henry's tomb to see and be seen.

Reports of "his majesty" soon came, and my hope was shattered. As one of the carcass collectors dragged a man's body from the sidewalk, he informed the weeping widow, who appeared frail and ready to join her husband, that the alarming threat of the plague had driven King Charles II and his family out of London with haste. The coward would rule from afar. Yet I suppose he had lost his throne once before and had determined this plague would not succeed where I had years before.

The Lord, it seemed, had a different plan, not yet revealed to me, or, I imagine, anyone. God have mercy on them all. The death toll was unlike anything I had beheld in battle—and as I recall, at my campaign at Dunbar I had led my men in the slaughter of three thousand Scots in just two hours. What angered Him so? Or perchance this contagion was a creation of the anti-royalists whom I had heard discussing virulent plans. A more direct attack would have been preferable.

The plague raged through London for more than a year. Late in the following summer, the scent of royalty cut through the filth as it drifted amidst the streets. The disease slowly began to retreat and King Charles II returned to his throne. Londoners who had fled followed his lead, and it appeared life would flow through the city once again. Or perhaps not.

Within a month terror returned with a vengeance, this time in the form of fire. Large conflagrations suddenly spread through the streets north of the Thames, which ran behind me. Whereas I suspected the plague may have been God's work to oust the king, this appeared to be the Devil's wrath, as the churches burned to the ground, and from what I could ascertain, thousands of homes. The furious flames soared high enough to burn the wings of pigeons refusing to leave their nests. Not only were properties and lives lost, but ideas of men held within the pages of books and expressions of art vanished in the scattered ashes. There were those within the walls of the tower who whispered the inferno may have been another form of Charles's revenge against the anti-royalists, but this I found unlikely. Disembowelment was more his style.

With the blaze growing in might, I feared God would take me again and my time on the post would come to an end by way of complete incineration. The flames looked as though they would soon reach the Westminster grounds and I, like so many buildings around me, would be left as ashes. It was indeed a strange sensation to face, to fear my own mortality while already dead.

The fire carried on for several days. Whilst anxiety grew within, Bradshaw, Ireton and I received God's blessing, for the winds picked up and fanned the flames in the opposite direction, back to where nothing remained to burn. The fire conquered all it could conquer, and thus surrendered to itself.

My afterlife upon the post was preserved. I very much looked forward to observing how London would fight back, and return to an even more glorious state. Men visiting the grounds spoke of a man named Wren who was to lead the planning. They said he possessed a brilliant mind, citing his experiments in transferring the blood of one animal into another, believing such work might someday benefit the health of men. I saw not how tampering with the Lord's creations in such a manner could do more than awaken His ire. But God willing, this fellow would have better sense with the task that lay ahead.

And so the years went on. We heads sat quietly, growing accustomed to the gradual erosion from the harsh winter weather and spring rains. Then, in June of the year of Our Lord 1684, our assemblage of repulsion undertook a new member: a fresh head was brought forth and given a spike between Bradshaw and me.

"Adding Armstrong to His Majesty's collection?" said a portly fellow with a sanguine complexion witnessing the impalement on his way to the treasury.

"Judge Jeffreys punishes high treason without mercy," said the sentry. "Three of his quarters are displayed here in towne, whilst the fourth is to be seen in Stafford."

Had this executed man tried to assassinate Charles II? I knew not what manner of high treason had earned him a position by me, but I hoped it had been worth it, and had brought some form of irreparable angst to the king. Ireton and Bradshaw by this point were in dreadful shape: Ireton's embalming offered little defence to the forces of decomposition, rendering him unrecognisable as anything other than the personification of death; and Bradshaw was simply nothing more than bone with scraps of dried flesh clinging wherever possible. Cooke and Harrison were also revolting, as their once fresh heads had been ravaged by excessive heat, rain, winds, maggots and that greatest of enemies: unconquerable time. I held up much better, still bearing many of my features. The new head, however, was freshly decapitated and still carried the look of shock and a full cap of hair.

"Welcome to Westminster!" Ireton said with cheer.

"Providence hath rewarded you my friend, you sit in good company," Bradshaw added. "The view is wondrous, and your fresh flesh will bring new frights to the people. 'Tis our daily entertainment!"

Armstrong was just discovering his afterlife; the trauma persisted.

Birds, insects and the elements had a new target, and soon enough he would fit in suitably with the rest of us.

IV

A WIND OF CHANGE

———

My good fortune atop the tower took a most unexpected turn one winter evening. After twenty-five long years of exposure to the elements, my wooden post finally succumbed to fierce winds and heavy rainfall. The storm snapped the rotting wood just beneath the back of my head and sent me crashing to the ground with the wind blowing through the solitary hairs that remained on my head. As it has been said, heads will roll. Mine made its way tumbling over the cobblestone road through puddles and mud mixed with the accumulated filth left behind from walking boots, rubbish and horse excrement. Yet when I came to a stop, I didn't stay still long. Above me stood a sentry on guard. He looked upon me with shock, having quickly recognised my face and realised I was not just another piece of fallen debris. The guard kneeled down, glanced to his left and right, and promptly placed me in his warm woolen cloak to provide not only shelter from the rain, but a secure hiding place as well. He knew my absence would not go unnoticed long and my return was sure to be in high demand. Suddenly, my afterlife changed forever.

When we arrived at the sentry's home, his wife and daughter were already in a slumber. He quietly retrieved a damp cloth from the kitchen and tenderly wiped the mud away from me. Rather than wake his family to share his prize, he once again gave me protection, this time tucking me away in an old chimney corner filled with blackened bricks, some barely secured in place, ash blanketing the ground. He wrapped me in a silk cloth and placed me in a box—a meagre casket. Blackness filled my minuscule quarters. While these accommodations lacked the wonders of fresh air, views of life around me and that most basic of all needs, light, I did find reason to be grateful: Charles II could no longer claim me as his trophy.

On occasion, this man, whom I had heard others call Henry Barnes, pulled the box out of the corner, opened it, unwrapped the silk and spoke to me. It seemed my ear, or what was left of it, interested him a great deal.

Henry looked to be in his fifties, with mostly grey hair and a tired, haggard face. A well-worn coat, waistcoat, breeches and hose shrouded his thin frame, while heeled boots gave boost to his rather average height. Kindness shone in his eyes. I had no occasion to see his wife and daughter yet, but he referred to the former as Margaret and the latter as Mary.

"Lord Cromwell, you will be safe here," he often assured me. "My family knows not of your presence. No one but me knows, and you will not be found."

Other times, he was less certain: "Lord Cromwell, should you be discovered, I fear I will suffer the same fate as you, though after decapitation, my head will likely be tossed aside. For it is a trophy to no one. I'm not ready to die."

With these fears, if possible, I would have suggested he return me to my chimney, rather than risk being found talking to a renowned and sought-after missing head.

But the temptation to open up to me, someone whom he had respected when I was still with my body, was too great. He could confess anything to me, and regularly did.

These confessions all too often involved his partaking in hedonistic activities, which only led to guilt afterward. Henry was an avid participant in cockfighting, a disgraceful sport that I outlawed during my reign. But the debauched Charles had allowed the matches to flourish once again. Henry lost a good deal of money in his wagers and feared Margaret's reaction should she find out. He knew no breeders and thus knew little of what to look for when cocking, betting on too many blinkards. At times, he said he considered pawning me off to pay his debts. I always ended up making a return to the chimney, each time wondering what I was worth.

Margaret, he believed, pursued her own sins as well. Henry shared his theories on her prurient activities, fearing he was being cuckolded. I had yet to behold her appearance, and thus withheld judgment. If possible, I would have offered to be placed at her bedside to provide any accounts of foul play. Of course, my very presence would have likely spoiled any adulterous moods.

When not discussing his woes and doings that directly contradicted my policies and beliefs, I took great pleasure in our visits, particularly when he brought me news of personal interest, which in early 1685 included the most glorious information of all.

"Lord Cromwell, Lord Cromwell! Have you heard?"

Naturally, I had not.

"Charles the Second is dead," Henry exclaimed. "He took ill just days ago and succumbed earlier today. Some have whispered tales of poison, for his health had been fine, and this sickness came on with unexpected suddenness. They say he's to be buried at Westminster Abbey, perhaps not far from where you were once interred."

Burial. This brought boundless joy. At some point, the deceased king will realise the magnificent favour he did me. Eternity will provide ample time to consider his entrapment and the unforeseen freedom he delivered to his worst enemy.

On other occasions, Henry shared information regarding the period immediately after my passing and before my impalement.

My funeral, which he had had the good sense to attend, deeply interested me. The ceremony did not involve my body, but rather a lifelike effigy made in wax, hence I had no awareness of the event until Henry's tales.

"It was a splendid affair, you were dressed in a rich suit of velvet and draped in a royal purple robe with gold lace, crown'd with a crown, and held a sceptre with a globe. You looked resplendent, like a king," he recalled. "Black velvet covered your chariot. It was drawn by six horses, also covered in black velvet, and adorned with plumes, from Somerset-House to Westminster. Officers carried guidons and pendants. Caparison'd horses embroidered with gold walked alongside the march to Westminster. Innumerable mourners attended, quite joyous, drinking and taking tobacco in the streets. It was indeed a most memorable event."

I expected nothing less than the grandeur he described; though I was not a king, I was treated very much like one. He then, however, discussed the events following my impalement.

"Your Lordship, the events at Tyburn truly brought you back from the dead. Much was written about you, imagining what you might have said at the gallows, and what your ghost might be experiencing," Henry told me. "I read one pamphlet entitled *A Parly Between the Ghosts of Oliver Cromwell and the King of Sweden*, in which the author depicts you in Hell, taking tobacco with the Devil before attempting to overthrow him. As punishment, Satan chains you up and lets the demons and all the condemned souls piss all over you. Quite an imaginative tale.

"Songs, too, have been sung with glee. 'From Tyburn they are bid adieu, And there is an end of a stinking crew...'

How surprised they would be to know how wrong they are, that you are right here, at my side. Safe and sound."

The physical degradation hadn't been enough for these royalists. They continued to attack me with words; a most formidable weapon. How had my son Richard allowed this to happen? How could he have let Charles II take the throne?

I soon learned my answer, as another session brought news of my family. Richard, I discovered, had indeed succeeded the Protectorate as I commanded, but not for long.

"Your son abdicated the position, Your Lordship," Henry said one day. "He had been neither statesman nor soldier, and lacked experience in public business. He often appeared feeble and showed little ambition, not suited for greatness as you were. So after just a few months, he chose to instead retire and live a private life. We've not heard from him since His Majesty returned."

This was distressing news, though I had feared my son had been overthrown, or possibly brutalised by Charles II. The vengeful king may have sought my own blood through Richard's body. Thus, knowing he had left on his own power led me to believe he was still alive and well, which was a source of comfort. I wished that Henry had the good sense to bring me to him, rather than tuck me back into the chimney after each of these confessional sessions. If I couldn't be returned to Westminster Abbey where my daughter lay, a reunion with Richard would suffice. Perhaps the spike in my head would finally be removed and I would rest peaceably upon his mantelpiece.

My dearest Elizabeth, I was told, did not fare well after this abdication.

"The Protectress fled the kingdom," Henry explained. "My sources claim she moved to Switzerland, then later retired to Wales. Your Lordship, she died more than twenty years ago. I am so sorry, she was a great woman."

How I wished I could learn more from Richard. Why had he abandoned his mother in her time of need? Where had he buried or, rather, condemned her?

※

"Lord Cromwell, today I saw the most wondrous sight! A German fellow by the name of John Valerius, who had no arms at all." Henry described his unusual figure with much enthusiasm as he pulled me from the chimney corner. "He demonstrated remarkable dexterity with his feet and toes, and exhibited little deficiency in his lack of arms and hands. I saw him perform at a small stage in London, where he played cards and dice, managing both with ease. His pliability allows his joints to raise a glass of liquor to his head for a drink. And while seated on a stool, he raised a musket and discharged it with the utmost agility and exquisite aim. I've never seen such skill. For a shilling I purchased a specimen of his footwriting upon the back of his portrait. This is how he makes his way, depending on the gratuity and generosity of those who witness him.

"It occurred to me that if an armless man could draw such a boodle, what of a man with no body whatsoever?

Lord Protector, do you suppose people would pay to witness you? Though you cannot regale a crowd with tales of your feats as Valerius did, your tale is already well known, and thus no words are necessary."

Henry's excitement grew as he arrived at this thought.

"One day, Mary can profit in such a way, perhaps after more time has passed. For I know not if James wishes a return to Westminster Hall's tower for you, as his brother did. I will not risk it."[1]

Would there come a time when people would wish to look upon me not as a deterrent, but as a wonder? An inspiration, not a horror? Curiosity lies deep within all men, a natural emotion that must be satisfied. And what could give rise to more curiosity than the embalmed head of one of history's greatest leaders? With Henry's intent, I suddenly found myself with something to look forward to. Someday, my power would be felt once again, and in the process, I could enjoy sunlight and the world around me.

These private sittings continued over the years, which brought enjoyment. Then one day, he came to me seeking advice, which he hoped my presence would influence.

"Lord Cromwell, I fear the worst. I gave insult to a gentleman whilst passing on the street as I made my way to Westminster. My shoulder brushed by his, without intention, but he did not see it as so, and rather took profound offense," Henry explained. "I was simply in a hurry, late for an appointment with Lord Arlington. The gentleman was accompanied by a young lady, beautiful, with a long, elegant dress and an angelic face. I believe it was her company that led him to feel his honour had been challenged. I apologised profusely yet he still demands satisfaction."

Though a soldier, Henry was not a fighter; especially not in these elder years. He monitored the grounds of Westminster with nary an incident to cause alarm. This perceived insult, however, clearly caused him much grief.

"Today I received notification that the gentlemen, called Baron Thomas Randolph, has demanded a duel, and I'm to choose my seconds and afford him satisfaction at a meeting at six o'clock on the morrow," Henry said with utter intimidation. "I've never faced a duel before, nor have I ever desired to. Still, I was left with no choice, except for selecting a weapon and a meeting place. I chose swords. And a secluded walk behind Boxworth Church."

If my faculties had still served me, I would gladly have comforted Henry with combat techniques and a plan for victory. One insulted gentleman was hardly a battle worthy of concern. Still, Henry was fearful, and thus, so was I. My whereabouts in the chimney remained unknown to anyone, and should Henry not return, it would stay that way for the unforeseeable future.

The next morning, much to my surprise, Henry lifted my box from the chimney and placed me in a dark canvas bag, then hurried out of the house without waking his wife or daughter. After a short time, he took me from the bag and removed the box lid, propping me up against an oak tree near the meeting place behind the Church. The sky was clear and a sparkly frost layered the grass. The golden leaves on the trees and the crisp temperature declared that autumn had arrived. I welcomed the fresh air, revelling in the breeze that whisked through the hairs clinging to my skull and twisting around the iron point. I wondered if Ireton and Bradshaw still felt the coolness of dawn, and if so, doubted they appreciated its splendour. For not until you've sat in a chimney for several years do you truly know the glory of a blue sky.

The church itself was very small, dark and austere. It appeared to date from the twelfth century. Narrow crenellations ran along nearly every edge of the white stone tower, porch, aisles and clerestory.

Accompanying Henry were two of his peers, sentries armed with sabers. In the distance another group of men prepared their cold steel, wiping the blades clean with rags, as if it were a contest of flamboyance. This Randolph gentleman was much taller, younger and quite stronger-looking than Henry. Dressed neatly in dark breeches, stockings and boots, and a blue waistcoat bearing a unique crest to boast his pedigree, he appeared ready to attend to other affairs after the duel, as if it were a mere errand on the way to loftier deeds. No other souls were to be found; the area was remote, and it was simply too early for anyone to be going to or fro. My spirits were confoundedly low.

But then I thought, Henry has brought me here for a reason. His seconds are present, like Randolph's, but unbeknownst to his adversary, Henry also had the Lord Protector of England, Ireland and Scotland in his corner. He would draw vitality and inspiration from me; I would be his muse. Of course, had Henry truly been bold, he would have gripped me in his hand, startled Randolph by the very sight of me, then thrust my spike right into his black heart. Satisfaction would be ours.

Instead, Henry slashed his rapier through the air, practicing his maneuvers and attempting to preserve his composed exterior, despite chattering teeth and the clear appearance of being overmatched. My plan of attack did not seem to be part of his strategy. Then one of Randolph's seconds and one of Henry's paced out the stretch for the duelists. I heard "Salute! Present!" and both Henry and Randolph crossed swords.

"Onset!"

With that, the steel flashed, glimmers of light bouncing off the blades. Randolph immediately took the offensive, with Henry striving to defend himself. My benefactor receded, fending off jabs, desperately attempting to land a strike. Randolph's eyes showed determination; it was a look I knew well, one that thirsted for blood and would not rest till it was quenched. The seconds watched eagerly, ready to jump in if needed, each looking as if he wanted to battle the other's and turn the duel into a fray. I had never felt so powerless, save Charles II's day of revenge.

This duel—all duelling—was barbaric. Combatants often place their faith in Providence to see them through unharmed; yet these matters that duels attempted to settle frequently involved the most trivial of offenses. For God to care about such peculiarities of social behavior is surely impossible. The death of a traitor king is the Lord's work; the perceived insult from a sentinel is man's own doing, and the parties involved need do no more than duel with words to find a solution. A loss of blood, or worse, of a limb or life, does more to create problems than solve them. This was an act I should have forbidden during my reign. Yet I could not affect the outcome with these ideas, so I merely rooted for Henry to draw first blood.

He managed to hold off the baron for what was perhaps no more than a minute before losing his footing on the slippery grass. Randolph, grunting, continued to wield and lunge with his weapon, finally wresting Henry's own sword from his grip. With Henry defenceless, a smile crept across the baron's wicked face. My dear friend's eyes grew large, like a beast knowing he's been defeated, succumbing to a predator. Randolph took a slow step, as if savoring the moment, then sprang forward with his weapon extended, aimed directly at Henry's abdomen.

"A hit! A hit!" shouted one of Randolph's seconds.

Blood dripped from Henry as his seconds rushed to his aid. Randolph, victorious, ceased his offensive, pleased to have preserved his honour. He sheathed his sword and reached for Henry's hand to shake it in a display of sportsmanship.

"Good fellow, perhaps next time you shall take greater caution in the presence of gentlemen," Randolph said. "Dress your wound and be well. Good day!"

He retrieved his hat from one of his seconds and promptly left. An ally of Henry's fashioned a tourniquet from his own shirt to stop the flow of blood.

Fortunately, Henry's strength held and he was able to

retrieve me without exposing my existence to his seconds. With my lid in place, we slowly journeyed home, though Henry's anguish grew throughout our approach. Upon reaching the front door, he could barely stand. Margaret and Mary greeted him there with pronounced concern, having been worried at his disappearance that morning, and now more worried at the sight of blood and weakness. Both still wore their white bed gowns. Margaret gripped her grey hair, yanking it back, stretching her wrinkled skin—a show of stress. Mary paced through the foyer. I was placed on a chair near Henry's bed, where he lay down and attempted to rest and gather strength.

Margaret had fetched a physician, but he offered little hope. A fever raged through Henry's body, so the doctor punctured a vein with a steel lancet and began letting his blood into a pewter bowl. But while the fever necessitated the balancing of his blood levels, it seemed to me that it was a loss of blood that had initiated the fever. I found it strange that this treatment might cure Henry.

"Margaret, Mary, come to me, there is something you must know," Henry said after the last of the doctor's treatments. He appeared weaker than he had during the wounded walk back from the duel.

Margaret and Mary stood at his side. Tears welled up in their eyes; they were visibly shaken.

"I love you both dearly, you are my life, my joy," he said, taking great effort with each breath. "But I have had a secret I must share, one I've kept too long."

They looked at him curiously, unsure of what it could

be. Their concern deepened.

"We three are not alone within these walls. For years, unseen to you, there has been another, a silent but powerful friend. He is with us at this very moment. Margaret, Mary, we are blessed, for we are graced by the presence of the Lord Protector of the Commonwealth. His head resides in the box seated there," he said, pointing in my direction. "Open it, and gaze upon the embalmed head of Oliver Cromwell."

Disbelief shrouded the faces of both Margaret and Mary, as Henry's claim sounded outlandish. But at his behest, there on his deathbed, they obliged, lifted my lid, and cried in terror. Memories of Westminster Hall stormed back, yet rarely has such a close look been taken.

Henry explained the circumstances of our meeting and the secretive affair we had kept over the years.

"These are my last few moments, dear family, for I am weakening. I have laboured to provide you with shelter and food, sustenance. And now, Lord Cromwell. Care for him, treat him with respect. Speak to him as I have, and he will reciprocate and look over you, protect you. This I know. This I promise you."

Mary's tears streamed down her cheeks and onto her white bedgown as she embraced Henry.

"Father, don't leave us! Let me fetch the doctor once more, he will let more blood!" she screamed hysterically. "Mother! Grab a knife, we will do it ourselves! I've seen the physician work, there is no time to waste!"

Margaret appeared dumbfounded, in a state of disbelief and confusion over her husband's bewildering condition. She knew nothing of the duel. When she had lain down to sleep the night before, life had been in perfect order.

"Get the bloody knife! Cut him, Mother! Now!" Mary yelled.

But Henry's breaths slowed, and before Margaret could bring herself to help, his eyes closed and one last breath escaped his body.

My benefactor had passed into my world. And I knew nothing of my new caretakers.

V

HEAD FOR SALE

———

T hrough the days that followed I remained in my box in Henry's desolate quarters, untouched and ignored. During this time, between bouts of weeping, I overheard portions of conversation between Mary and Margaret as they discussed Henry's burial arrangements. A small number of friends would attend his funeral, but the respect shown by those who loved him was far outweighed by the unintentional effrontery that would ensue with his interment. Had they only known the truth of death, they would have severed his head, placed it upon a fine silk and lowered it into a small box positioned next to mine, allowing our frequent discourses to continue forevermore. Admittedly, this would benefit Henry far more than me; spending eternity chatting from a box was not my vision of the future. New adventures lay ahead which, God willing, would prove more fulfilling.

I cannot be certain, but it felt as if several fortnights passed before Mary retrieved me from the bedside and we went on a short journey together. Her silence throughout the carriage ride prevented me from having any idea about where we were directed. Yet the message was clear: I would not be returning to Henry's chambers, or the chimney I had called home.

Some time later, the sound of the horse's trot ended and our carriage came to a stop. A gentleman opened the door and greeted Mary with great exuberance.

"Bonjour, Miss Barnes! It is my distinct pleasure to welcome you to London," the man said with a French accent. "I trust your travels were pleasant?"

"Oh, indeed! Quite pleasant, thank you, Mr. Du Puy," Mary said.

"S'il vous plaît, call me Claudius. Now, let us step inside. I am most anxious to show you the collection, and even more anxious to see its latest addition."

After a few steps, I heard a door open, and Mary immediately gasped at what she saw.

"Madamoiselle, allow me to introduce you to the wonders of the universe!"

The Frenchman spent the next hour colourfully describing many of the unusual items he displayed on the walls and hanging from the ceiling of his private museum, his theater of curiosity, sharing their fascinating tales: a mummified Egyptian head believed to be that of a relative of Cleopatra; a brick from the Tower of Babel and a splinter from the remains of Noah's Ark (balderdash, at best); the upper jaw of a whale captured by Scots after a mighty weeklong battle at sea; jarred specimens of frogs that reportedly rained over Bromley and terrified the townsfolk to the point that at least one elderly woman perished from fright; many stuffed birds, among them, a hummingbird, which was said to buzz like a wasp; an automaton of a peacock that walked and pecked, influenced by sketches from Leonardo da Vinci (I found this to be quite an enjoyable marvel); various musical instruments, many from foreign lands, such as an elegant Indian organ made entirely of lacquered flutes or pipes, one longer than another, and able to emit an agreeable sound; a goblet of magnificent workmanship, on which Bible stories were elegantly engraved; a preserved human tail removed from an unfortunate infant just days after its birth, caused by the constant sight of rat tails during an infestation at the pregnant mother's home; anatomical waxworks demonstrating precisely how the Lord above designed our internal organs; life-sized wax figures fashioned with expert craftsmanship, including one of Rosamond Clifford, a mistress of King Henry II, kneeling before Queen Eleanor, who extended a dagger and a poisoned cup; a wooden Ammonite idol of an ass's head called Moloch, to which children were sacrificed; botanical samples of nearly every flower gracing France, Italy, Russia, India and Bermuda; insect specimens from every corner and crack of the earth delicately pinned to white boards, some of the pests once poisonous enough to kill a horse with a single bite; Oriental footwear that stunted and

distorted the feet of women; exotic shells plucked from the
sea; precious glimmering stones believed to possess magical
abilities; a snakeskin hanging from the ceiling, sixteen feet
long and one wide; and, much to my delight, a vial of blood
from my old friend Charles I. A small descriptive label accompanied each piece.

Let it be known that there are two types of men: those
who do, and those who benefit from the former. Among the
first, I speak of men such as myself, who do God's work to
create a better world for those who inhabit it: the architects
who provide shelter and cement our legacies in stonework;
the scientists who give us understanding and physics; the
artists who bring joy and warm the heart; and the revo-
lutionaries and soldiers who rid nations of kings. Claudius
was of the other sort; a collector who basked in the achievements of others, whether men or the wonders of creation.
These things, these masterpieces of nature and designs of
mankind, gave his life meaning. That which once made
others who or what they were have now made him someone: a caretaker, an impresario of the unusual. This collective effect revealed to me that Du Puy did not own these
unique items at all, but rather, they owned him. On this
day, I was to become his latest owner.

Mary had little to say regarding the exhibits, she
clearly wanted nothing more than to rid herself of me.

"Mr. Du Puy, I thank you for the gracious tour," she
finally said, assuming he had completed his account of the
entire inventory. "But let us discuss our transaction."

She set my box upon a table, removed the lid and

carefully unfolded the silk, revealing me to Claudius.

His face glowed with delight as he gazed upon me. I reciprocated, though with far less delight. This eccentric fellow had tufts of white hair protruding above both ears, rather unkempt, and but a few loose strands reaching over the top. Where the devil was his periwig? His wide eyes were aged, surrounded by lines that seemed to mark the many paths his objects had taken to arrive here. As he grinned at me, his mouth offered its own display of curiosities and I wondered if his missing teeth could be found in a dingy jar within these walls.

Claudius was tall with a thin frame, covered by a white linen shirt, a brown justaucorps and breeches. His dress hoped to portray him as an aristocrat, but its well-worn appearance and a few missing buttons spoiled the illusion.

"Miss Barnes, this is a truly remarkable specimen!" he said as he lifted my box off the table, holding me close to his chest, as if I were his newborn son.

"Then you have the money we agreed upon?" Mary asked.

"Oui! Oui! Indeed! Indeed! I shall retrieve it presently," Claudius responded enthusiastically. My ears were not privy to the amount of the exchange, but I prayed that Mary received a generous sum. This was precisely Henry's intention; this was my protection over her and Margaret.

"Oh, Lord Protector, you will be my star attraction," said Claudius as he handed over a thick envelope. "My chef-d'œuvre!"

※

A simple oak shelf positioned in a glass display case along the far wall of the museum served as my new home, with some manner of marine creature to my left, and a giant Caribbean conch shell to my right. Ireton and Bradshaw they were not. These and other insignificant gewgaws surrounded me, not a one worthy of my presence; yet here I sat, awaiting curiosity-seekers to willingly hand over their pence to Claudius for the privilege of laying their eyes upon me. It was as Henry had predicted; like Valerius, the man without arms, I became a legitimate attraction. Once feared by all who opposed me, I now entertained six days a week, sunrise to sunset.

Looks of wonder, awe and disgust filled my weeks. Everyone from scholarly patrons with their tailored black trousers, pocket watches chained to waistcoats, and finely waxed moustaches to mere peasants in faded rags journeyed to see this gloriously grotesque embalmed head of mine. Curiosity is truly an innate mark of mankind. It, along with thrills and prurient desires, has proven to be one of three unwavering businesses throughout history. Du Puy quenched this curiosity by entertaining each and every visitor with my storied history, from the beheading to my fall at Westminster. As he promised, I was the greatest attraction London had to offer. This brought a measure of joy, to know that even in death, I captured the attention of the people like no other.

This pleasure continued uninterrupted for many

months, until one wintry day, as snow blanketed the streets of London, the routine came to a momentary halt with the entrance of a squat, rotund German fellow. He was heavily clothed with a large woolen coat, thick fur-lined hat, grey gloves and old squared-toe boots that tracked dirt-filled slush across the floor. With snowflakes melting into his coat he handed over his eight pence to Claudius and proudly announced himself as Zacharias Conrad von Uffenbach. His tone implied that his name should have already been quite known. Without hesitation he took eager footsteps toward me, explaining along the way to Du Puy that he was a visitor of Europe's finest scientific collections and "wunderkammers," writing about each for publication. His intent here was to add a new entry, focused around Du Puy's latest and most renowned acquisition. Von Uffenbach leaned in close to me for a thorough inspection. I, in return, got a close view of his thick, greying muttonchops, double chin, dark piercing eyes and damaged skin. This man looked as though he'd suffered various flesh ailments, with scars showing on both round cheeks; the muttonchops worked hard to cover as much as possible, but the follicles found limits in their reach. Perhaps he, too, had warts and felt a connection to me. Von Uffenbach, however, unquestionably lacked my handsome countenance.

"Take a good, close look, sir. He is indeed the Lord Protector, Oliver Cromwell," Claudius said politely, though our visitor had certainly not waited for this invitation.

"Indeed?" von Uffenbach said with a note of skepticism as he continued to scrutinise my every feature. "I do wonder, what is the basis for the authenticity of your claim, Herr Du Puy? This wooden stake from the impalement poses an inconsistency with the iron posts upon which severed heads are displayed, would you not agree?"

A wave of regret fell over me for not conquering Germany.

"Herr von Uffenbach, I guarantee the head is genuine," Claudius quickly responded. "Wooden posts have been replaced by iron in more recent years to avoid such catastrophes as what you see before you. Never again will a storm snap such a twig and send a head tumbling to the ground."

Du Puy explained the circumstances under which he had acquired me, but von Uffenbach remained cynical, suggesting I was an impostor. This insult was unforgiveable, and if I could, I would have promptly impaled this arrogant German with one of Claudius' narwhal tusks.

I am certain Du Puy shared my anger, but he refrained from violent measures, instead attempting to interrupt von Uffenbach from his feverish note-taking by shuffling him over to less interesting relics. This did not appear to be a plan for success.

Despite the unabashed nerve of our visitor, he raised a curious notion: imitation.

It was an idea that would not remain exclusively his for long.

VI

FAMILY REUNION

___

Von Uffenbach's assessment of his visit did not please Claudius. The morning of its publication, before opening his doors, he read it aloud. I, along with the countless other marvels and novelties, served as his audience:

> "Herr Du Puy also showed us, as one of his greatest curiosities, the head of Cromwell, just as it fell down with the wooden spike that is broken off—unless, indeed, they had palmed off the head of some other dead man on Herr Du Puy."

His anger escalated and blood rushed to his face with each word:

> "For it seems to me most suspicious that it is stuck on a piece of wood, which is said to have fallen

down with the head, while the heads of malefac-
tors are generally stuck not on wooden, but on
iron, pins or spikes. Herr Du Puy assured us that
he could get sixty guineas for it. I was surprised
that these English could still have such affection
and respect for this monstrous head; for there are
still many such heads to be found in England,
many of them too quite ready for such an elevated
position. With this head of Cromwell there was
also the head of a mummy, which I should infinitely have preferred."

Claudius threw the paper to the ground in disgust.
"He prefers the head of the mummy! The mummy?! Absurd! Nothing more than a forgery! And this—this he believes to be authentic?!"

Despite its ignorance, the article produced no ill effect on admissions to the museum, though I began to wish
it had. My people came in droves to witness me year after
year, and Claudius' perpetual storytelling grew unbearably
tiresome. I was doomed to hear the tale of the king's revenge until the day Claudius died or closed the doors to
his collection. Remarkably, Du Puy spoke with glee during each retelling, never growing weary of the repetition so
long as a fresh set of pence were deposited into his hand.
Women gasped and men nodded as he spoke, their wide
eyes always stretching from their sockets to secure a closer
look.

This was a new chapter of punishment: first impalement, and now the sharp edge of words. Though I missed the companionship of my fine fellow heads, and even Henry, my current quarters were indeed preferable; I, the Lord Protector, enjoyed admiration from the masses and protection from the harsh elements in Du Puy's inimitable shelter.

Still, I very much wanted to plot an escape. Powerless to do so, I merely sought hope in the arrival of new guests, believing that one would carry a familiar face, someone who bore a relation to me. I felt certain that a grandchild would hear of my presence and wish to see the head of the family, perhaps even claim me as his rightful property. I understood the lack of visitations during my impalement, as my kin were certainly not welcome in London, and even had they been, my visage would only have served to tarnish their final memories of me.

But had not Richard, the Protector who was anything but, taken a lover in hiding to give him a son of his own? Mary, Bridget, Frances or Henry surely had broods of their own to carry on the Cromwell line. It was very much to my dismay that without the sentry's chats, I knew not of what became of my progeny. I knew not whether they still lived, or if they and their families had been victimised by Charles II and James II in their vigorous quest to terminate any remaining vestiges of my line. Ignorance is the plight of the dead.

To this existence, I was afforded rare moments of respite with the occasional new acquisition, new oddities that allowed me to stay abreast of the recent state of things, both political and cultural.

One particularly peculiar arrival was a witch mark from a town in the Massachusetts colony called Salem. Du Puy spread the tale of a young woman, Susannah Martin, who was found guilty of witchcraft and hanged in 1692. This brown-coloured mark, not much larger than a wart, was allegedly left by the Devil himself after the woman agreed to serve him. Cut from her cold flesh, it was preserved in the small jar now seen upon the shelf adjacent to mine. The very same colonist who peddled the witch mark also sold Claudius a recipe for witch cake, of which the ingredients included rye and the urine of those accused of witchcraft. The cake was to be fed to the accused witch's dog. This concoction followed English folklore, which posited that the witch's urine retained invisible particles that she used to attack innocents. As the dog ate the cake and bit through the particles, the accused would scream in pain and prove herself a sorceress needing to be hanged. All this twaddle succeeded magnificently in arousing the curiosity of visitors.

My own place of birth, Huntingdon, had a similar outbreak of witchcraft during my years battling Charles I which resulted in the extermination of numerous accused witches. Though I knew her not, Lady Susan Cromwell, my own aunt, was said to have perished at the forces of bewitchment several years before I was born. Three suspects were executed for their alleged roles.

I questioned the veracity of all these claims, as reason suggested that a true witch, with the Devil beside her, would not be so easily captured and killed. I suspected that

quickly overtook them and their faces twisted and contort-
ed in the most grotesque manners. I had nearly forgotten
how nauseating I had become.

"Lord have mercy!" shouted the woman whom I assumed to be his wife. "Appalling! Frederick, I demand you
have that, that frightful thing removed immediately!"

"But Eunice dear, he is family! This is the *Lord Protector*, Oliver Cromwell!" said Frederick. "Have you any
idea what it took to find him?"

"I do not care! It's rubbish is what it is! Simply dreadful! Please, I cannot bear it, take it away!"

"Absolutely putrid!" said another woman, who had
already turned away from me.

A small child began to weep, whereas an older lad
took a closer inspection, intrigued by what lay before him.
To my dismay, Frederick granted his wife's wishes; he
promptly replaced my lid and rushed me to another room.
I heard the sound of a wooden drawer creak open, and then
felt my box placed carefully inside. The drawer shut softly
and Frederick's footsteps scurried out of the chamber. I was
cast into total darkness once again, like a common corpse.
Just yesterday I was embraced by all, a sight to behold, a
cherished treasure; today, I was shunned by my own blood.
But Frederick would return. The family would soon reconsider their fears and respect my presence. Of this I was certain.

✳

Alone, I found company in memories triggered by my return to Huntingdon. God Himself delivered me here on April 25th, in the year of Our Lord 1599. My mother was thirty-four years of age at the time, having already given birth to four children. In all, she bore ten, though only six sisters survived: Elizabeth, six years my senior; Catherine, two years older; Margaret, two years my junior; Anna, three years younger; Jane, six years younger; and Robina, eight years younger. Joan, my eldest sibling, was born in 1592 and died when I was a wee lad. A brother, Henry, perished before my birth and another, Robert, was born nearly ten years later and died almost immediately; I was the only male strong enough to carry on the Cromwell name. As such, I grew up with great responsibilities. Looking back, I see that the Lord had been preparing me; my destiny was foreshadowed. Mother, though very loving, was aging, and her body had grown weary. I had little choice but to help care for and support my sisters. I was, at an early age, a protector.

We dwelt within a modest home and shared rather crowded chambers, despite my grandfather's status as one of the wealthiest men in Huntingdon. But Father was one of many siblings, and one of the younger sons; thus he inherited only an average measure of land. A gentleman, he became a Member of Parliament for Huntingdon several years before my birth, and in 1600 held the title of Justice of the Peace and Bailiff. Aside from his duties, we Cromwells were a family of farmers and brewers. I toiled on our land and began an apprenticeship in the brew house as a

✳

Blackness smothered me as it had long before at Westminster Abbey. Footsteps broke the occasional silence, oft accompanied by dull conversation, witless banter and the arousing sounds of affection, which escalated as Frederick and Eunice (and perhaps other women) took pleasure in each other. Much was taken. I missed my Elizabeth dearly.

Frederick had searched long and hard for me, threatened Du Puy and paid him a handsome sum, only to leave me hidden away at the behest of a lady. Female charms had a way of conquering the strongest of men and the greatest of states. Such is the power of a woman.

This nephew of mine had secured me within a chest of drawers that he could safely claim as his own, private from his wife's garments and intrusions. Yet this particular drawer held nothing else of need, for it stayed closed whilst others were opened and shut regularly. I was either alone or amidst unneeded items or old, unwanted attire. I had not the fortune of being stored alongside his frequented undergarments or other necessities. I suppose this had its merit, for my dignity, what was left of it, had been spared.

As time passed, affections between Frederick and Eunice grew less frequent, replaced by the arguments that come with age. The tedious dialogue, however, did not subside. Talk of a German fellow named George who'd become king, unpleasant weather, new clothing, daily dining with something called a fork and other drivel carried on. Throughout it all, my name went unmentioned.

Vast boredom overcame me. Until one day, the chatter stopped. Only sobs from Eunice could be heard. Soon, to my delight, her whimpers ceased. Frederick, and perhaps Eunice, it seemed, had crossed over to my realm. Despite having little sense of the years gone by, I believed he had simply grown old and died. Good riddance to him. May he spend eternity contemplating his ignorance.

VII

INHERITANCE

Grief over Frederick's death gave way to joy over the spoils of his estate. The rustle of furniture and parade of footsteps indicated that his possessions were being rapidly dispersed amongst his kin. Frederick's beneficiaries were like soldiers looting a conquered land, only these were not warriors, they were scavengers. Was it his death they mourned, or simply that he'd lived so long? One of these vultures finally made his way to the dresser, eager to explore what riches Frederick secreted in his private bureau. He began opening the drawers and shuffling their contents about piece by piece. When he at last opened my drawer, I eagerly awaited witnessing his greedy face metamorphose into one of horror when he peered into my box. But instead, he lifted the lid and gave no look of shock. To my astonishment he radiated with a sense of wonder and surprise. It was a look I had seen once before, years earlier upon my arrival to Huntingdon. This man was none other than the young lad who had inched closer with curiosity as others recoiled when Frederick gave my introduction. Years of darkness suddenly yielded to the splendour of light, and I found new hope. With a smile, the man closed the box, tucked me beneath his arm and dashed out of the room.

When he finally came to a rest he set me down, removed the lid once again and gathered a crowd.

"Have a look, lads!" he shouted with glee. "Found him hiding in my uncle's drawer!"

We were in a tavern. Carousing dullards lowered their heads around me. Their fingers crept closer and began to poke and tap my face.

"Back off, ya buggers!" my new caretaker said. "Look, don't touch. He's very delicate. D'ya know who he is? D'ya have any idea?"

The group of imbeciles indeed had ideas, each exceedingly daft.

"That's William Shakespeare. That's who!"

"No, it's that science fellow, what's his name? Isaac Newton!"

"King Charles! Now you know, Brother Joe! End of story, Cory!"

"No, no, 'tis your mum! Right, Samuel? Dug her up, did ya?"

"The whole lot of you muttonheads haven't got a

clue!" the man called Samuel said angrily. "Do you not see
the spike running through his head? You've had too much
to drink, ya poor sots."

This is why I outlawed alehouses during my reign.
They lead to immorality and, as these men demonstrated,
a rotting of the brain. These buggers knew nothing of mod-
eration.

"Well, who is it, then?" one of the idiots asked.

"'Tis Oliver Cromwell! He's my uncle. Or my uncle's
uncle's uncle's uncle. Something of that sort. He's family."

Family, perhaps. A Cromwell, not even close. The
light that had energised me began to dim.

✳

Samuel obambulated from tavern to tavern, basking in his
newfound glory and giddy as a young lad newly in love.
These watering holes were all similar, aside from the occasional cockfighting venues—usually called The Cock Inn,
The Cock Pit, or The Cock and Balls, which also served
as a meeting place for firearms enthusiasts. Nevertheless,
each reeked of alcohol and offered beer-stained wooden
benches, filthy floors and soiled bars, all of which were
scarcely detectable under the poor lighting. Inside, I'd see
boisterous men playing cards and dice, drinking merrily
and conversing about most everything, of which I caught
only brief bits upon our entry.

Some spoke of a war with the American colonies,
which now called themselves the United States and de-

clared independence from the king. Had the Devil and his witches conquered those loyal to England and led these creatures to resist the monarchy? If Hell had risen from the depths of the earth, better it be on the other side of the seas. More likely, though, the colonists had found inspiration from my own rebellion and were prepared to overthrow the king. With God on their side, his majesty's head would soon cross the Atlantic. The latest to take the throne, another George, apparently fought in order to continue collecting taxes from the Americans. I wished these people well in their fight, for their quest kept my spirit alive.

Others discussed their new cocked hats and methods of powdering their periwigs. Battle appeared to be of little concern.

At times, men spoke of strange and unusual things they had seen; oddities on exhibit, like those at Du Puy's museum. One story, told by an old drunkard who claimed to have just returned from Prussia, involved a chicken with a human countenance. The body of this particular fowl, he explained, was covered in variegated feathers and appeared as any other chicken, with the exception of its face, which was completely bare. Its skin had a bluish colour, the sockets of its eyes resembled a human's, the upper part of its bill was bent and blunted off in such a way that it formed the shape of a nose, and its mouth was complete with lips, two rows of white teeth and a rounded tongue. Every bizarre word of his tale engrossed the small crowd, since English fowl look like fowl and nothing more.

These tales were mere asides from everyone's favou-

ally shook from the screaming and shouting below. It was
a place to sleep, but little else. I presumed he had a meagre
inheritance barely supporting him. The living conditions
did not concern me, as comfort was no longer a luxury I
required. My one extravagance came in the form of travel
between this dwelling and the inevitable pub, when Samuel would carry me to the taverns in his hand with no box
to hide me. He garnered looks along the way as he surely
desired, but for me, it was an opportunity to witness the
beauty of the city. I had scarcely seen it since my impalement. The work of Christopher Wren proved honourable,
for London had fully recovered from the flames and the
new architecture brought a fresh magnificence. He had
come a long way since attempting to drain blood from dogs
and inject it into men. His rebuilding of St. Paul's Cathedral was most commendable. Its dome reached toward the
sky; no building stood taller. The western façade featured a
portico flanked by two impressive towers, creating a dominant stance between the Heavens and earth. God had allowed London to burn, but in His wisdom, he left a blank
canvas for Wren's masterly art.

As Samuel and I spent more time together, the bond
between us grew stronger. This became evident during a
visit to Westminster Hall, though he had no specific business there. He simply looked up at the tower where I had
sat, looked at me and continued on his way. It was the first
time I had returned. None of my companions remained.
Now only stonework decorated the tower. Who had removed the heads, and when? Had they been discarded?

Or might I run into one of them at the tavern? When Cox approached us at one of our preferred watering holes, I imagined he'd been on a quest for all the regicide heads and needed me to complete his grotesque collection. Instead, he and Samuel engaged in the usual discourse.

"Samuel, good to see you, my friend!" Cox said. "Cromwell is looking quite nice. Still has one ear left, I see. Let me give you a hundred pounds for him."

"Thank you, James. But I'm not selling."

"And are you prepared to repay my loan?"

"No," Samuel answered. "In fact, I'm in need of a few more quid if you could be so kind. I will repay you, you have my word."

Samuel had no means of repaying Cox, yet neither man showed any concern.

*

Seasons passed and our notoriety grew with each tavern visit. Cox remained interested, but Samuel had earned more attention now than ever and continued to reject purchase offers. Many learned men sought him out for a chance to study me. Of note was an enterprising surgeon and collector of the unusual, John Hunter.

Samuel knew much about this man, for he had built a reputation on his peculiar activities and mastery of anatomy. Hunter educated himself by retrieving corpses from the grave, and he claimed to have dissected thousands of human bodies, all in his quest to better understand how the body worked and to perfect miraculous procedures to heal men. It was through this manner, not through the books of old, that he gained a thorough understanding of every muscle, organ, blood vessel and tissue the Lord gave us. Amputation became a last resort rather than a common necessity to repair wounded limbs, and Hunter postulated that bloodletting was an erroneous form of treatment, meaning our fathers and forefathers had been mistaken in their remedies. This was a flawed and far-fetched theory. Yet his work earned him a position in the Company of Surgeons and he currently served as the appointed surgeon to King George III. However, had the Americans succeeded in removing his majesty's head, even Hunter would have been powerless to reattach it.

Having heard tales of my head rolling through London's taverns, Hunter invited us to his wondrous home in Leicester Square. We took our visit on a pleasant autumn evening, making our way through the busy quarter bustling with residents taking one final sort through shopkeepers' goods as dusk settled in. The address led us down a small, quiet by-street for several blocks before we came upon Hunter's two-storey house. Samuel knocked and was promptly welcomed by the doctor. Upon entering we were greeted by a remarkably tall creature he called a giraffe; I knew not whether this was God's work or a monstrosity crafted by hand. Hunter had, he explained, performed many experiments that bastardised the Lord's imagination, such as grafting the leg spur of a fighting cock onto its head and attaching a cockerel's testicle to the stomach of a hen.

Hunter planned to open his home to the public as a museum. Indeed, it was worthy. His décor was unlike anything I, or anyone, had ever seen. Massive rooms allowed space for bones of whales, elephants and camels, joined by parts of zebras, hyenas, leopards and other exotic creatures. Hundreds if not thousands of skulls and bones of numerous sorts—including the bizarre skull of a young boy with a second, imperfect skull attached at the crown—filled shelves, and live toads, silkworms, hedgehogs, pheasants and other beasts scurried in cases and cages as they awaited study and experimentation. Glass jars held the foetus of a rhesus monkey, the head and hand of a chimpanzee, a cancerous scrotum (which even now made me tingle with discomfort), the enormous foot of a patient with elephantiasis, organs of pangolins, fetal kangaroos, squids, insects of all sorts, heads of a woodpecker, a puffin and other birds, human foetuses at every month of development (some looked peaceful, others slightly disturbed) and diseased body parts. There appeared to be hundreds more of these jars. Paintings adorned the walls and featured exquisite likenesses of even more unusual creatures, such as an ape, a rhinoceros and an albino baboon. It all made for a wonderfully haunting and morbid display.

Every inch of this assemblage would have made Claudius ill with jealousy. Hunter's phenomenal collection had everything. Except me.

The doctor himself looked to be in his late fifties, about my age upon my death. He had a dishevelled beard, and despite his eminent status, he wore no periwig, instead

Samuel, like a mouse cornered by a vicious cat, cowered, then sprang to his feet with a quickness that caught Hunter off guard. In full stride he snatched me from the table and dashed out of the laboratory back through the drawing room. The eyes of every creature seemed to follow us.

"Go! Go far from here!" Byrne shouted to me as we passed. "But know he shall follow relentlessly!"

Samuel threw the front door open and, without slowing a step or loosening his grip, ran.

✳

escape a madman is one thing, but to dodge debt is te another. A week after fleeing Hunter's house of wons and horrors, Samuel faced a new, unforeseen foe.

"Samuel, my friend, the time has come," James Cox with a smile as he pulled up a bar stool next to us. "You me precisely one hundred and one pounds. I am here llect."

"I've got nary a pence, Mr. Cox, you know that."

"I do know that. I also know what happened with unter," Cox said. The smile disappeared. "You were ate to leave that house with your head—Cromwell's urs."

I'll not part with it."

Which? Either Hunter will, how should I say it, u down and add it to his collection, along with your ll, and maybe an organ or two after he plays with

tying his yellow hair in the back.

Hunter led us through his extraordinary drawing room to the marvelous centrepiece of his collection: the giant skeleton of Irishman Charles Byrne. It stood nearly eight feet tall and looked down upon us or, more specifically, me.

"Please, get me out of here," Byrne whispered.

"I'm as dead as you," I replied. "Utterly powerless."

Hunter explained with great delight that Byrne had wished to be buried at sea, but Hunter had offered a dishonourable undertaker five hundred pounds to substitute the contents of the coffin with stones and give him the body. As he continued to tell us about his quest to obtain Byrne in order to gain an understanding of gigantism, the giant continued to speak to me; I was a new soul to confide in.

"I cannot stay," he said.

"This doctor has done you a wondrous favour," I told him. "Look around, the world has been brought right before you. You see things here few men have witnessed or will ever witness. The sea would have been nothing more than darkness and decomposition. Your soul merely nibbled away by persistent fish."

"He's a madman. He vowed to own my bones the first time he laid eyes on me in London. It wasn't just him, other physicians and anatomists waited for me to die. They could sense my illness, like vultures circling," he said. "So I wished to be dropped to the bottom of sea, where no one would find me. I would not let them dissect me and pick at me like a piece of meat. They all wanted to know what made me grow so large."

I, too, wished to know. I had never seen his equal. He didn't know the origins of his exceptionality, either, only that he'd been nothing more than a freak, earning a living with one showman after another, including James Cox.

"This life depressed me," he said. "So I took to drinking. First I drowned my sorrows, then myself. I was but twenty-two years old. Now I spend my afterlife knowing Dr. Hunter has won, he kept his vow against my wishes. He shouldn't have the satisfaction."

Just then, Samuel, having imbibed much before our visit and standing too close to the giant, nearly tripped over Byrne's large foot. He caught his balance before Hunter could notice; fortunately, his attention had become overly occupied with me.

Hunter's tour took us next to his back room. This was his laboratory, filled with filthy bloodstained tables, benches, chairs with restraints, sharp tools and blades, and discarded bits of flesh and bone. Several candles offered a dim glow. A discreet second entrance sat at the other end.[2]

"Sit down, Samuel," Hunter said. "Let me see the head."

Samuel sat in a rickety wooden chair covered in deep scratches, each undoubtedly a mark of a macabre story that had taken place in it.

Hunter clutched me in his coarse hand with a firm grip. "The embalming work is commendable. The head has held up well considering the circumstances it has been through. Samuel, I must study Cromwell and add him to my collection."

"Sorry, Doctor, 'tis not for sale," Samuel s____ ing to his integrity.

"It's missing an ear," Hunter said, not____ cerned with Samuel's rejection. "The Lord Pr____ not be missing an ear."

Hunter slowly approached Samuel, sti____ With an idea and a devious smile, his eyes gl____ stared at Samuel. He paused at one of his t____ the instruments and selected a small, sharp____ free hand.

"But this is easily remedied."

Samuel looked as if he'd seen the ____ vival instincts took over immediately____ Hunter, I'll sell you the head! Five h____ it's yours!"

I hitherto expected curiosity, ____ took us both by surprise. Did I belie____ giant? Was Hunter's collection inde____ tion? The exhibits fascinated and ____ unique companion, but Hunter w____ was great, yet was at the cost of ____ destroying their souls and med____ Lord's punishment would be for____

"The monetary offer ha____ said calmly as he continued to____ sually resting in his palm. Ar____ hand, he gently placed me ____ "Now, if you please, turn y____

your innards. Or you'll sell Cromwell to me to settle your arrears."

"And if I refuse?"

The feeling of being wanted never grows tiresome, whether it's by a nation, a beautiful woman or a purveyor of curiosities.

"You have no other means to pay. If you refuse me, I'll work with Hunter until we both have satisfaction," Cox calmly explained. His stare pierced Samuel's soul with tiny daggers. The cunning jeweller had been planning this moment for years; each penny loaned, another carefully laid piece of the plot. Poor, foolhardy Samuel looked lost, with no means of escape. His hand trembled, and beer splashed gently onto his trousers.

"Allow me to rephrase the proposition," Cox said. "Give me Cromwell, and you get to keep my money and both of your ears."

"I believe the head to be worth more than one hundred one pounds," Samuel responded with a note of concession in his voice. "I suspect I could fetch more from other interested parties, perhaps even Dr. Hunter himself, should a more civilised arrangement be possible."

Silence.

Finally, Cox, wishing to end this game after years of one-sided play, nodded. "One hundred ten, then. Will that suit you?"

"Mr. Cox, you're a jeweller. Your desire for this decaying, flaking impaled skull escapes me. It is as frightful as your gems are radiant. Desires aside, you're a man of means, thus surely a bit more is within reason."

In the years I'd spent with Samuel, moments of intelligence had been scarce. I, too, though, wondered what Cox aimed to do with me. A man does not sit patient for years, biding his time until the opportunity is right to pounce without grand designs.

"My intentions are not of your concern. I will, however, offer you one hundred eighteen pounds.[3] Accept it, or I return with Dr. Hunter and my earlier, less attractive offer."

Samuel extended his hand, and the men shook.

"I will have the proper papers drawn up," Cox said. "We shall meet here again within a fortnight's time to make the exchange." He tipped his hat, grinned at us both and triumphantly left the tavern.

VIII

OF MACHINE AND MAN

─────────

My afterlife has now lasted twice as long as my time among the living. In it, I have witnessed the world passively, noting its evolutions in architecture, fashion, science, speech and more. Kings have come and gone. Advancements in machinery using steam power have lessened the labours of men and created significant efficiencies. The American colonies have been lost in an embarrassment to the empire's once mighty military; yet George III retained his obviously incompetent head.

Today, my adventure takes a new turn, one I hope never leads to another tavern, for I have seen all anyone— alive or otherwise—ever need see within an alehouse. This, God willing, would be my last moment in such establishments. Cox had arrived with his documentation and a witness, and Samuel would henceforth be left to his own wits.

We sat in a quiet corner of the pub.

"Please read it and ensure it is to your satisfaction," Cox advised as he handed over the contract and seventeen pounds.

Samuel held the document in defeat and muttered the contents aloud:

> "Know all men by these presents that I, Samuel Russell of Keppel Street, in the Parish of Saint Saviour's, in the County of Surrey, as well for and in consideration of the sum of One hundred and one pounds heretofore advanced to me by James Cox of Shoe Lane in the City of London, Jeweller, as for and in consideration of the further sum of Seventeen Pounds, making together the sum of One hundred and eighteen pounds, to me in Hand paid by the said James Cox at and before the sealing and delivery of these Presents the receipt of which said several sums of money I the said Samuel Russell do hereby acknowledge and thereof and therefrom and of and from the same respectively and every part thereof do acquit release and discharge the said James Cox his executors and administrators for ever by these Presents have Bargained and Sold released granted and confirmed and by these Presents do bargain and sell release grant and confirm unto the said James Cox all that skull or head supposed to be the skull or head of Oliver Cromwell to have and

to hold the said skull or head unto and to the
only use and behoof of the said James Cox his
executors administrators and assigns absolutely
for ever free from and without and interruption
or disturbance whatsoever of from or by me the
said Samuel Russell or any other person or persons whatsoever and I the said Samuel Russell
for myself my executors and administrators do
by these Presents covenant and promise that I
the said Samuel Russell shall and will warrant
and for ever defend the said skull or head unto
the said James Cox his executors administrators
and assigns against me the said Samuel Russell
my executors and administrators and against all
and every other person or person whomsoever
and I the said Samuel Russell have put the said
James Cox in full possession of the said skull or
head by delivering him the same at the time of
the sealing and delivery hereof. IN WITNESS
whereof I the said Samuel Russell have hereunto
set my hand and seal the thirtieth day of April in
the Year of Our Lord One thousand seven hundred and eighty seven.

SAMUEL RUSSELL

Sealed and Delivered and Livery and
Seisin of the said skull or head given to the said
James Cox by the said Samuel Russell delivering
seisin thereof to the said James Cox in the pres-

ence of F. Magnial."

Samuel gripped my wooden post and extended his arm to Cox, just as he might have handed over a mug of beer.

"It is in no way to my satisfaction, Mr. Cox," he said. "In fact, I must say I am barely able to comprehend it. However, I find little choice in the matter and wish to preserve what is left of my honour, and more importantly, my flesh. Therefore, I hand you what remains of Lord Cromwell. Please do take better care of him than I have."

Cox couldn't fare much worse.

※

Without hesitation, Cox carried me to his London workshop on sinewy Shoe Lane, teeming with vendors and lively crowds. Inside, it became quite apparent that Cox was no ordinary jeweller. This man, who looked to be in his late sixties, had surely spent his life perfecting his craft, as had the dozens of skilled men under his employ who were busy fashioning their own elaborate creations. Of note within immediate view was a jewel cabinet mounted in gilded copper and brass and set with painted enamel plaques and fruitwood. Two playful cherubs and a woman's bust surrounded a watch upon the box. An automaton in the form of a chariot being pulled by a Chinese attendant also struck me as particularly impressive in its intricacies. The piece was cased in gold with diamonds and other jewels set in silver, pearls, gilded brass and steel. Mandarins and flying dragons were perched atop a metallic bouquet of gem-set flowers, which sat above a two-tiered parasol. A clock rested on the side of the chariot, which could be set in motion by a complex system of springs and coils.

Cox was more than an artist; he was a genius. At last, someone I could relate to.

He summoned several workers, who quickly appeared before us, and made the proper introductions. Apparently I had been expected; these men were well aware of Cox's plans and showed no expression of disgust upon making my acquaintance.

"Have you assembled the pieces?" he asked.

"Yes sir, Mr. Cox," one of the men answered eagerly. "It's downstairs, we've only been awaiting this final piece. Come!"

Had Cox built one of his intricate jewelled casings for me? My thoughts raced with ideas. Perhaps I was to become a clock, not unlike those I had just witnessed; my skull would be filled with a series of gears, levers and coils, while my face would hold the hands to tell the time. Exquisite details telling the stories of my life would be designed around my head: a small brass body of Charles I on one side and his head on the other; myself triumphant upon my horse with an enamelled sword, set with gemstones, raised in victory; a silver Parliament with paste-jewel accents forming the base of the casing; and ideally, the dates of my rule as Lord Protector to finalise the monument to the Commonwealth's greatest period. Cox's skilful inventiveness would undoubtedly bring elegance to my hideousness.

We made our way down a slender, dimly lit staircase into the bowels of the workshop. Cox's assistants illuminated the room with candles and led Cox to the pieces they had spoken about. My imagination had steered in a much different direction than his, for it became quite clear that I was not to transform into a clock. To judge from the shapes of the complex constructions of coils, counterweights, levers, gears, rods and countless other details, Cox had a much better idea: I was to receive a torso and limbs. I was to be more than a head; I was to be a man once again.

"We are about to embark upon the greatest automaton the world has known," Cox said enthusiastically. I could feel his excitement and knew that he'd waited many years to speak these words. "We will surpass Jaquet-Droz's musician and writer automata[1] and go beyond the wonders of von Kempelen's Chess Player.[2] We will leave men, women and children with a sense of wonder and disbelief! They will insist a real man is concealed within the machinery, just as they did in regard to the chess contraption. Our Cromwell will stand before kings and queens—no, walk before them—and they will marvel at our ingenuity and reward us for our efforts!"

I marvelled already. If, as Cox promised his men, I could walk before royalty, they would see me as a novelty, a mere afternoon of entertainment. Yet if I could have any control, I would walk methodically over to the unsuspecting dictators until I was close enough to see my reflection in their eyes, and use the sharp edge of the jewels lining my mechanical arm to slice their smiling heads right off in front of all attending the show. What a grand finale it would be! Could this be Cox's ultimate plan? I, a Trojan horse of sorts, built to do the bidding of this aspiring regicide. Success, I suppose, would lead to a hanging once again followed by a beheading from my automaton body. Strange, this cycle of afterlife. Cox, too, would dangle at my side and his head would join me just as Ireton's and Bradshaw's once had.

Whilst I dreamt of what could be, Cox's men began fitting me with my new limbs. Each locked into the torso, with gears properly aligned to allow precise, coordinated movements. Rubies covered the arms and torso to create the illusion of a red jacket; pearls coated my new legs to complete the uniform motif.

The assembly was a swift process, ending with Cox's finishing touch: the placement of my head on the body. He left my wooden post intact and set it directly into a hole in the torso; a tightened screw kept me firmly in place. As I stood complete, for the first time in more than a century, I looked down upon these craftsmen, for they had built me tall, perhaps more than seven feet in height. It was a resurrection of sorts, a miracle that would have made God Himself proud. Save for my head, I was beautiful.

Without delay, and with eager and excited eyes, Cox inserted a large brass key into an opening in my chest and rotated it numerous times, over and over again, before finally removing it and taking a step back to watch me come to life. Indeed, the set of coils began to unwind and set my gears in motion. I felt the vibrations through my wooden post—a pulse. Slowly, my left leg rose off the ground and moved itself forward. My right leg followed. I took one step a time, one small victory followed by another. By the time my machinery slowed to a halt, I had made it across the room, approximately ten paces. I felt like an amalgam of a somnambulist and a bumbling moppet, rising from a crawl for the first time—only my legs weighed hundreds of pounds and were coated in riches.

Cox and his men rejoiced with smiles and cheers; I was not unlike the Son of God, returning from death to walk the earth once again. I would have a powerful effect on all who were to witness my majesty and the brilliance of man: the Lord Protector, reborn as an embalmed, mechanical Messiah.

Now, how did these talented fellows intend to hoist me from the depths of this basement?

✢

Just as I had been carried in a lead coffin to my vault at Westminster Abbey so many years before, a team of men once again gathered their strength to lift and relocate my body to the ground level of Cox's workshop. After further testing, it took very little time for my creator to arrange an initial performance at the newly opened Theatre Royal Drury Lane. Covered in a dark shroud for secrecy, I was transported in a horse-drawn carriage through the narrow, circuitous streets to the show. As I was moved inside, I heard a voice outside the entrance singing my praises in an attempt to lure an audience:

"Ladies and gentlemen! Inside these doors the great-est wonder of the known universe awaits your eyes for tonight's headline performance! A marvel of hitherto un-discovered riches in mechanical miracles and resplendent jewels will amaze and enrich your mind as London wel-comes the return of Oliver Cromwell from the mysterious realm of death! For here, within these theatre walls, the Lord Protector's embalmed head is reunited with an au-tomaton body fashioned by the one and only James Cox! You may hate Cromwell's head, but you will love the rest of him!"

I failed to understand why my head would be hated. Its appearance was far from pleasant, but disgust and ha-tred are hardly brethren. Perhaps these modern Londoners were in love with their latest monarch, forcing history to view me with disdain. The garrulous chap out front was correct, though, in his final thought—love or hate my head, the rest of my body was undeniably a spectacle for the ages. Well worth the two shillings admission. Soon enough, I had no doubt they would love me in my entirety—warts, flak-ing flesh, cracked skull, missing ear and all.

Inside the theatre, behind the curtains, Cox removed the shroud and began tests to ensure I was in pristine work-ing order whilst preliminary acts entertained the crowd. These routines, including a farce called "Catherine and Petruchio," offered mild amusement through follies and capers, as far as I could detect from the scattered chuckles. The stage, flanked by thick iron columns, stretched approximately eighty feet in length, allowing abundant space for whatever movements Cox had devised for me; I had not been privy to his plans, though he had tinkered heavily with my precious metal innards.

After an hour's time, "Catherine and Petruchio" concluded and Cox stepped through the curtains to introduce me. I eagerly awaited my moment in the spotlight; though wooden, the stage would permit my walk upon water. This audience would become believers in the power of science as evidenced by my every movement, and the sight of my deteriorating countenance would rekindle revolutionary stirrings buried deep within their souls. The Lord viewed me as another son, kept on earth to continue the mission I had begun so long before: as I rose on mechanical legs, the king would fall to his flesh-and-bone knees. Applause interrupted my reflections, and the curtains spread.

There I stood, centre stage, with an enormous crowd gazing directly at me. The cavernous theatre supported five tiers, which proved not enough, considering that each seat was filled with curious eyes. The stunned, confused looks showed they knew not what was presented before them, for I had no equal.

"Welcome, welcome! I thank you so very much for joining us this evening. I am James Cox, and *this* is Oliver Cromwell. Yes, the real, one-hundred-percent-genuine head of Oliver Cromwell, resting upon a body which I have conceived. Tonight I will present the reanimation of the Lord Protector through a meticulous and wonderfully precise series of mechanisms. He is my masterpiece:

the Cromwell automaton, or as I fancy to call him, the *Cromaton*. You've never seen the likes of such a creation, this I promise you! Now, let us begin with a simple demonstration."

I, like those in attendance, was eager to see what I would do. If I was a new Son of God, Cox was my divine puppet master, pulling my strings at his will. He stepped behind me and adjusted a series of levers before winding my coils. It appeared that he had fashioned not just one series of movements, but several, which were interchangeable at his command. Set into motion, I was about to discover if Cox's intentions were as well thought out as his designs. My metal foot took a step forward, clanking down harshly on the wooden stage. The lights glimmered on my jewels as I slowly approached the audience. After several steps I came to a rest, which triggered my torso into a bowing motion, as one might greet another. Cox, however, heightened the drama with a grisly twist. Just as a gentleman would remove his hat during such a gesture, my arm swivelled to my head, clutched it from the top and lifted it away from the body. I then stood upright again, with my head gripped in my extended hand. This brought cheers mixed with shouts of fright, and certainly fulfilled Cox's promise. My gears, though, were still turning and sent my arm back in motion to return the head to my shoulders. With a remarkably gentle motion, the wooden stake slipped perfectly back into its slot and I was whole again.

Cox continued to showcase a variety of movements that sent me walking in circles, lifting items, and writing my name upon a piece of parchment; the signature was a fair replica of my own. By this point, the crowd had grown fond of my abilities and any fears had been mitigated.

"Now, for one last grand demonstration of precision, I should like to request a volunteer," Cox announced. "Someone with a tender neck, if you please."

Silence filled the theatre. Cox surveyed the audience, but not one hand reached up. Growing impatient, he took control of the matter. "You there, madame," he said with a smile to a young lady seated in the third row, whose neckline was exposed by her gown. "Please step up onto the stage. I assure you, no harm will come your way."

She stood hesitantly and made her way to the stage, unaware of what she had just involuntarily volunteered for. Either she possessed commendable bravery or she feared not being brave in front of all those seated around her. Cox greeted her with an open hand and learned that her name was Lily. He lured her to a position toward the right of the stage, blindfolded her and asked her to position herself on her hands and knees. "Stay still, Lily. That is all I request, stay very still," Cox told her. Lily did her best to oblige, but she trembled in her uncomfortable pose.

Cox walked toward me and once more wound me enthusiastically; only this time he inserted a large hatchet in my left hand. As the gears fell into place, I slowly took my first step toward Lily. I could hear the gasps and whispers amongst the spectators; fragile women held on to their husbands tightly and some, unfortunately, covered their eyes—a shame, indeed. After several loud footsteps I stood

before Lily and my arm began to raise the hatchet. Was this
Lily a queen, or perhaps a princess? My hand slowly start-
ed its descent; Lily grew visibly more troubled as shrieks
could be heard from the galleries. Then, like a clock whose
gears have ceased to turn, I came to a sudden stop just before the blade was to touch Lily's soft neck.

Cox took Lily's hand, pulled her to her feet and removed the blindfold. "Well done, Lily! Give this woman a
round of applause, for she has survived another execution
attempt by the Lord Protector, Oliver Cromwell!"

My intelligence in mechanics would never match
Cox's, but in terms of confidence, we were true equals. No
man would risk the life of a young woman for the purposes
of entertainment without absolute certainty that his work
was to perfection. I led the revolution with the same as-
suredness and won a nation. Tonight, Cox won the ado-
ration of the crowd. The performance would soon be followed by many similar engagements throughout London.

✶

News of France's growing revolution became a frequent
topic of conversation, particularly the thousands of heads
lost at the drop of a razor from some contraption called the
guillotine.[3] The French king had been an early customer
of the blade, and a young lad who seemed to be leading
the cause, Maximilien Robespierre, was ruthless with any
who opposed the revolution.[4] If my soul had not remained
within my head I would have supposed I had been reincar-

nated. Cox may have physically reanimated me, but this Frenchman, unbeknownst to him, performed the same feat for me spiritually. I heard no reports of what became of the severed heads, though I imagined if they were skewered across the streets of Paris many gruesome stories would have travelled with haste. Instead, they were likely tossed into the depths of a pit, all left to lie eye to eye, exchanging complaints about the overcrowded accommodations, unattractive faces, Robespierre's revolutionary tactics, the failure of tyrannical rule and the unpleasantness of the ubiquitous maggots.

Cox, shrewd as always, capitalised on the news without delay by rightly promoting me as the "Original Revolutionary" and adjusting his stage banter to offer a more accurate description of my triumphs. The hatchet I held in the final act was subsequently referred to as the "Original Guillotine." Attendance rose, bookings increased and Cox's fame grew at such a rapid rate that he soon received an invitation to perform before King George III and Queen Charlotte. I found this most interesting, given the portrayal of me as a revolutionary during the current political climate, yet I commended them for showing bravery and quenching their curiosity. Would my initial hopes and dreams of a second regicide come true?

After weeks of preparation, Cox and I were received by George and Charlotte on a pleasant summer afternoon at her residence, called the Queen's House.[5] This home must have been recently acquired by the monarchy, as no queen I had known of lived in these quarters. The expansive lawn and brilliant gardens were intersected by a slender canal sparkling in the sunlight, which offered a slender bridge for us to cross as we approached the impressive red brick mansion. Inside, the king and queen descended from a grand staircase to greet us. We were led to the music room, where an extensive collection of paintings dressed the walls and crimson velvet covered numerous chairs and tables. A large piano rested in the middle of the chamber; the sculpture of a man's head sat upon it, with a label stating his name as George Frideric Handel. This clear appreciation for the arts further explained our presence. Charlotte was dressed in a rather simple white frock that highlighted her dark complexion and wide nostrils, which were accentuated by wrinkled skin; she appeared to be in her fifties. A glimmering fringe necklace offered a touch of sophistication. In George, who attempted to look his part in a dapper double-breasted coat, I could see only an old, stubborn man stained by defeat; his loss to the Americans had not escaped me. Various guards, who were as stiff as I, and staff attendants accompanied them, along with another fellow introduced as Prime Minister William Pitt.

Pleasantries were exchanged, and Cox introduced me with new words, prepared especially for this occasion:

"Your Majesty, Your Highness, it gives me great pleasure to stand before you today with what I regard as the unequivocal height of science, art, beauty and history. My Queen, you will see I have spared no expense in embellishing the Cromaton with jewels. He is second only to you in such riches. These gems, however, mask my true art, which will dazzle you with an array of talents. I am well aware of your affinity toward the musical arts, and though we cannot promise to exceed the talents of Mozart, who once shared his genius in this very room, or Handel, whose bust graces your piano, I do hope you find joy in witnessing a man who was beheaded nearly one hundred fifty years ago fill the room with the splendour of an original piano concerto."

"I am glad to hear it," George said with little expression. Charlotte's eyes were fixed in a more expected state of disbelief.

Cox positioned me at the piano and wound me vigorously, setting my arms and fingers into motion. My system of mechanics could not compete with God's superior system of flesh and blood, and therefore I played very slowly, unable to match the skill of this Mozart or Handel, both blessed with the ability to strike keys with speed and dexterity. I sounded very much like an amateur, and though Cox attempted to stress the fact that I was a rotting head with a metal body laced with jewels, the king and queen looked displeased with the melodies. Pitt, too, showed signs of irritation, though I did not suppose he could fare much better seated at this sprawling instrument. Cox recognised the situation. Growing nervous, he fiddled with my settings to begin a new demonstration, the one we had previously used to open shows in which I simply walked forward and took a bow. The intimate setting allowed me to step very close to my royal audience. I had come to a stop just two feet away and could see their pupils widen and small goose pimples arise on their arms. Charlotte's face was dotted with several small moles, to which I offered my silent sympathy, but even from a distance one could detect that both she and George offered more favourable expressions at my movement. Indeed, this routine extended a show of respect and bore no comparisons to other musical prodigies. Cox looked relieved for the moment, but then the gears continued their arranged sequence and I removed my head after the bow. Matters immediately took an unfortunate turn for the worse. Shock rattled Charlotte; George appeared equally disturbed, perhaps suspecting that a beheading of his own awaited him. As I reached my head forward, it grazed Charlotte's protruding nose and offered her a flake of worm-riddled flesh. Though she had been too stunned to move out of my way, she suddenly shrieked and jumped from her seat, as one might at the sight of a scurrying rodent. Cox had slightly miscalculated the distance needed for this act. This sort of miscue, this slip in precision, was exactly what I had hoped for during the routine in which I held the hatchet. At this point, there would be no such opportunity, though no moment during any performance thus far had entertained me more.

Charlotte covered her eyes and looked away as George rose from his seat and barked, "Enough!" Pitt stepped between the king, queen on one side and me on the other as if serving as a shield during an attack. Cox rushed to my aid and pulled me aside, creating a more comfortable distance from the squeamish queen and her frail husband.

"Mr. Cox, your creature, this '*Cromaton*' as you wish

to call it, has offended my wife, the Queen, and therefore offended your King as well," George said angrily.

Cox was quick to grovel, "Your Majesty—"

"Silence! You bring before us a regicide for our amusement, and it nearly assaults the Queen in what could be considered a premeditated attempt at a second murder. I will not allow it. Prime Minister Pitt, please see to it that Mr. Cox removes the Cromwell head from this, this unholy machine. Ensure the body is quartered and never reassembled again. You shall then draft an act, call it what you like, the Anti-Reanimation Act or something of that nature— use your wits—to further ensure that no others who possess or may exceed the cleverness of Mr. Cox should ever find opportunity in such a venture again. Now please escort this man and his filthy, evil head off the premises of the Queen's House."

Pitt plucked my head off the mechanical body and shoved me into Cox's hands with no regard to the delicacy of my features or any respect for me as the Lord Protector. We were shuffled through the front door and cast away, back to the workshop for a full disassembly. A short time later the Cromaton sat in pieces just as it had my first evening there.

Upcoming bookings were cancelled and Londoners were forced to find their entertainment elsewhere, particularly in the works of Shakespeare, which remained popular all these years later. Pity his head hadn't been preserved to witness the longevity of his success. I do believe he would have taken much delight in the passion for his little plays.

Cox retained his immense wealth, but no sum of money could repair the damage done. As for me, I had seen the king as I desired and been beheaded once again, as I suspected. If only it had been for the proper reasons.

✷

Though I missed the glory of the theatre life and the wonder I saw in the eyes of men, women and children of all ages—for even the eldest, most well-travelled of persons were treated to a brand new experience—I was truly grateful for my brief time in the spotlight. My days were now spent as they had often been in decades past, upon a shelf, with me left to stare at whatever lay in my line of sight and hear things spoken within earshot. In Cox's studio, that meant his magnificent creations and general blather about sales and finicky customers. Little was said about me or my discarded metal, bejewelled body. What had become of it? Cox had shown phenomenal vision in creating the limbs and could pursue such endeavors for the benefit of the living; many men who fought for me lost limbs in battle, and I had no doubt such casualties persisted in the current day's military. I remember one soldier who suffered a devastating break in the leg, which was entirely crushed from the knee down with bone protruding from the flesh. The doctor called for his amputation instruments; he placed his hand on the thigh, just above the wound, took a sharp knife and drove it into the thigh beneath the bone, then swept it outward swiftly. He then grabbed a saw to sever the bone, taking about two minutes to complete the cut. When the leg dropped to the ground he sewed the flaps of skin together to close the gash. That soldier, and any other victim, would rejoice with a new arm or leg whether it shimmered with rubies or not.

As I watched workers craft exquisite new pieces of jewellery I became inspired with ideas for how Cox could use me, and hoped he, too, had been formulating other plans for us. Surely I could still be a muse for this artist. As evidenced all around me, Cox was a master at producing clocks with animated creatures, not unlike the remarkable cuckoo clocks I remember seeing during my time in power. He built mechanical birds and animals into his work, set to move in various ways upon the strike of a new hour. I imagined ways in which I could be the focal point of such a clock, well beyond my initial thoughts before receiving my automated limbs. I could replace the cuckoo bird, resting behind a large clock face; each new hour the face would open and I would spring forth on a small platform to announce the new time. Cox could employ sculptors to mimic my head and mass-produce these "Cuckoo Cromwells." They would serve as true conversation pieces, enliven any cabinet of curiosity and perhaps even help wake their owners in the morn; my macabre countenance, face-to-face with theirs at sunrise, would force even the weariest from the comforts of bed. Cox could continue to capitalise on me and renew his happiness as my caretaker.

Neither Cox nor God, however, had such grand designs for me. Perhaps it was for the best, as I began to ques-

tion my own ideas and contemplated whether or not a form
of insanity was beginning to set in: I, the Lord Protector
of the Commonwealth of England, Ireland and Scotland,
withered down to a cuckoo clock? Woe to a head with nothing but ideas to pass the time.

Cox, in fact, had very different plans for me. Unable to get over our failed venture, he decided to seek out
a buyer while he could still capitalise on our brief success
and the potential to continue promoting me as the Original
Revolutionary; upheaval apparently continued amongst
the French. On occasion, he invited prospective buyers
into the workshop to inspect me and make an offer. Many
came, yet I remained, until one day when three men arrived
and announced themselves as brothers named Hughes. A
date etched into a newly designed clock informed me the
year was 1799. Cox made his sales pitch, ensuring my authenticity, and reminded them of the extraordinary nature
of my preservation and the importance of my role in our
nation's glorious history.

"Exhibition of this specimen will draw attention with
great certainty, as he is a true crowd pleaser and is still revered by thousands to this day," he explained. "After our
shows came to a sudden halt, many were deprived of the
opportunity to see him."

The Hughes brothers nodded in agreement. They
each held me, surveying me closely before passing me
along. The three looked alike, each appearing to be in his
forties with handsome, clean-shaven faces and grey locks
peppering their black hair. The spark of entrepreneurialism

could be detected in their eyes.

"Mr. Cox, we would very much like to purchase Lord Cromwell and are prepared to offer you two hundred thirty pounds," one of the brothers said.[6]

Cox, not surprisingly, accepted the offer. It was nearly double what he had paid for me. During our years together, I had proven myself a sound investment, and I had little doubt I would continue to be so.

I just had to be me, if it was still to be believed.

IX

BOND STREET

———

To bid farewell to a friend is never easy. In life, we say our good-byes knowing we may see each other once again or at the very least enjoy written correspondence. At death, we are stricken with the sorrow of finality; there will be no more hellos, no future exchange of thoughts, ideas or emotions. Yet here I remained, somewhere in the middle. I was forced to part ways with James Cox and was unable to show appreciation or gratitude for the time we spent together. This was a great man, blessed with creativity and ingenuity; it was indeed an honour to have observed his work and been a centrepiece of it. Providence, though, shows mercy to His faithful subjects, for this departure was an emotionally driven business transaction, not a funeral, which meant I very well might enjoy Cox's company once again, so long as blood gave his body warmth and I was not lost in a drawer or chimney for the next several decades.

I left the workshop that day with the three men, prepared to see where my journey would lead next. It was the first time I had experienced multiple possessors and I wondered how I would be shared amongst them. I did not suppose they lived communally; therefore only one brother could enjoy my company within his home at a time. Would I be rotated from one residence to another after an agreed-upon number of days had passed? Would struggles, be they physical or verbal, arise from untamable jealousy?

Our carriage rode straight to the home of an acquaintance of theirs. Since they had not wasted a moment stopping at one of their own homes first, I determined these brothers had no interest in clearing gimcrackery off their personal shelves to make room for my dusty old head. This bode well; a plan was afoot. Concealed in a large cloth bag, I could hear a man greet the Hughes brothers and eagerly usher us into his residence, ready to discuss business.

"Very good to see you John! Allow me to quickly introduce my brothers, Thomas and William," one of the Hughes said. "Lads, this is John Cranch. Painter, antiquarian, historian, and best of all, publicist."

"Pleased to make your acquaintance, gentlemen, and brilliant to see you again Richard," Cranch said.

"Pleasant fellows, of course, same mum as m'self," Richard said. "But we've not come to dillydally in formalities, let us instead introduce you to the man of the hour, or shall I say, a part of the man of the hour!"

He chuckled at his poor attempt at a jest then slowly opened the bag and pulled me out by my spike.

"This, John, as promised, is the Lord Protector, Oliver Cromwell," Richard announced. "What's left of him, that is."

Cranch took hold of me for a closer inspection. My gaze lifted from his inquisitive eyes directly to his slightly conical, tall hat, which covered either his greying hair or an unusually lofty, powdered periwig that may have been disheveled and unpresentable. His high-waisted coat was topped with a standing collar that climbed upward along his neck, as if it wished to reach the heights of his hat. Long, dark breeches were tucked into his tasseled boots. I was not impressed with this manner of dress and would not wish to emulate it, given the opportunity. I presumed Cranch was not admiring my headgear, either, unless he desired a skewer to amplify his hat's elevation.

"What do you say to that, then? Quite a specimen, is it not?" Richard spoke with jubilation, obviously quite proud of his acquisition.

"Marvellous, just marvellous," Cranch remarked as he continued to look me over meticulously. "Exhibition space at Old Bond Street is available, now that the showing of the rattlesnake has closed."

"Make the arrangements. Surely those who witnessed the exhibit of the slithering beast will be eager for a more stimulating display," Richard said.

"Let us include a few artefacts to accompany the head, billed as Cromwell's own possessions. It will enable

Cranch's original handwritten advert, with notes.

us to command a greater admission fee. I shall hasten to write a brief history of the head's journeys and place a bulletin in the *Morning Chronicle*."

The brothers left me with Cranch. Energised with their plans and anticipating a touch of fortune and fame, he promptly carried me to his writing desk to begin work. The bureau was crafted with a handsome moulded-edge top composed of three planks, outfitted with several graduated drawers with brass pull rings. Sketches of women, creatures and architecture lay scattered across the surface; most demonstrated nothing more than meagre talent. I reckoned his skills in publicity were his stronger asset.

As Cranch sat assiduously with his ink and began penning the advert and designing it for the printer, I rested in the far left corner of the desk next to a burning candle, as if I were to offer further illumination:

THE REMAINS OF THE REAL
EMBALMED HEAD OF
THE POWERFULL
AND RENOWNED USURPER,
OLIVER CROMWELL,

Styled Protector of the Commonwealth of England, Scotland and Ireland; with the original dyes for the medals struck in honour of his victory at Dunbar, &c &c—are now exhibiting at No. 5 in Mead court, Old Bond Street. ADMITTANCE, and printed copy of a genuine narrative relating to the acquisition, concealment and preservation of the articles exhibited, two shillings and sixpence.[1]

Next, he took it upon himself to write my posthumous biography, this "genuine narrative" entitled, *Narrative Relating to the Real Embalmed Head of Oliver Cromwell, Now Exhibiting in Mead-Court, in Old Bond-Street.* He knew of my early history at Tyburn and Westminster Hall, but beyond that, he had heard only the tales passed down from Richard; the other brothers offered nothing more. I watched his pen ink what few facts he was privy to, then suddenly come to a stop. Cranch wore a look of concern and left the room.

Days later the Hughes brothers returned at Cranch's request. He retrieved me from the desk and held me before the three men. "My friends, as I've begun considering the history of this head, I must ask, how do know it is truly Cromwell?" he said in an accusatory manner. "What provenance have you to speak to its authenticity?"

The brothers glanced at one another, unsure of the answer. Doubt hadn't taunted me since von Uffenbach at Du Puy's museum of curiosities.

Suddenly, Thomas, who I had thought mute, spoke with wisdom: "'Tis simple, for what other historical character is known to have been embalmed, beheaded and spiked? There is none other."

William and Richard agreed, forgetting Ireton as the only possible response. Cranch ignored these facts and remained skeptical.

"But Thomas, pray tell me, could one not have let

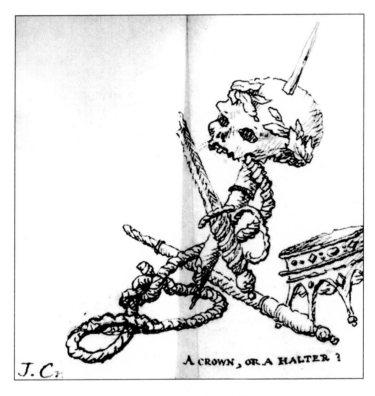

An original Cranch scribble.

an embalmed head lie in its tomb, attached to its body, for many years before removing it and propelling an old rusted spike through its skull?"

"Cox assured us this was the one true head of Oliver Cromwell," Richard adamantly responded.

"Just yesterday I conferred with colleagues regarding the head's travels and learned that a shop along Butcher Row held a skull recently shown as Cromwell," Cranch said, to everyone's surprise. "A doctor witnessed it and confirmed it as genuine."

"Hogwash!" Richard exclaimed. "Absolute rubbish!"

"Perhaps. Probably just a huckster capitalising on Cox's recent success with the head. But as I began writing the pamphlet, it occurred to me there are many gaps in the trail of ownership. Write to Cox and let him know you require further information regarding the manner in which the head found its way into his possession. Let him offer proof beyond his word. And ask what he knows of this Butcher Row madness."

The brothers agreed and left with haste. I appreciated Cranch's integrity as a historian, and wondered how many other false heads were advertised as my own.

Cranch returned me to the desk as he awaited word from Cox. He could write nothing more till then. During this time, the notion of an impostor swirled through my empty skull, spinning around the spike like an acrobat around a pole. What soul stirred within the head at Butcher Row? Did he revel in the idea of becoming the Lord Protector? Or did he find anguish in having his entire past, his full identity, wiped away and replaced with mine? If other counterfeit heads were being exhibited, were they at least from worthy men? Perhaps a decorated general or learned man of science. Or would they be from executed criminals, poorly disguised with dried flesh, who suddenly found their punishment turned into the blessing of becoming England's greatest political figure? And what of the simpleton? A head that had no notion of who I was could be easily shown to equally dull persons who knew no difference. A true waste. It then occurred to me that perhaps there actually had been another genuine Cromwell head shown—just not mine. I know not what became of my son Richard, but if he had been embalmed, exhumed and beheaded, he, too, could be displayed as the Lord Protector Cromwell. My son Henry also could have been the victim of greedy ghouls wishing to exhibit a Cromwell head of their own. These thoughts persisted, interrupted only by the realisation that I sorely missed the days when I had more important thoughts to consider.

In a week's time Cox responded to the Hughes brothers' enquiry. Richard delivered the news to Cranch; it was scarcely news at all.

"Cox claims it is genuine, and that it had passed through Russell's family over several generations, and that Russell himself is a distant relative of Cromwell's," he said. "He had never heard of the Butcher Row impostor and offered nothing more."

"'Tis unfortunate, indeed," Cranch said with a sigh

as he paced the room. "But alas, we have this head. It may very well be real, so we will treat it as such. I will write the biography as I see fit. His history will henceforth be known as I craft it. Is this not the manner in which all history is recorded? It is written, and it is so."

"I have no doubt it will be splendid!" Richard winked and left Cranch to his work.

I, however, had my doubts. "Splendid" would not be an option, unless it were to be judged as a creative work of fiction—and Cranch was hardly Cervantes.

My misinformed yet entrepreneurial historian immediately set out to complete the task, ignoring the details he lacked and attempting to weave together a cohesive story. In reporting on my years with Henry after my fall from the tower, Cranch simply said that I "was taken up by one of those many persons whom the flagitious conduct of these monarchs, had by that time converted to a less unfavourable opinion of Cromwell. By this person it was soon after presented to one of the Russell family." My time at Du Puy's museum was entirely absent, and nothing whatsoever was made of my grave within Frederick Russell's drawer. Despite his failure to uncover the truth, Cranch did put forth much effort in supporting my authenticity, though I could not be certain of his argument's veracity. He stated, in regard to my head:

> In the year of Our Lord 1775, the learned and ingenious Doctor Southgate, late librarian to the British Museum, had been applied to for his opinion of

its identity, and that after a very attentive consideration of it for twenty minutes, and comparing it
with medals, coins, etc., he had delivered his opinion in these words—"Gentlemen, you may be assured that this is the real head of Oliver Cromwell."

I had no recollection of an encounter with a Dr.
Southgate, though it is within the realm of possibility that
this "learned and ingenious" librarian witnessed me under
the influence of libations at a tavern with Samuel—and
perhaps even kept a piece of me for further study. I failed
to comprehend, however, how a comparison with medals
and coins offered clues of any sort in his examination. They
certainly featured my likeness (which was particularly satisfying on those made from the Crown Jewels), but they
were hardly as detailed as any of my painted portraits.[2] I
was further perplexed with the source of Cranch's quota-
tion. Whether it was genuine or a product of the publicist's
imagination, he, too, appeared unsure of the relevance of
coins and medals, and thus supported it with another statement from a "celebrated medalist" named John Kirk to
add credibility:

> The head shown to me for Oliver Cromwell's, I ver-
> ily believe to be his real head, as I have carefully ex-
> amined it with the coin, and think the outline of the
> face exactly corresponds with it, so far as remains.
> The nostril, which is still to be seen, inclines down-
> wards as it does in the coin the cheek bone seems to
> be as it is engraved, and the color of the hair is the

same as one well copied from an original painting by Cooper in his time.

Cranch cited this report from the same year as the Southgate account. It is true that Samuel Cooper painted many portraits of me; he was indeed my favourite artist, and it pleased me to believe the likeness he produced was so striking that it could still be used to identify me. Yet given my state after more than a hundred years of death, in which I have been exposed to the elements, been juggled in taverns and had an ear pilfered, I questioned whether even Cooper's mastery could allow such a testimony.

As I watched Cranch continue his attempts at verification through medals and other such nonsense disguised as evidence, I became most appalled when his ink ran dry at page twenty. The ignorance within caused enough outrage, but for Cranch to abbreviate my afterlife so drastically, despite his efforts to ascertain more information, was, in his own words, "flagitious." London desperately needed a guillotine of its own.

✳

Much fanfare besieged the opening of my exhibition at Mead Court. I rested upon a brass ring protruding from an impressive plinth, decorated with an exquisitely carved relief of me standing over a kneeling Charles I with his severed head lying peacefully on the ground as cherubs hovered above. Sufficient sunlight shone through surrounding windows to illuminate every gruesome and artistic detail. A decorative artificial wreath was placed around my cranium to match my appearance on the coins of my era and to conveniently mask the cincture cut by the embalmer, and a glass casing shielded my head from the expectation of curious fingers, clumsy hands and potential nasal drippings from children and ill folk. The medals Cranch was so fond of hung nearby. Large prints filled out the room, each featuring vivid illustrations depicting my journey through the decades. I took pleasure in staring at the many images of myself, which included my triumph at the execution with Charles praying futilely to the Lord, and my conquests on the battlefield, where I was seen victorious upon my horse with sword held high. Even images of my current self spiked at Westminster brought delight. The work was commendable; Cranch had certainly commissioned it to a finer artist.

Thomas and William Hughes stood nearby, presumably to act as both guards and guides whilst Richard and Cranch worked outside to draw people in and collect admission. I was prepared for the rush of wide eyes and disgusted looks, just as I had grown accustomed to at Du Puy's. When the doors opened, however, there was no mad dash, but merely several curiosity-seekers studying the imagery and leaning in close to my glass shield. Excellent strategy by Richard and Cranch, I thought, to control the long line and let guests trickle in slowly so they could stare at their leisure and let the sight of me soak in. A large crowd would only lead to chaos, anger and possibly another lost ear. Yet as time passed, the trickle weakened to a dribble, until it became clear there was no line control because there was no line *to* control. Commentary from visitors offered reasons for the ignominy:

"Two shillings and six pence for this? For a grimy old head?"

"It just sits there! No prancing about on stage?"

"My dear, did we not see one of these horrible Cromwell heads last month?"

By the third day, I heard a disturbance from outside the entrance.

"Thieves! That's my head in there! The Cromwell head belongs to me!" It was the unmistakable voice of Samuel Russell, inebriated as usual. "Cox swindled me! How much did he sell it for? Greedy bastard! Give me back my head!" This was bad for business; our meager crowds grew even more scarce as the spectacle carried on. Cranch and Richard tried to calm Samuel and steer him away from the exhibit. After nearly a half-hour's time, the shouts subsided, meaning he left the premises, got arrested or passed out drunk. I reckoned the latter.

And so it went over the course of a week. People found the exhibit overpriced or questioned its authenticity, or both. Unfortunately for the Hughes brothers and Cranch, these realisations typically occurred before potential visitors paid the fee.

I had hoped Cox would make a visit, since he could easily afford the admission and might wish to see me. Perhaps it would have only brought him sadness to see me on display without my artificial body and to hear skepticism from Cranch.

King George and Queen Charlotte also declined to visit.

In my two hundred years of existence, this was the first time I had tasted failure. 'Twas an admirable streak.

X

A NEW MODEL FAMILY

———

There is a small victory to be had in knowing when you are defeated. Cranch and the Hughes brothers recognised this and rather than continue to lose money, they ended the exhibit after one unsuccessful month. As they packed up the illustrations, medals, pamphlets and my head, their disappointment manifested itself in anger and blame toward each other. Cranch believed the Hugheses had been swindled by Cox and left them to clean up their mistake, whilst the brothers argued that Cranch had failed miserably in his role as publicist. I felt much like a helpless child between two parents engaged in a senseless verbal battle, but I embraced the moment; it was as close to feeling like a child as I could experience.

Cranch, convinced that the three men were hopelessly ignorant, offered the brothers his well wishes and farewells, then left the exhibit with no desire to see the four of us ever again. Failure had gotten the best of him and undeniably confirmed his weak character. Marmaduke Langdale's royalists would have destroyed him at Naseby.[1] Cranch simply lacked the imagination to address the flaws surrounding the exhibit and try once again. This was a man who failed at failing.

The Hughes brothers fared no better. Left without their publicist and "historian," and lacking the acumen to put a new presentation together on their own, they chose to retire from the embalmed-head exhibition business. Richard, who had demonstrated himself as the alpha brother, elected to privately display me at home upon his mantel, where he could bask in my presence at his leisure.

My time on his narrow wooden shelf was, to my dismay, an utter bore. To my left sat a pair of brass candlesticks overly decorated with foliage, superfluous scrolls and etched lettering; a well-used toastmaster glass accompanied my right side. I passed many days studying the candlesticks to determine the exact nature of the shrubbery and floral designs and wondering if the script around the scrolls was merely indicative of letters for aesthetic purposes or a language I was unfamiliar with. If the latter, was the messaging of significance, possibly details regarding the foliage, or simply foolishness? A seldom used crimson settee with floral needlepoint resting in the corner near a dainty table highlighted the chamber's furnishings. Simple and rather flat moulding lined the perimeter of the room, creating a border for the cochineal-toned wallpaper that had been smothered with a pattern of golden thistles and fleur-de-lys. Poor taste had conquered and stubbornly occupied this dismal place. Fortunately, a window on the opposite side of the small, dank room invited the sun and moonlight in and provided a glimpse of the passing seasons. On occasion, Richard's plump daughter, called Edith, would take a close look at me, but only because she needed to take the candlesticks and toastmaster glass to the table for a formal meal. I remained on the mantel; there was no place for me at supper. Edith looked to be about sixteen years of age. Her homely appearance and thick figure repelled suitors and thus she rarely left the house. I suspected Richard's wife was deceased, since I never caught sight of nor heard a peep or shriek from her. William and Thomas visited on occasion, but only to see Richard. They had by then seen enough of me. These were my days, but to elaborate further on my doldrums would only lead to greater tedium.

Fortunately, my afterlife with the Hughes brothers was short-lived. Each, quite strangely, suffered an early, unexpected death. It began with Thomas, who showed up with unusual rashes attacking his flesh and often complained of severe stomach pains accompanied by effervescent bursts. Despite the incessant grumbling, Thomas stubbornly refused to visit a doctor; bloodletting, he claimed, made him feel squeamish and faint. Suffering was preferable. With each visit his pain worsened and the rashes spread, reaching along his arms, inching up his neck and smearing across his face. Soon, I imagined, his visage would rival mine in grotesquerie, though I never had the opportunity to find out. After a short while, visits from Thomas ceased.

William continued to stop by, but he, too, took ill. Heavy coughing and lingering high fevers joined forces with alarming rapid weight loss. A doctor soon diagnosed him with the dreaded consumption and ordered him away from the house to avoid spreading it to his brother and niece. Shortly after his banishment, word arrived that the disease had claimed his life.

Months later, Richard was out doing whatever tasks filled his day; I no longer knew how he occupied his time. One night, he did not return home and later there was a knock at the door. Startled, his daughter opened it and found herself listening to the local constable explaining that Richard had fallen from his horse after suffering a fatal bout of apoplexy.

Within the span of what I estimated to be six months, this poor young lass had lost her father and two uncles. All three, like all unimportant men, were now decomposing in the earth; the scent of death emanating from their corpses, signalling an invitation to eager parasites and busy worms. For this, I did pity them momentarily. Edith, however, wept frequently; no shortage of tears afflicted her during this period of mourning. When she at last came to peace with her circumstances and gathered her senses, she came to the mantel and addressed me for the first time:

"This is your fault, you wretched thing. You have put a curse upon this family, and I will not allow you to remain in this house another moment!" Anger filled her eyes, and veins protruded dangerously from her forehead. "I will not wait around until I, too, succumb to disease and find an early grave. Oliver Cromwell, you are a murderer! You have always have been a murderer—alive *and* dead! Come now, let us find you a new owner. A wealthy one at that."

The rant was long overdue and quite welcomed, though I wondered if the eruption might prove overly stressful and fatal, thus adding validity to her theory of a curse. Edith snatched me from the shelf and wrapped me in a black sheet, and we left the house. Things were finally becoming interesting again.

✳

When the lass finally unravelled my sheet, I sat in a spacious, dimly lit office where books dutifully lined the walls, and several terrariums joined forces with an array of scientific instruments and detritus to clutter tables and a simple desk. An elderly gentlemen, whom Edith addressed as Sir Joseph Banks, leaned in toward me with a smirk. "Miss Hughes, I am a botanist," he said. His voice was sharp, with an air of condescension. "What need do I have for this rotten head?"

Rotten I may be, but Banks was heavyset, with exceptionally bushy eyebrows.

"Sir Banks, please, I beg your pardon. I only requested this meeting because you are a master of the natural sciences and I believed this relic might appeal to your inquisitive disposition." Edith spoke with true sincerity, and I

knew not how Banks could disagree with her. "Not simply
for its historical significance, but as a study in human decay
and the longevity of the embalming process. If, sir, if I am
wrong, would it at the very least interest you to plant seeds
within the skull's cavity? Perhaps there are new lessons to
be learned in the growth of flora?"

"Miss Hughes, I appreciate your persistence, and my
condolences on your recent sorrows, but I assure you, I have
no desire to own, let alone spend another moment looking
at, this old villainous republican," Banks said. "The mention of his very name makes my blood boil with indignation. Please, wrap it up and be gone. Good day to you."

The girl folded the sheet around me and bid farewell
to this most unusual scientist who favoured hatred over
curiosity. We made our way through town to the next appointment; Edith proved as persistent as Banks had commented, and resourceful as well. At our destination, I was
once again presented to a potential buyer. This time, the location was a main room inside a new museum on Piccadilly
called The Egyptian Hall. I found myself surrounded by
ancient symbols and artefacts representative of the Egyptian culture. Unintelligible hieroglyphs abounded on the
pilasters throughout the hall. An excited fellow with high
cheekbones and short curled hair peered into my eye sockets.

"Miss Hughes, welcome! I thank you for your visit,"
he said.

"And I thank you, Mr. Bullock. Your museum is absolutely brilliant! I have never seen such clever architec-

ture. The Egyptians present much to fascinate."

"Indeed, indeed. My entire collection is housed here. The artefacts you see around you represent only a portion, for aside from Egyptian pieces, I've acquired oddities from my extended travels through Central America, South America, Africa, the South Sea and other places around this wondrous and mysterious planet of ours. But perhaps, I dare say, none as spectacular as this vestige of the revolution, which you acquired right here in London. This head of Cromwell is a true gem."

Bullock brought back memories of Du Puy—a wealthier, more sophisticated Du Puy. He showed promise.

"It certainly is an intriguing curiosity, regardless of political opinions respecting Cromwell's character."

"Then you should like to purchase it?" Edith asked, pushing me a bit closer for Bullock's inspection.

"Indeed I should. But alas, I cannot. Goodness, no."

"Pray tell me why, Mr. Bullock!"

"Miss Hughes, I am honoured to have witnessed this skull with my own eyes, and I admit, I wished for nothing more in accepting your meeting. At your initial request, I shared the news with Lord Liverpool, who is intimately associated with the museum, and he regretfully declined to acquire the Lord Protector. Human remains of any gender or age are no longer to be exhibited within these walls or those of other museums. Had Cromwell been beheaded today, this rule would extend to his punishment as well—no heads upon spikes, not in today's learned world."

Edith's disappointment spread across her face like

emotional leprosy. I shared in her anguish and wondered
why this man called Liverpool determined it was not proper to display human remains in a museum. Was the human
body not God's greatest creation—His masterpiece—and
worthy of study, observation and appreciation by all? Was
it not blasphemy to worship artefacts created by men over
He who created Man? Bullock and his cohort Liverpool
would have a very quick change of opinion when death
brought their turn to rot in a grave, far away from the beau-
ties of this museum and the world that had helped fill it.

"I do thank you very much once again for sharing
him with me. It has been wholly satisfying. Just splendid!
Would you care for a tour of Egyptian artefacts or my Aztec display? Fascinating people, the Aztecs—very skilled
craftsmen. There's a thirty-foot-tall statue of a serpent you
simply must see. And if you should like, I also have fifteen
thousand species of quadrupeds, birds, reptiles, fishes, insects, shells and corals on view."

He could add another fifteen thousand, but no other
singular treasure could elevate the collection more than I.
Despite my disappointment with Bullock's rejection, I welcomed the opportunity for a tour, for unless the girl had
more appointments, we had nothing more to do but return
home. I had never travelled to the Egyptian or Aztec lands,
and unless my seller found a buyer there, a trip promised
to be unlikely.

"Mr. Bullock, I do appreciate the offer, but I must
decline," Edith said, clearly in no mood for a jaunt through
history. "I do wish you would reconsider, though. Perhaps

for your private collection?"

"I am afraid not. Lord Liverpool would have my head—though it would not qualify for an exhibit, either!" Bullock found himself quite whimsical.

Edith wrapped me up without feigning a smile, and we departed.

✳

I cannot be sure how much time passed since meeting with Banks and Bullock; one loses track of the days, hours and weeks quite quickly when wrapped in a black cloth with no sounds, save the occasional indifferent footsteps. It was only when a second pair of footsteps arrived that opportunity presented itself. Edith had taken ill and called for her doctor. Fortunately for me, medical men are an inquisitive sort by nature; that is what compels them to seek out cures for whatever ailments they encounter. It is also the very trait that forced this particular doctor to ask questions beyond those related to the lass's well-being.

"Edith, you must take care of yourself, especially during this time of mourning," the doctor said. "Your father, your uncles, they need you to be strong and carry on. They've no need for you to join them in Heaven just yet, my dear. Now then, I have with me several leeches—a dozen should suffice—imported directly from France to cure your discolouration and chest pains. Just remain still and relax while they sip away the blood."

"Oh, thank you, Dr. Wilkinson. You're very kind.

You've always been so good to my family."

"It's my pleasure, Edith. You will swoon in no time and I will remove them. Until then, I must ask, if I may, what ever became of that head of Oliver Cromwell your father tried to exhibit some years ago?"

"It remains in this house. Have you leeches for it? Can they suck evil from a dried-out skull? That head is likely the cause of my illness! Do you know it murdered my father and uncles? I'm certain it's after me now. I have tried desperately to sell it and must try again. My father always told me it had great value. It's rubbish to me, but I need the small fortune it should fetch, if it does not kill me first."

"Might I see it?" enquired Wilkinson.

"You might," said Edith. Her voice began to sound faint. "It is there, in the corner, wrapped in the sheet. I could no longer bear to look at it."

A moment later the doctor raised me off the ground and unfolded the sheet. He gave a thorough, studious look at my entire head, as if I were a patient and he were giving deep thought toward a diagnosis. His grip was firm, warm and purposeful. The distraction I created was disturbed only by the thump of Edith hitting the floor. The leeches had finished their work.

Wilkinson quickly set me down to attend to Edith. He deftly removed the well-fed parasites, placed them back in their ornate gilded jar, then lifted Edith and laid her upon her bed. While she lay recovering, the doctor once again focused his attention on me at her bedside. His fingers caressed my face, poking into my eye sockets, scratching my remaining bits of hair. He leaned in close to let his nose in on the examination; his deep whiffs around my head soaked in the unique scent of death spiced with the armour of embalming chemicals and the passing of time. He seemed to rather enjoy it.

When Edith awoke, she appeared groggy and weak.

"How are we feeling, my dear?" Wilkinson asked.

"Quite tired, and I still ache," she said.

"Give your humours time to find balance, by tomorrow you'll have your strength back."

Edith struggled to smile as her eyes shifted toward my head in the doctor's hand.

"Edith, if I may, I have one more thought which may offer healing," Wilkinson said.

"But of course. What is it?"

"This head. I believe it may heal you. I shall purchase it from you if you will allow it. It fascinates me as much as it angers you. And the transaction will relieve your anxiety surrounding it."

Edith smiled, effortlessly this time.

"Yes, yes, please!"

Wilkinson and Edith settled on a price of one hundred fifty pounds, which included the price of the leeches: a handsome profit for her, a bargain for him and renewed appreciation for me.

As an old friend of the family, I wondered if the physician had long awaited, and perhaps planned, this moment.

✳

Upon my arrival at Wilkinson's home I felt a sense of enthusiasm mixed with trepidation. The doctor, who still enjoyed the pleasure of youth, was a tall man who wore a chinstrap beard, perhaps to appear older and wiser, and was outfitted with a fresh waistcoat and exceptionally long breeches that reached directly to his feet. He beamed with passion for his purchase, meaning his intentions would be not to keep me a secret as Henry had done, but to share me generously with his family and friends, as Frederick had planned. But would they share in his elation, or banish me as the Russell family had?

Wilkinson called for his wife, son and daughter and introduced me, effusing with joy. To my surprise, their faces showed delight. I was welcome. This was home.

"Father, can I have it?" his son asked. The precocious boy reminded me of my Richard when he was ten years of age.

"Someday, William," the doctor answered. "For now, Oliver Cromwell belongs to me."

"Who was he? And why do you have his head?" His daughter showed a more pragmatic inclination.

"Yes, Josiah. You left with leeches and sucked a head off a corpse," his wife, called Jane, keenly noted. "Where exactly have you been?"

After a colourful explanation of Wilkinson's encounter with Edith satisfied his wife's enquiry, the doctor proved himself quite knowledgeable by enlightening his daughter with a response to her initial question. Unlike others who had claimed to tell my tale, Wilkinson went deep into my history, rather than beginning with my execution of Charles. A true scholar, he remembered my entry into politics as a Member of Parliament for Huntingdon in 1628, then for Cambridge in 1640. As he continued, he reminded me that we all live on through the memories others retain and pass along. Only the Lord above knows how long I shall continue to roam this world, but my prolonged physical presence is not my road to immortality; Wilkinson demonstrated that that path has already been paved. His son joined his attentive daughter as he continued the story. I, too, listened gladly.

"King Charles, may God bless his misguided soul, favoured himself over us, the good people of England. Taxes were levied wherever possible for his personal gain. He enforced old forgotten laws, such as the Distraint of Knighthood, which had been suspended for more than a century. It stated that any man who earned more than forty pounds a year from land must be knighted—and anyone who failed to appear for the ceremony was fined. Why, he even brought back the ancient Ship Tax, which was only meant to be collected under the threat of invasion to provide ships for combat. Even inland counties were forced to pay a tax on the Royal Navy. Those who protested the tax, citing its illegality, were fined, generating yet more money for the crown. He sought riches wherever they were to be found—even giving orders to rob Spanish treasure ships!

"The king also offended those who considered themselves religious—which were a great many. Though Protestant, he married Henrietta Maria of France—a Roman

Catholic. Oh, the people did not approve at all! The Puritans were especially angered, not just because the queen would be free to practice her religion, but also because the king began introducing rituals into the churches, then railed off the altars and put the ministers between the worshippers and God. It felt quite Roman Catholic! The conflicted king also sent ships with the initial plan to battle Louis the Thirteenth in his fight against the Huguenots, but then had a change of heart so as not to upset his wife, and instead ordered his men to fight alongside Louis against the French Protestants. It was a despicable act, and God Himself surely withheld His own strike against Charles.

"So Parliament fought to stop the king. In 1629, it made a peaceful attempt to correct his policies through three resolutions, the first of which condemned a change in the state religion—imagine that, a king with the power to overrule God. Secondly, it condemned any taxation levied without its authority, and finally, any merchant who paid illegal taxes would be a traitor to the liberty of England. But the tyrant adopted his father James' nonsensical belief that kings were 'little Gods on Earth,' and so he ignored the resolutions and wrongly arrested members of the Commons. The king imprisoned three of them and justified these proceedings by stating that 'Princes were not bound to give account of their actions, but to God alone.' Such a god was not the god the rest of England would abide by, and thanks to men like Oliver Cromwell, we did no such thing."

Truly there are many rewards in being a hero, but

hearing my tale passed on with such pride was among the finer ones. Be it known to all that the afterlife is undoubtedly enriched by the actions and deeds we perform during our time among the living.

"Tensions mounted between Charles and Parliament, leading to civil war in 1642," Wilkinson continued. "Conflict often brings out the best in men, it forces us to reach deep into our souls and tests our resolve, our mettle. Remember that, my children, hold tight to your spirit and it will guide you to victory. Your mind and heart are gifts from God—He has armed you with the greatest weapons needed to survive in life. Let Cromwell's head remind you of this, for despite his plumb lack of military involvement, he found a way to raise troops in the Cambridgeshire region and a cavalry in Huntingdon and devised a strategy to defeat the Royalist army."

"But Father, what then happened to his body?" his daughter asked.

"Patience Maria, you must allow me to finish the story."

"He can't have fought without a body!" William added with a chuckle. He thought himself quite clever, as children oft do.

"Hush now, William! Cromwell was a man who believed in the will of God and the power of an idea."

Wilkinson knew me well, for many an eve before battle I sought a moment of peace riding alone, smiling out to the Lord in praises, knowing He would assure victory.

"Our friend here shared a new notion with Parliament, a new kind of army, one that would be responsible for battle anywhere in the country as opposed to being tied to a specific area. Imagine ten cavalry regiments of six hundred men, twelve infantry regiments of twelve hundred men and a regiment of one thousand dragoons ready for battle at all times. Every soldier was disciplined—perfectly devoid of the temptations of drinking and gaming. They called it the New Model Army, and this head of ours was in charge as Lieutenant-General. By 1645, troops defeated the king's men at the great battle of Naseby and continued finding victory after victory, even after Charles fled and formed an alliance with the Scots."

It was none other than the hand of God that brought forth our success on the battlefield. After Naseby, we marched three thousand prisoners through the streets of London. A happy victory, indeed. The royalist newspaper, *Mercurius Aulicus*, was baffled by the defeat and in such a state of shambles it failed to publish an edition for weeks.

"Parliament and Cromwell triumphed, and finally Charles was put on trial to pay for his crimes."

Wilkinson spoke of the trial and justice brought forth by the executioner's cold steel blade. The climax to the story, naturally, was my rise to the position of Lord Protector.

"Royal blood does not make a leader, always remember that," he stressed.

The discussion of my reign eventually led to one of my death and exhumation, which at last satisfied the children's curiosity. Wilkinson, however, offered a curious tale about my body:

"Some believe a conspiracy was afoot and doubt that the body hanged at Tyburn was Cromwell's. The body was taken to the Red Lion Inn in Holborn, where it stayed for two days, during which time a switch may have taken place. Cromwell's body was wrapped in a cerecloth, so it could have been substituted with a fresh corpse. The gorget found upon his breast identifying him as Cromwell when he was disinterred could have easily been placed on the changeling. This, some believe, explains why Cromwell's body was described as being so fresh when it was hanged, when the real body should have been in far worse condition. If this were the case, then the body tossed away at Tyburn was not Cromwell's, and this is the head of some poor innocent wretch whose grave has been forever disturbed. Cromwell's body would have been buried at Holborn. If there be truth in this tale, and the family made such secretive arrangements, it explains why no descendants beyond Frederick and Samuel Russell ever laid claim to the head. Ah! 'Tis a load of hogwash if you ask me."

It could be nothing more. This notion of my family's silence intrigued me and offered a sorrowful reminder of how I am forever bound to ignorance, save for whatever enlightenment I can gather from those around me.

"A fine story, Father!" said William. "May I play with the head now?"

"Wait! This, you see, was but one claim!" Both of Wilkinson's eyebrows arched. "One of our great historians—John Oldmixon his name was—wrote of another possibility way back in 1730. He told the story of an old gentlewoman who attended Cromwell during his final sickness and stated that the day after his death there was much consultation on how to swiftly and safely dispose of his corpse. Those present wished to prevent any desecration that avenging Royalists might take—like plucking him from his grave and chopping his head away—by wrapping it in lead, placing it on a barge and sinking it in the greatest depths of the Thames. The woman claimed this occurred the night after, led by his closest, dearest relations and most trusted soldiers. Her tale, though, is the only evidence of such an event, so we shan't concern ourselves with it.

"Another theory says Cromwell's body was never at Westminster! There was a diarist at Tyburn—chap by the name of Samuel Pepys—who noted that during his lifetime, Cromwell transposed many bodies of kings from one grave to another, meaning, he believed, that it was possible the exhumed corpse was that of a king, not Cromwell. And *that*, children, would mean our head is that of a monarch!"

Pepys. I had no recollections of this madman, nor did I care for the ravings he had committed to paper. No king was placed in my vault before I took residence therein, nor did I leave instruction for anyone to swap my carcass for that of a tyrant's. As for this gentlewoman, hysteria is a likely culprit for her fabrications. Several good women offered care during my final days, but I agreed to no such underwater horrors.

"So, Father, is this Oliver's head or not?" Maria asked anxiously.

"I believe it to be," Wilkinson answered. "But I will

make enquiries to be certain. Now, run and play—but William, please, not with the head. Cromwell is our guest and you will treat him with respect."

Just as the doctor had done for my life, he now placed my head on a pedestal—one built of polished red oak, four feet high. I was set in a snug silk-lined oak box to complete the presentation. Appropriately, I was positioned at the head of the chamber, which was otherwise filled with an abundance of complementary furniture and an arrangement of panels and shelves supporting knickknacks, such as petite porcelain figures of children holding mandolins, tambourines and flowers, along with novelty taxidermy items, including a ferret adorned in a hat and spotted dress. Perhaps these amused the youngsters. Gaudy pomegranate-patterned paper coated the walls. The styling indicated the doctor was a man of wealth and rather particular taste. The many mahogany armchairs and the two burgundy buttoned-leather settees, however, should have been turned in my direction, allowing all to comfortably sit before me.

✷

John Flaxman declared himself an expert on me. I failed to understand how this guest of Wilkinson's could be so bold. After all, death claimed my body a hundred years, if not more, before he was born—what wisdom could he possibly profess? Regardless of his true knowledge, the doctor's efforts to confirm my authenticity were praiseworthy. Wilkinson chatted gleefully about me, but Flaxman showed tremendous audacity in expressing skepticism.

"Mr. Flaxman, I respect your opinion, which is why I have extended this invitation to you," Wilkinson said with an air of confidence, for he hoped this foolishness his guest spewed would soon be dutifully retracted. "I do very much admire your work and the manner in which you capture the likenesses of men. I've not seen a sculptor equal your abilities. So I ask of you, kindly do me this small favour: Tell me how you would describe Cromwell's face. Impart your knowledge, then examine the head in my possession and see for yourself if it meets your vision."

"Very well, Dr. Wilkinson, very well," said Flaxman. His voice had a tinge of defeat, a note of acquiescence that obliged the request simply to prove his point. "Oliver Cromwell had a low, broad forehead, large orbits to the eyes, a high septum to the nose and high cheekbones. But there is one feature which will be with me a crucial test, and that is that instead of having the lower jawbone somewhat curved, it was particularly short and straight, but set out at an angle, which gave him a jowlish appearance."

Admittedly, this sculptor had researched me with admirable vigour; his description was akin to one perhaps only my mother would have been keen enough to provide.

Wilkinson led Flaxman through his festooned living chambers to my display for the much-anticipated comparison. It took no more than a single glance for the sculptor to recognise my visage as that he had just so aptly described. A smile crept across his face, wiping away all doubt. His sinewy fingers gingerly caressed my skull, as if his mind needed the physical confirmation to appease its disbelief.

"Dr. Wilkinson, I must say, I am indeed quite satisfied. As you believe, I believe. This could be none other than the Lord Protector. Is it, dare I ask, for sale?"

The doctor was in no need of money, though verification from Flaxman made him feel profusely richer.

In the nights and days that followed, Wilkinson entertained friends and neighbours, revelling in the joys of being host to such a marvel. Frequent dinner parties and merrymaking revolved around discussions of and gawking at my head, along with the occasional debates over King George's sanity, which was apparently fading quickly in his old age.[2] (I questioned whether it was ever present to begin with, but alas, I had no say in the discussions.) Wilkinson spoke so passionately about me that it became infectious; friends told friends, and they wanted to see me for themselves. William and Maria, too, took pleasure in frolicking near me and at times included me in their imaginative play, though minding their father and never laying a finger upon me. I was grateful for their enthusiasm and respect; someday they, too, might surround me with curious acquaintances in their own homes. This was quite preferable to Edith's disdain.

Wilkinson's felicity fuelled an appetite to discover my posthumous history, which led to a surprise visit one afternoon from John Cranch. The doctor had entreated him for knowledge, which Cranch viewed as a profitable opportunity. It was he who held possession of the contract between Samuel Russell and James Cox, and it was now for sale. After a short conversation, Cranch leered at me when Wilkinson declined to purchase the parchment, as if I had once again stymied his designs for a taste of prosperity.

At times, the entire family gathered round to read the latest printed stories aloud; I began to feel much like Uncle Oliver rather than a foul severed head. One popular new tale, in particular, created quite a stir in its thoughts and ideas for all of us: *Frankenstein; or, The Modern Prometheus.* Its main character, a Dr. Victor Frankenstein, created a monster from the bits and pieces of deceased men. "After days and nights of incredible labour and fatigue, I succeeded in discovering the cause of generation and life," the character states early in the book. "Nay, more, I became myself capable of bestowing animation upon lifeless matter."

This notion had its origins in the laboratories of prodigious thinkers; ideas are all linked, they do not spawn from nothingness. Early in the story, during his time of study and research, Dr. Frankenstein mentions his need to read the works of the notorious occultist Paracelsus. I recalled tales of this so-called physician, whose demise occurred just a half-century before my birth.[3] His real name always challenged my tongue: Philippus Aureolus Theophrastus Bombastus von Hohenheim; most people remembered him more succinctly as the Devil's Doctor because they believed he sold his soul to Lucifer in exchange for a wealth of unholy knowledge. But those who did were but jealous fools angered by his intellect and enraged at their own ignorance. Paracelsus looked up to God for inspiration. When he sought to transmutate lead into gold, he argued against naysayers by questioning their own belief system:

> Some will say this is pagan or superstitious and witch-craft. As though conjuring could achieve anything! They ask how metals, in conjunction with characters and formulas, might have such power if not through the Devil? To such skeptics I say: My friend, can't you believe that the Lord is powerful enough to give such virtues to roots, metals, stones and herbs? Dare you say that the Devil is more artful than God?

This Dr. Frankenstein character studied Paracelsus primarily for his belief in the homunculus—a small man that could be brought to life through what I always considered the absurdity of magic, not nature, as he posited. Paracelsus had concocted a formula requiring the sperm of a man that was to be putrefied by itself in a sealed cucurbit for some forty days, until it came to life. At this point, the homunculus would take the shape of a man, though transparent and lacking a body until it was fed with an elixir of human blood, and so nourished for the length of forty weeks whilst kept in the warmth of horse manure. Thence a human child grew—one who could be educated and obtain reason like any other. Success, of course, remained elusive, unless Paracelsus described a pile of reeking, viscous filth after nearly a year's work a satisfactory achievement.

But *Frankenstein*'s author, an unknown scribe, surely drew inspiration from more than Paracelsus and his occultist contemporaries.[4] Science had presumably evolved to a most impressive state over the past century and a half. If this was as I suspected, I feared our most learned men were doing God's work without His consent, dangerously overstepping the boundaries of our terrestrial domain and tempting His immeasurable wrath. Punishment would be swift and fierce, perhaps applying to the story's author as well. Or, contrarily, if Man could renew life where it had been lost, had we become angels of God? Had the Blessed Almighty, in fact, allowed for such discoveries to create new hope for me? The wonders of the natural sciences very well might proffer me a new pulse as Cox's automated limbs artificially had.

When I considered this possibility, I recalled the philosophical writings of one of the more intelligent Frenchmen of my time, René Descartes, who gained a measure of renown for, among other cogitations, proposing the mind-body dichotomy. In his words, "*Cogito ergo sum.*"[5] My body is long gone, yet I continue to think; I exist. I am proof of his theory, which he assuredly discovered for himself upon his own death. Oh, I cannot conceive of the torture that poor, trapped soul has since endured and thenceforth will face for eternity. The nature of this afterlife has been most unexpected, and though fortunate in the circumstances that have given me much to appreciate, I had in life expected to be with God after death. Death, however, is a mystery to all who live, so why should it not be a mystery to those who die? Is it possible that a meeting with the Almighty still awaits? I have made the bold assumption that this afterlife is all there is, but perhaps this conclusion is erroneous; this afterlife may, like life, be limited in nature and eventually lead to a third phase in God's Kingdom. Certainly this opportunity to eventually reach Heaven would bring great relief to those many souls imprisoned in graves; those designated for Hell I truly pity, for I could imagine nothing worse than the suffering all dead currently withstand.

For now, I could only wait and wonder what would come of me. Should a real Dr. Frankenstein take hold of my head, would I be less like Cox's creation and more akin to the book's monster—a part of a whole—married to the limbs and organs of others, with another's brain fitted within my cranium to form some scandalous, unholy beast? And just how would my soul connect with that strange, damp brain? Would other souls be present in the gathered parts, and if so, how could they co-exist? Descartes had not explored the concept of minds merging with new bodies, at least not whilst his own body lived.

As *Frankenstein* progressed, the monster faced much animosity and experienced extraordinary grief. I supposed this was to be expected and would be no different for me, should it come to pass that I, too, took on such a state.

At times I envied the children, who listened carefully to each word, yet returned to their Bilbo catchers, quoits games and dolls once Wilkinson closed the pages of the book.[6] I had no other such distractions. Not until a letter arrived from Edinburgh, sent by another doctor, who had been busily cutting up fresh corpses in a classroom, that is.

XI

CURIOUS ENCOUNTERS

———

Dr. Robert Knox was, according to his letter, a Fellow of the Royal Society of Edinburgh and an eminent anatomist and lecturer from Surgeons' Square at the anatomy school. His courses included a full demonstration on fresh anatomical subjects to study the structure of the human body and a history of its various parts. Word of my head under Wilkinson's possession reached Knox and piqued his interest, despite the obvious fact that I was hardly a "fresh" subject. The doctor, however, found potential for other learnings, as he stated in his note:

> I beseech you, Mr. Wilkinson, as a fellow practitioner of the medicinal trade, to take journey to Edinburgh with the full head of Oliver Cromwell and allow me the privilege of a comprehensive

examination of the specimen. It is my earnest belief and immeasurable desire to discover the extended effects of embalming and time on the human skull; whence I may compare the Lord Protector's skull to that of a freshly acquired skull, and that the scientific community may uncover further secrets therein and celebrate new knowledge furthering the subdiscipline of osteology. On behalf of Surgeons' Square, I am pleased to offer a fee of £5 for this honour; in addition, arrangements shall be made for your living quarters, which I assure you will be most acceptable.

The anatomist is an inimitable creature. Since before my own time anatomists have been known to work surreptitiously with villainous gangs of grave robbers to retrieve subjects for study. These men, whose trade lent them the name "resurrectionists," worked in the dead of night, when the moon was but a sliver, silently digging with an array of wooden tools to avoid the lurid clank of iron on stone. A canvas laid next to the grave received the soil and preserved the uniformity of the grass. Once the coffin was reached, these ghouls would affix iron hooks to the lid and pry it off. Bodies were stripped of their burial clothing (as if not pilfering that with which they were interred offered an ounce of respect) and put into a sack. With the dirt neatly replaced, the miscreants sneaked away quietly to avoid any attention in those wee hours and to reap their reward from the anxiously awaiting physician.

Wealthy families feared this fate for their deceased loved ones; no privileged husband, wife or child was to be launched into eternity only to be disturbed by heathens and destroyed by scalpels. This created a market for ghoul-proof coffins—thick and secured with heavy stone slabs—and left the poor more vulnerable and even more miserable. Yet as the rich lay rotting in their safe stone-lined coffins, their confined souls assuredly prayed not to God but to some form of ghoul to release them, whilst the souls of the poor likely rejoiced at those initial glimmering rays of moonlight until they witnessed their bodies being ravaged in public, then buried again, shredded and mangled in a rubbish heap.

The bastards forming these resurrectionist gangs oft resorted to violence to defend their territories and operate as monopolies in any given area, for any given anatomist. Should an entrepreneurial scoundrel seek entry into the field, he was beaten to the point where he could no longer dig up a body, but might instead offer himself as a perfectly fresh corpse. Any anatomist seeking a better price from competing gangs also risked an early trip to a colleague's dissection table.

Executed criminals constituted the only alternative, as their bodies were made available for study as soon as the ropes were cut. Henry VIII granted the Company of Barber-Surgeons access to four such felons a year, but this hardly proved enough.[1]

The term "resurrectionist" always warranted a negative connotation, which indeed matched the character of the pitiful lowlifes who engaged in the activity. Yet had they acted with more noble intentions that sought to do what the term suggested—resurrect—these men would have provided an afterlife for the soul amongst light and life. In a sense, they would offer that which man has sought since Adam discovered the silent body of Abel—a cure for the dead.

Earlier in these pages I suggested the dead be kept with loved ones or posted in public to forever bask in the wonders of nature and Man's creations therein, realising, of course, the hopelessness of such change. As my thoughts turned to the notion of resurrecting bodies to free souls from the earth's darkness, I contemplated a new, more rational idea that might please the living. Rather than bury our dead six feet beneath the surface, graveyards and cemeteries shall be inverted; bodies will instead lie six feet *above* the ground, placed in caskets of glass. Such elevated coffins would welcome the sunlight and catch the twinkle of a midnight star—all whilst staying perched above the sight of average men. It is with sincere hope that those who read these words will one day incite this revolution and end the tyranny of the subterranean tomb. Even in death, one must dream.

Dr. Knox was not a man whose acquaintance I wished to make. Wilkinson, though, spent far less time considering the matter.

"My dear, Oliver and I are off to Edinburgh!" he announced to his wife, barely finishing reading Knox's letter. Any opportunity to dote upon me could not be denied; his affection for me grew with each day. "Have we biscuits, cheese and meat pudding to pack? 'Tis a long journey ahead!"

I had not peregrinated to Edinburgh since 1650, when the Scots pledged allegiance to Charles II and my men and I paid a visit to help them reconsider. We made bit of a shambles at the Palace of Holyrood by lighting its eastern range afire, but I later instructed Sir William Bruce to draw up plans for a new design. I hoped Wilkinson would find time for a visit, as the project surely had long been completed and I would be pleased to see Bruce's results.

✳

Two and a half days aboard a two-horse-drawn carriage to Edinburgh offered a plethora of bumps within my silk-lined box, but fortunately the top was left open, affording me a refresher in the Lord's majesty. For without the Almighty's artistry painting the landscape with golden fields of ripened wheat, autumn colours gracing the trees and floral delectations to complement the magnificent blue sky, I would have been left only with Wilkinson's dreadful songs as entertainment.

When we arrived at No. 10 Surgeons' Square, Dr. Knox had just completed an afternoon lecture. Hundreds of students abuzz with their newly gained knowledge of practical medicine, organ functions and surgery made their way out of the classroom into the thick, foggy air. In my school days I had never witnessed such a popular course, for the room could scarcely hold two hundred students, but easily double that had filled its steeply ascending rows of seats.

"Good afternoon, Dr. Wilkinson, I presume?" Knox said.

"Indeed! A pleasure to meet you, Dr. Knox! Many thanks for your letter and thoughtful invitation."

"Yes, of course. Though I expected you sooner."

"Pardon?"

"I expected an immediate visit, Dr. Wilkinson. It is not often one receives a note from a Fellow of the Royal Society, after all, is it?"

The anatomist may have excelled at his craft, but he was hardly the affable type.

"Dr. Knox, I assure you, we left shortly after receiving your letter."

"Very well. You brought the head, then?"

"Why, yes, but of course," Wilkinson said as he pulled me from the confines of my box. Knox greeted me with a slight grin and a piercing stare through his wiry spectacles. Aside from a bald head, with scraggly, unkempt hairs lining its circumference at the rear, he appeared youthful, though unattractive. A periwig would have served him well.

"May I?" he said with an extended hand eager to receive me.

"Yes, yes, I travelled many miles so that you may," Wilkinson said. "The Cromwell head stayed right at my—"

"It is extraordinary," Knox interrupted. He grabbed hold of me and turned away, caring not at all for Wilkinson's travel anecdotes. Friendships clearly lacked the importance of studies. He walked me over to the centre of his classroom and sat me upon his dissection table. Quick flicks of his finger scattered away excess entrails and viscera from his earlier lecture, yet the dark wooden table remained damp with the fluids of his most recent subject. I suppose the surface had once been much lighter in colour.

"Indeed, which is why, as I was saying—"

"Dr. Wilkinson, what you were saying is of little consequence," Knox quickly informed us, disrupting Wilkinson's line of thinking once again. "The important matter here is the preservation of this remarkable head and what osteological learnings are to be discovered. I'm indeed fascinated about how it has retained its character thus far and how it shall continue to do so."

Knox wasted no more time with superfluous chatter. His industrious fingers set out to survey the topography of my head by stroking my skull, fondling my flakes and gently combing his nails through my lonely hairs. His calculated touch had me wishing for the softer, more sensuous affections of my long-lost Elizabeth. The caress of a curious man, though, was Fate's desire. Wilkinson stood quietly and kept a watchful eye on Knox, which brought me comfort. Wilkinson's soul shone with goodness, whereas Knox gave every appearance of having ice course through his veins.

Afternoon acquiesced to the shadows of twilight and the darkness of night. Under the illumination of candlelight, Knox hastily scribbled pages of notes and sketches in his journal as he thoroughly examined every surface of my being. Wilkinson patiently looked on. The lecture hall was silent, save for the scratches of pen striking paper, the whistles of the blowing wind and Wilkinson's occasional yawn. The sudden creaking of a door, accompanied by footsteps, disturbed this peace. Wilkinson jumped, snapping out of his near slumber, whereas Knox remained calm, as though intruders were expected.

Two men entered the hall from a tunnel, struggling to carry an old dirty tea chest.

"'Ello Doctor! Got 'nother for ya! Quite fresh she is!" said one of the men. He was a squalid little wretch, not more than five and a half feet in stature, round-bodied, with hard, fiendish eyes and a truculent smile.

"Quite fresh, indeed! 'Ave a look, then. Well worth the ten pounds, I reckon," said the other fellow. He was taller and bonier than his companion, with dull blackish eyes set wide apart, sunken cheeks and a thin-lipped mouth, all of which shrouded him in misery.

They gently lowered the chest to the ground as Knox approached them with brisk, purposeful steps. The shorter man scurried to open the crate, looking entirely pleased with his offering.

"Yes, yes, she will do just fine." Knox noted with pleasure. "You lads have had good fortune in finding such superb bodies."

"Not dead more 'n a few hours I'd s'pose," said the bony man.

"Could be less—even less than a few hours!" his

partner added merrily.

"Mmm. Yes, perhaps." Knox reached into a pocket and handed over their payment. "Bring more as opportunity allows it. Now be gone, quickly."

The ghoulish pair grinned at the glimmer of their profits and scampered away, like rats back to a hole. Did Knox have resurrectionists working on a daily basis? The corpse was, as they had promised, remarkably fresh. The girl was perhaps no more than eighteen years of age, finely proportioned. She arroused Wilkinson's interest and he joined Knox near the voluptuous body for a cursory examination. The anatomist was caressing her curves, as he had my skull, but perhaps with different intentions.

"She's quite young. No signs of trauma. Strange, the body is cool, but not even stiff or emitting an odour yet," Wilkinson remarked.

"Yes. She will be put to good use, this I assure you," Knox responded.

"Did the men say how the lass died? Had she been ill?"

"No, they never say. They never know a thing—except that a body's life has expired. And that they should deliver that body to me. Sometimes, my friend, the things I do not know are just as valuable as that which I do know."

"I see," Wilkinson said. "These bodies arrive on a frequent basis, then?"

"Dr. Wilkinson, you were invited so that I might ask the questions," Knox responded tersely, refusing to look him in the eye throughout the brief discourse.

"Perhaps I shall direct my questions to the men whose services enable your lectures," Wilkinson said with a deserved note of irritation. "I do imagine they would gladly accept additional payment for a few simple answers, would you not agree?"

Knox sighed. "Let us retire for the evening."

If Wilkinson was not to ask questions, I certainly could. The girl had so recently passed into the realm of death that I believe I quite startled her with my initial contact.

"What happened to you?" I asked. "And do you know why you're here?"

"I, I don't know," she answered. "Who are you? Where are you?"

"I am here—the embalmed head upon the stained table. I am Oliver Cromwell, Lord Protector of the Commonwealth of England, Scotland and Ireland."

"What mean you by an embalmed head? Take me for a fool, do you?"

"Look at me," I said.

"I'm still drunk is all!"

"Tell me, what happened to you today?" I asked again.

"Very well, Lord Cromwell, very well. First, you oughta know me name is Mary Paterson. I s'pose it was foolish, but this morning me girlfriend and I was out looking for a drink. We came into William Swanston's spirit shop and purchased a gill of whiskey. As we sipped, a fella approached us, William Burke he called himself.[2] Friendly little man he was, full of conversation. Kept filling our glasses and adding gills of rum and bitters till me eyes grew tired and I wished to sleep. He told me his place was right nearby and we could head off there straight away. Me friend declined, but I thought him a nice enough chap so I went. A dark, uneven staircase led up to his home, which was but a single poorly furnished room. A truckle bed sat before a window with tattered curtains. Crude pictures adorned bare, ugly walls. I expected more, for William seemed a man of greater means. Another woman was home and makin' a fuss, maybe his wife, but I cared little about it. I just lied down on the mattress and fell into a slumber. Some time later, I felt pressure on me mouth and throat, which woke me, but then I fell right back asleep. Now here I am. D'ya know what this place is? Where are me clothes? I'm so cold! And who are these bloody old buggers starin' at 'n' touchin' me bristols?"

"The hairless gentleman is Dr. Knox and the one wearing the face of concern is Dr. Wilkinson," I said.

"Am I sick, then? What are they to do with me?"

With hesitation, I answered, "I do not know."

Knox began to pour whiskey into the crate, presumably for its preservation qualities.[3]

"But know this, Mary Paterson," I added, as alcohol drowned her lifeless body. "God is with you."

As Wilkinson saved me from this lecture hall of horrors, Knox looked up and made one final request for the evening: "Join me for tomorrow's lecture. You shall see what necessitates bodies such as this one. I also wish to spend one more evening with Lord Cromwell before you make your return home. For this I would be grateful."

Wilkinson and I left the anatomist to Miss Paterson.

The next morning, Wilkinson paid a visit to the nearest constable to share what we had witnessed. He needn't have heard Mary's story to suspect how the two men had acquired such a fresh specimen. The constable nodded along but informed Wilkinson of Dr. Knox's respected reputation and Mary Paterson's troubled ways. She had, we learned, spent a previous night detained in the watch-house. Her death, the officer believed, was not terribly surprising. Burke and his diabolical friend had outdone the resurrectionists; they produced their own cadavers rather than going to the trouble of digging them up. Wilkinson had seen enough and determined that Knox had as well, and thus there were two fewer heads than expected at the day's lecture. Our journey home began. To my dismay, the Palace of Holyrood was not on the itinerary.

※

Incorrigible bumps and joggles along our return to London had me fearing that part of my skull would splinter and fall away. I would appear as if I had been poorly trepanned, like some hapless sufferer of seizures or mental illness. At least I am dead—I remain perplexed about the reasons one would allow, nay, desire, a trephine to bore a hole into the skull whilst one was still breathing.

After several long days, the mighty hand of the

Lord led us home safely, both of us fully intact. Jane and the children were eager to hear of our experiences, which Wilkinson shared with discretion. No further letters from Dr. Knox were received in the weeks and months that followed.

My dominant position within the living chambers remained unchanged as the years went by. Maria and William were growing at a rapid rate, as children do; life surged through them, leaving a trail of radiant smiles on glowing faces. They reminded me of my own brood—those who survived me—who have each retained their beauty and youth in my memory, but as I considered the time that had passed, I envisioned them ageing through the decades into their elder years and grew dismayed at the thought of them each buried in a box, eaten away by parasites and reduced to mere bones. Maria and William, so full of life now, would soon enough be two more buried skeletons as I continued to exist, always observing the next generation.

Wilkinson worked diligently to write my tale, but unlike Cranch, he put care into his words and studies to preserve it with eloquence and corroboration to support my authenticity. Friends and neighbors continued to visit for a glimpse of me. Wilkinson even invited the occasional patient to gaze upon me as a distraction from his illness, as if I possessed some sort of mystical healing power. I witnessed no proof of my effectiveness; the treatment was more likely another excuse to flaunt my splendour.

By all accounts gathered from those around me, it was the year of Our Lord 1838 when the therapeutic qualities

Wilkinson believed I held failed us most, for the doctor had grown ill himself and I was powerless to aid him. Though my faith in the Creator was unwavering, I struggled to understand why He had chosen to take Wilkinson now. What services could a physician offer the soil?

My sadness was mitigated only by William's inheritance of me and his shared passion for my existence. He, too, enjoyed exhibiting me to intrigued parties and discussing the unusual path I had taken. His interests, beyond me, weighed heavily in the sciences, particularly in recent inventions and new methods of understanding the human character. In regard to the former, William was especially smitten by an apparatus called the telegraph, devised by a clever American.[4] He raved about its ability to send messages through wires, though I understood not how this miracle was made possible without the guidance of an angel. Just as my ideas furthered military tactics, the ideas of others enhanced communication tactics, which could in turn strengthen the New Model Army through heightened efficiencies. As for my pacifist owner, he made frequent use of the device by speedily tapping out messages, probably with the intent to extend invitations to visit me.

A new branch of study, palaeontology, also drew occasional interest. British men of science had uncovered wonderfully large bones from the depths of the earth and initially believed they belonged to an ancient race of giants, but as more specimens were found, it seemed they had no relation to any living creatures, though they did appear to resemble members of the reptilian family. William referred to this group as "Dinosauria" and spoke of it frequently to whoever would listen. An arresting find, indeed, but I heard nothing in regard to the nature of these creatures' appearance, their absence from the Bible, or why they no longer roamed the earth. The latter concern, perhaps, is best explained through Noah, for if he had not room for such colossal creatures upon the ark, they would have perished in the flood. But why would God have created Dinosauria only to allow their extinction? I would have very much liked such a beast at my side; its massive jaws could surely have devoured my enemies.

Palaeontology and the telegraph were fascinating, but it was a very different science that found itself drawn to me. William called it phrenology.

Frequent phrenological discussions between William and his companions proffered entertainment on many days and evenings. This newfound science, as it was revealed to me, purported to explain the intellectual and moral character of a man through the special elevations and depressions of the cranium, formed by the physiology of the brain. The brain is the organ of the mind, and each faculty of the mind has its own special organ in the brain. These faculties, they claimed, could be improved by cultivation and deteriorated through neglect.

The amateur but enthusiastic phrenologists ofttimes gathered round measuring and fondling one another's heads for rudimentary examinations and readings. There was much conjecture surrounding the form of their skulls and the girth of the cerebrum and cerebellum, all of which led to beliefs of individual characteristics involving Amativeness, Inhabitiveness, Adhesiveness, Philoprogenitiveness, Benevolence, Veneration, Mirthfulness, Ideality, Conscientiousness, Alimentiveness and other simple traits described in excessively long words. William received high marks in the Benevolence, Wonder and Acquisitiveness categories. The Lord did not grant me the gifts of scientific cogitation, but as I observed these phrenological follies I questioned the accuracy of their methods. I reckoned the only certain outcome of the readings was a well-massaged scalp.

As a head of inordinate historical significance, I offered great stimulation for these budding scientists. As with the anatomists, most skulls provided to the phrenologists were those of executed criminals. The intellectual and moral characters of such scoundrels were generally known and accepted, but, the phrenologists wondered, how did my skull differ? The head of a religious man, a faithful man, a man of conviction and power was a prize to be rejoiced. William employed an entrepreneurial spirit and offered a local and supposedly respectable professional phrenologist, Cornelius Donovan, the chance to perform a reading on me for a small fee.[5] In so doing, he would not only profit, but also theoretically offer further evidence and advance the science.

Donovan demonstrated no hesitation in accepting the offer, and so a glorious summer day found us travelling to his office in the Strand. As our carriage made its way under the blue sky into the City of Westminster, William clutched

the great Oliver Cromwell?"

"I am. And who, pray tell me, are you?"

"Why, I am Franz Joseph Haydn."

"I do not know this name. When did you die? What measure of fame are you known for?"

"My death was in May of 1809," he said. "I am an Austrian composer. A rather successful one. The Esterhazy family, one of the wealthiest and most powerful in all of Austria, employed me for more than thirty years as their composer and musician."

"And by what good fortune did you find yourself salvaged from the grave?" I asked.

"Good fortune, perhaps. But reprehensible intentions," Haydn responded. "I owe this peculiar existence to a young man whom I considered a marvelous friend, Joseph Carl Rosenbaum. He was an accountant for the Esterhazys and offered his services to me as well, along with pleasant companionship. His wife, Theresa, had the voice of an angel—it was the finest in all of Austria. Joseph was a predecessor to this Donovan quack. He fancied himself a pioneer in phrenology—with me to thank."

"How so?" I asked as Donovan continued his jabbering to William about the summitary curve and roundness of my head.

"After my death I lay in my coffin, resting in pure silence. The funeral had been small. An extravagant service could not be arranged while my country was under siege by Napoleon. There, nestled away in the darkness, I reflected on my many gifts to world: symphonies, string quartets, music that stirred the soul, all playing silently within this skull. Then, several nights after my interment, came noise. Though it was nothing more than the sounds of tools breaking into my casket, each strike resonated like a wondrous instrument: the gravediggers' concerto. A wretched little man took his blade and struck my stiff, lifeless neck, stabbing and sawing rhythmically, releasing my vile stink as he worked tirelessly. His ability to remain undaunted during the process indicated that he had experience in this lowly line of business. I watched helplessly, unable to offer any resistance as he yanked and pulled at my head to finish the task. His face of determination shifted to one of victorious relief as he replaced the lid and soil and wrapped my decomposing dome in a sheet. Shortly after, to my surprise, I heard Rosenbaum's voice. He had come to collect me and sounded quite pleased to do so. As he escaped the cemetery in his carriage under the black sky, he opened the sheet to ensure that it was I. The stench of my rotting, shredded flesh overpowered him and caused him to vomit into my face. If possible, I would have done the same to him for these actions.

"The carriage delivered me to a group of doctors who accelerated the decomposition process by extracting my decaying brain—it lay beside me, the engine of all my achievements, pulverised by their pointy instruments— and boiling my head to cleanse away my flesh with chemicals until I became the immaculate skull you see before you. This misery lasted for an hour's time. All this, so he and his cohorts could rub their fingers over my head and map out what they believed were the grooves of my genius. Do not let Donovan or his peers subject you to the chemical treatments—for even after all these years you still have hairs upon your head. Men alive today are less fortunate with their follicles."

"The Lord has blessed me in all manners," I said. "Please, continue."

"But of course, my embalmed friend! After the phrenologists had their ways with me, Theresa displayed me in her home and paraded me amongst her socialite companions as she hosted soirées. I believe she and Joseph prized my head more than my music. I had become something greater than a departed friend—I was her trophy."

"I, too, have been treated as such," I interjected. "Our owners are quite proud of their acquisitions. It is as if they can achieve our level of virtuosity simply by association."

"Oh yes, yes. Now, years later," Haydn explained, "after the war, Prince Esterhazy exhumed my body to offer me a more ceremonious funeral. When I was discovered headless, the prince was outraged and set off to find me. Although reports led him to Rosenbaum's house, the clever accountant proved too shrewd and had Theresa hide me under the bedsheets with her. I had, at one time, imagined myself in such an erogenous position with her, but never in this manner. The police dared not peek under the sheets where a lady lay. And so I remained with the Rosenbaums. My only joy within my casing was the sweet sound of Theresa's singing, which was all too frequently interrupted by the banalities of her conversations with Joseph. At their eventual deaths, I was bequeathed to an accomplice, Johann Peter, who also wasted his intellect through phrenology. Though I have heard more readings than perhaps any head, alive or dead, I still fail to understand its usefulness and objectivity, and see in it only one trait which they've mapped to a small region of the cranium: Mirthfulness.

"I eventually was received by the Austrian Institute of Pathology and Anatomy. It is that organisation that has allowed Donovan to study me for what has been a prolonged examination. And so I sit. I marvel at the world evolving around me—for both its achievements and its stupidity. But alas, I have been nearly as garrulous as Donovan. I know of your legacy, Lord Protector, and what Charles II did to you. That iron spike looks terribly painful. Perhaps I shall give count to my blessings. Oh, my apologies, let us not discuss your discomfort. Tell me of your journeys since being freed from Westminster. And what advice do you have for a young severed head like myself?"

I obliged, sharing my experiences, struggles and beliefs surrounding our state of existence. Donovan was polite enough to continue discussing such matters as the development of my perceptive regions and the integuments over my superciliary ridge, which afforded me the opportunity to complete my tale for Haydn and expand our conversation into future events. As we delighted in our time together, we imagined the possibilities of gathering other renowned heads—with or without body—to form our own Society for the Betterment of the Afterlife, in which we would all share ideas, stories, hopes, dreams, miseries. Since we possessed no means to organise, the society might be left to men like Donovan, seeking out heads like us, to unknowingly arrange. Haydn expressed interest in reuniting with Mozart, the fellow who had created wonders on the piano before George and Charlotte. Haydn had learned much from this master. He also desired a meeting with one of his talented young students, Ludwig van Beethoven, who had died several years earlier, he had heard. Our futile plans were soon foiled as the phrenologist neared the end of his exploration:

"That he was a man of strong social, self-regarding moral and religious feelings, such an organisation places beyond a doubt. But the scientific observer does not find that elevation of the region over the organ of Comparison, which would encourage the hope that Cromwell's was a mind which could sympathise deeply with the afflictions of his fellow creatures. These broad and strongly formed heads are rarely found with very benevolent dispositions, however capable those endued with such organisations may be of performing acts of kindness to friends, or to those whom they make use of."

Donovan took a breath, at last.

"William, in this present reading, I have merely sought to bring whatever knowledge I have been able to acquire of the laws of cerebral organisation to bear upon the subject, in order to test the pretensions of this head to stand accepted as that of so very remarkable a man. I am most gracious for the opportunity you have provided me."

"This has been most enlightening," William said, brimming with admiration. He was much like a student smitten by his professor's brilliance. "Thank you, Dr. Donovan, thank you. Your work confirms for me the studies my father conducted and the opinions he gathered regarding the head's authenticity."

This proof that William enjoyed, though welcomed, was at its core quite flawed. If William had presented another embalmed skull with a spike in it belonging to another poor soul, and introduced it as me, would the phrenologist have given the same reading? For this gentlemen knew my traits well, so it would be a simple task to ascribe my characteristics to whatever terrain the cranium offered. To discover whether he would have offered such a reading or quickly identified the skull as an impostor would have meant successfully determining the authenticity of the phrenologist. And this, I believe, would have offered greater value to the world.

As William continued to thank Donovan and delivered a superfluous valediction, I bade Haydn farewell and gave prayer to the Lord for both him and me: that the composer should never reunite with his ravaged buried body, and that I should be forever grateful to experience a symphony.

XII

LETTERS AND SPEECHES

———

D r. Knox, Cornelius Donovan and William's friends
and neighbors received me enthusiastically, but
I felt certain that this small group were the indi-
viduals most intrigued by me. The world was moving forward, and my mark in history had settled into its place; it
was no longer a fresh memory for the people of the Commonwealth. Oliver Cromwell had become news of the old.
However, in the year of Our Lord 1845, that changed considerably. My extraordinary lore hastily made its return to
the forefront of the masses with the publication of *Oliver
Cromwell's Letters and Speeches: With Elucidations*, by
Thomas Carlyle. This Carlyle had acquired an astounding
collection of my most eloquent pronouncements and correspondences. The elucidations, I can only assume, were
necessitated by the gradual deterioration of the English

language. Over the centuries, proper manners of speaking have declined, hence my use of formal language challenges the untrained mind. I dread what I shall have to endure in the latter years of the millennium.

As my guardian, William had grown into an avid collector of Cromwelliana (having managed to acquire a plaster copy of my death mask and a few coins from my Protectorship) and he wasted little time in purchasing Carlyle's work. He read select letters and proclamations whilst company gathered in our chambers. For at the Wilkinson house, Carlyle's publication was not simply a book, it was an event. Assorted phrenologists and other interested friends joined for an evening of readings. William had since left his father's home and settled nearby in his own dwelling outfitted with several rooms, including a spacious dining room visible from the parlour in which I resided. He possessed fewer knickknacks, opting for a slightly more sparse décor. A collection of paintings brought colour to the walls, oak furniture accommodated his guests, and I remained planted in my usual box.

With a hushed crowd, William read select passages from Carlyle's introductions—elucidations on his elucidations, I suppose. From these selections I learned that the author had scoured more than a hundred repositories collecting prints and manuscripts of my words. He also made it quite clear that he feared proper diction and spelling, preferring instead to cater to a new generation with modern spelling and syntax.

"'They stand in their old spelling; mispunctuated,

misprinted, unelucidated, unintelligible,—defaced with the dark incrustations too well known to students of the Period,'" William read aloud. "'To collect these Letters and authentic Utterances, as one's reading yielded them, was a comparatively grateful labour; to correct them, elucidate and make them legible again, was a good historical study.'"

The attendees listened closely, sipping tea and nibbling on biscuits as they admired the brash nature of Carlyle's words and occasionally glanced at me, as if I were guilty of poorly crafted correspondences, a criminal scribe of sorts. Not a single soul present had ever written a word whilst engaged in battle, with dying men around him, with bones chilled in the wintry frosts or flesh weeping in the sweltering sun. Carlyle, whose own writing I had not had, or would ever have, the opportunity to publicly critique, continued as William read: "'I have corrected the spelling of these Letters; I have punctuated, and divided them into paragraphs, in the modern manner.'"

The modern manner is rubbish. 'Tis an embarrassment to the Commonwealth. I found solace knowing I could not witness the corrected spellings myself, leaving me blissfully ignorant of these egregious changes. I shall wish for the same should these very words within this memoir be edited before publication.

"'Oliver's spelling and pointing are of the sort common to educated persons in his time,'" read William, "'and readers that wish it may have specimens of him in abundance, and of all due dimness, in many printed Books: but to us, intent here to have the Letters read and understand, it seemed very proper at once and altogether to get rid of that encumbrance. Would the rest were all as easily got rid of! Here and there, to bring out the struggling sense, I have added or rectified a word,—but taken care to point out the same; what words in the Text of the Letters are mine, the reader will find marked off by single commas: it was of course my supreme duty to avoid altering, in any respect, not only the sense, but the smallest feature in the physiognomy, of the Original.'"

Enough of Carlyle's words! Thus far they offered little value beyond insulting the very man who was now bringing him fame. William's friends seemed to agree; several of them urged him to begin the important readings. Despite Carlyle's editing, I recognised my remarks. Each page breathed life into me as William recited them aloud— my own words heard through another's mouth. All my thoughts, beliefs, convictions and passions brought forth to guide others. Through the blessing of the printed page, an idea never dies.

As we listened, each word validated my greatness, my leadership, my faith in our Lord and Saviour, and—with this letter to Bridget which I had written so long before on the 25ᵗʰ of October in the year 1646—begat undeniable emotion and joy in my role as father. She was with Henry Ireton at Cornbury in the General's Quarters:

> Dear Daughter,
> I write not to thy Husband; partly to avoid

trouble, for one line of mine begets many of his, which I doubt makes him sit up too late; partly because I am myself indisposed at this time, having some other considerations.

Your Friends at Ely are well; your sister Claypole is, I trust in mercy, exercised with some perplexed thoughts. She sees her own vanity and carnal mind: bewailing it: she seeks after (as I hope also) what will satisfy. And thus to be a seeker is to be of the best sect next to a finder; and such an one shall every faithful humble seeker be at the end. Happy seeker, happy finder! Who ever tasted that the Lord is gracious, without some sense of self, vanity and badness? Who ever tasted that graciousness of His, and could go less in desire,—less than pressing after full enjoyment? Dear Heart, press on; let not Husband, let not anything cool thy affections after Christ. I hope he will be an occasion to inflame them. That which is best worthy of love in thy Husband is that of the image of Christ he bears. Look on that, and love it best, and all the rest for that. I pray for thee and him; do so for me.

My service and dear affections to the General and Generaless. I hear she is very kind to thee; it adds to all other obligations. I am

Thy dear Father,
Oliver Cromwell

I missed Bridget dearly, she was but twenty-two at the time, which Carlyle respectfully shared with the reader. Whilst I very much enjoyed hearing my words to her once again, it was a peculiar experience to hear them through William's soft, timid voice. His tone also lacked a certain quale that was neither fatherly nor capable of commanding men and earning their unquestionable respect.

"He certainly does like Jesus, does he not?" said one of William's guests, managing to besmirch Christ's name with the tone of his simple observation.

"Cromwell was deeply religious, so yes, indeed, he invokes the Lord's name in nearly every letter," William wisely explained. "He believed it was God who drove his mission to overthrow the monarchy. Have you no sense of history?"

"I have, but of course," the man responded. His smug face formed around an elongated head, similar to a potato with nary a hair atop it. Spectacles rested upon a pointed nose, which at the moment darted around the room like a compass settling on a new direction. "It's just that, well, can any one of you here tell me where God was as Cromwell's men slaughtered thousands upon thousands of men? What kind of God works in such violent ways? If the Lord, with His mighty power, wished for a disposal of the monarchy, could He not have conjured up a more humane method of change? And what of the Restoration? After Cromwell's death and his son's abdication of the pro-tectorship, did God suddenly change His mind and wish for a king once again? A fickle Supreme Being, is He not? Or was the sheer will of Charles the Second so forceful it overwhelmed, nay, overpowered our omnipotent Creator? 'Tis incongruous with what I wish to believe. Oliver himself had siblings, children and grandchildren that perished at too young an age. And why, pray tell me, would God allow a man so close to Christ, a man who carried out His missions here on earth, to be treated so harshly after death? No soul can rest in Heaven whilst the body is tortured terrestrially. What can I say? I am a curious fellow!"

"The Lord makes no mistakes," William responded. "Have faith, for who are we to question His ways?"

"William is right, you would be wise to listen to him," said another fellow. "Lest you suffer the consequences of blasphemy!"

"And what consequences might those be, Dr. Gully? Hush now!" said another.

Murmurs filled the chamber as the discussion grew heated. My forced silence proved excruciating.

"Who are we? Yes, who are we?" retorted the pointy-nosed man. "William, my dear friend, we are the living. We are His creations, seeking to better our lives and the lives around us. Not end them!"

The crowd's eyes were fixed on this outspoken man, who seemed so enraged by my letter to Bridget. Ignorance is the genesis of anger.

"We must accept one of two things," William countered gently. "Either the Lord has a master plan yet to be revealed unto us all, which may have required the brief cessation in the monarchy, or He simply set us all in motion, and has given us freedoms, opportunities, decisions, to make our way, be it good or evil."

"Thank you for that, Reverend," the man said, extending his sarcasm. "If it is the latter, which I prefer to believe, then God is an observer and chooses no sides. This, in turn, proves Cromwell's foolishness, for Christ is not whispering 'Kill the king!' into his ear."

The man stood up, pacing as he continued to command the room's attention. "The Lord is sitting there, somewhere in the Heavens, looking down upon His creations slaughtering one another in His name and wondering where He went wrong in the construction of the brain and the conscience. As innocent souls rise to the Pearly Gates, He must be greeting each one with a long philosophical explanation of why they have arrived so prematurely. Imagine it! 'Hello my child, welcome to Heaven! My deepest apologies for having not been granted more time with the living and an opportunity to grow in adulthood. But you must understand, evil people will do evil things, and I merely watch it happen. Now, please, run and play with the angels. I have millions of people running amok on the earth squealing their prayers at this very moment, which I will now go and not attend to.' William, what say you to that?"

"I say trust in God," William answered with a weak sigh. "We shall leave it at that."

I pitied this poor fellow, who finally returned to his seat. Indeed, I question why God hath taken loved ones from me too soon. I fail to comprehend why our souls remain trapped within our rotting shells. But when life flowed through my body, faith rewarded me with a set of mores. God gave my life purpose and direction, even though brutality was oft a result of it; those who lay on the battlefield perished so that countless others might enjoy a better life. This misguided man does not understand that achieving an ideal often requires less than ideal means. He is but a fool. Yes, I do believe he must be nothing more than a sad fool, with a long head.

"Right, then! Let's hear more from Ollie Cromwell!" the fool shouted with a facetious smile.

William gladly flipped the pages and selected my proclamation given during our assault on Scotland in 1648. I take pride in my scruples exhibited here, lest anyone believe my battles were fought without regard for the enemy:

> Whereas we are marching with the Parliament's Army into the Kingdom of Scotland, in pursuance of the remaining part of the Enemy who lately invaded the Kingdom of England, and for the recovery of the Garrisons of Berwick and Carlisle:
>
> These are to declare, That if any Officer or Soldier under my command shall take or demand any money; or shall violently take any horses, goods or victual, without order; or shall abuse the people in any sort,—he shall be tried by a Council of War; and the said person so offending shall be punished, according to the Articles of War made for the gov-

ernment of the Army in the Kingdom of England, which punishment is death.

Each Colonel, or other chief Officer in every regiment, is to transcribe a copy of this; and to cause the same to be delivered to each Captain in his regiment: and every said Captain of each respective troop and company is to publish the same to his troop or company; and to take a strict course that nothing be done contrary hereunto.

Given under my hand, this 20th September, 1648.

Oliver Cromwell.

Indeed, I recall one soldier who neglected this proclamation and pilfered rations from a civilian family. The victims were issued an invitation to forgive the aggressor as he swayed from the gallows and became sustenance for carnivorous birds. Justice would have been better served had the ravenous fowl been caught and served as supper to the family: an eye for an eye, or more specifically, rations for rations.

"Not a single mention of Jesus," William noted. "I do hope this entry pleased us all."

There was no dispute.

William read several more passages before concluding the event by allowing each of the guests to hold the author of the words spoken throughout the evening. I could sense the energy I invoked in each, for in a sense, my very being brought the past directly to the present in a most unique manner. History lay in each of their hands. Eventually, I was passed along to the fool, who lowered his spectacles and stared directly into my eye sockets, as if he wished to communicate with me. It was a shame I could not oblige. I need not have defended my beliefs, but had I been able to speak, it would have afforded me a chance to help him understand God's ways and set him on a proper path. Instead, I rested upon the man's cold, dry hand; his blasphemy had invited a thin layer of death to creep upon him. For it was clear that a part of his soul was already dead.

※

Not long after William's reading, one of the men who had attended, Dr. Gully, paid another visit. Gully was middle-aged, but exhibited a youthful vigour through his wide eyes and optimistic facial expressions.

"William, your father worked diligently to provide provenance for Oliver Cromwell." He gestured excitedly toward me. "And you yourself have acquired the statements from Dr. Donovan. But would not the opinion of Thomas Carlyle further confirm his authenticity? What other living historian could offer a more informed judgment?"

"I suppose Carlyle is a connoisseur of all things Cromwell," William said.

"I can reach him by letter," Gully continued. "And I shall!"

Several weeks later, Gully returned with a response. The doctor certainly was a resourceful chap. Having waited to sit with William, he ripped open the envelope and silently browsed its contents as William waited eagerly to learn when Carlyle's visit would be.

"William, my friend, it is with great regret that I must report Mr. Carlyle's response," Dr. Gully said. He looked at the letter again, as if a second perusal might change its contents. "He has declined the invitation on account of a fraudulent Cromwell head he has already visited. He does not wish to be bothered once again and believes the existence of such a head to be an impossibility, stating that no embalmed head could withstand the years of exposure to rain and winds whilst impaled upon the tower."

"Write him once again," William said confidently. "His research into the life of Oliver Cromwell was thorough, his efforts into his afterlife should be no different. Assure Mr. Carlyle he will not be disappointed."

O Lord, grant me the ability to write one more letter for Carlyle to collect! One proclaiming my existence and exposing his erroneous beliefs. Despite my futility, I had the good fortune of having William at my side.

"Of course, it shall be done," Gully responded. "I promised you Carlyle, and I do not wish you to be disappointed, either."

As we awaited the historian's response, William continued to host friends and enquiring acquaintances, offering the usual tales and granting the privilege of fondling me. One evening, which could not have been more than a fortnight after Gully sent another plea to Carlyle, an unexpected visitor knocked at the door during a gathering.

William opened the door to find a thin, young man with sunken cheeks and tired eyes.

"Thomas Carlyle, I presume!" William said, elated.

"No, I am Mr. Chorley," the man replied.

The chamber fell silent, and there was an awkward pause until the stranger continued.

"I am here at the request of Mr. Thomas Carlyle to examine the alleged head of Oliver Cromwell which is believed to be in your possession. I assist Mr. Carlyle in his writings."

"Do come in!" William said. He seemed pleased to have gotten a response from Carlyle, even if it was not a personal one. "The head is right this way."

William's guests cleared a path for Chorley and followed his every movement. Standing before me, he leaned in close and circled my display as his darkened, sleepy eyes performed the examination to the best of their abilities. A dark hat fit snugly atop his head; lint, in turn, clung tightly to the brim, presumably collected during his apparently long, exhausting journey here. Loose buttons struggled to hang on to his tattered brown jacket. It gave the appearance of having provided warmth over many treks. His lips were chapped and in need of aid. For once, could not these inspections be performed by a woman?

The hushed room amplified every sound emanating from Carlyle's lackey. His heavy breathing wheezed through his nostrils, causing stray hairs to shudder with each exhalation. Unlike most visitors, he declined the opportunity to behold me in his own hands. Instead, his fingertips were busy scratching commentary into a dainty notebook with ragged edges and soiling on its pages. Much use had been made of this journal; perhaps its other pages were filled with notes regarding my letters.

The silence was at last broken by Dr. Gully. "Well, Mr. Chorley, what is your opinion?"

Chorley sniffled, slowly straightened his posture and let out a deep sigh. "It is a most intriguing specimen, I grant you that. I shall share my findings with Mr. Carlyle and if he should wish to make a visit you shall be notified."

He jotted down another thought, then flipped the book closed and returned it to his coat pocket. With that, he tipped his hat at William, thanked him for his hospitality and promptly left us.

The quiet chamber erupted with chatter. Yet Chorley had left a lingering echo of doubt.

✻

Anticipation stirred within the household in the days that followed Chorley's visit. As the months cycled through with no word from Carlyle, optimism waned. William would not have the pleasure of meeting an author and adding his expert approval to my list of credentials. Still, he entertained visitors regularly and joyfully shared the wonder of me.

I had nearly forgotten the entire affair, when one day Gully burst through William's front door shaking his fist furiously and clutching a periodical in his other hand.

"Bloody fool! That Carlyle is a bloody fool!" he

shouted. His hair and dress were dishevelled. One would
expect that Gully had just engaged in fisticuffs with the
scribe, which appeared to be a possibility should the two
ever meet.

"He's not coming, then?" William asked.

"Coming? Oh no, he shan't be coming anywhere
near us, I tell you! He hadn't the courtesy to write me, but
he did mail the paper!"

Gully unraveled the periodical, scurried through its
pages frantically until he landed upon Carlyle's words:

> There does not seem the slightest sound basis for
> any of the pretended Heads of Oliver. The one at
> present in vogue was visited the other day by a
> friend of mine: it has, hair, flesh, beard, a written
> history bearing evidence that it was procured for
> £100. (I think, of bad debt) about 50 years ago; it
> now appears to have once had resinous unguents,
> or embalming substances in it, and to have stood
> upon a spike: likely enough the head of some de-
> capitated man of distinction; but by the size of the
> face, by the very width of the jaw bone, were there
> no other proof, it has not any claim to be Oliver's
> head. A professional sculptor, about a year ago, gave
> me the same report of it: "a very much smaller face
> than Oliver's, quite another face." The story told, of
> a high wind, a sentinel, etc., is identical with what
> your old neighbour heard, long since, of the Oliver
> Head in the shape of a Scull. In short the whole af-

fair appears to be fraudulent moonshine, an element not pleasant even to glance into, especially in a case like Oliver's. I remain always, Yours with sincere thanks,

T. CARLYLE.
5, Cheyne Row, Chelsea.
21ˢᵗ Feb., 1849. A. L. F

"It's rubbish," William said calmly. He paused, then clarified, "*Carlyle* is rubbish."

"Will you send a retort, then?" Gully asked. "This letter, it's slander, it is! What will people think?"

"They will think what they wish to think, and if they wish to judge the head for themselves, they shall be welcome to do so."

What other embalmed, decapitated head of distinction did Carlyle suspect I might be?

✳

Carlyle's commentary raised questions amongst its readers that persisted over the ensuing years. It was an irritant, but one I had grown accustomed to over the centuries. God knows the truth, and I have faith He shall make it evident to all in good time.

Time with the Wilkinsons, however, brought welcome distractions from rumors. William found a wife, a beautiful lass called Ada, who accepted me with only slight trepidation. She referred to me as "that wretched thing," until William chronicled my full story, which effectively imparted upon her a sense of appreciation for my presence. Finally, William had another to whom he could extend his heart.

Ada wore blonde hair in curls, which framed her glistening blue eyes, aquiline nose and thick lips that formed a smile more often than not. Her supple locks and full bosom bounced rhythmically with every step that her svelte figure took. I was pleased for William, and though her beauty was second only to that of my dear Elizabeth, I took pleasure in the competition.

As is usual with the newly wed, a child soon followed; the lad was named Horace. His cries were at times insufferable, but as with my experiences during the plague, I was quite relieved that my sense of scent was no longer with me. William and Ada coddled him with love. Without Ada's knowledge, William brought Horace before me and shared tales of my exploits; my life had become a childhood storybook. This was not merely William's way of continuing to spend time with me, it was his method of ensuring that Horace would care for me as well one day. Affectionately called "Uncle Ollie," I became one of his first and likely most impressionable memories.

Young Horace grew to be a thin, gangly lad with unruly shocks of auburn hair, wide hazel eyes and a precocious nature. High energy levels apparently prevented him from allocating time to eat. He did, however, find plenty of occasions to share his thoughts with me and develop a friendship, much like my first guardian, Henry. Naturally, the innocence and curiosity of a child made these moments much more lighthearted than the tales and troubles Henry had divulged to me. Flatulence was the boy's preferred theme, accompanied by the breaking of wind and giggling commentary on its force. Horace eagerly relayed stories of a French youth who was gaining renown for his abilities in this arena.[1] He spoke of him like a hero, and as with any enamoured child, he aimed to mimic that idol. Horace's interest in bodily functions extended to discussions concerning the joys of sneezing, for their mucus-excreting powers; demonstrations frequently occurred within uncomfortable proximity. On occasion, the boy ventured into more philosophical topics that proved more stimulating. Thunderstorms oft spurred these sorts of suppositions. "Maybe God is bursting with tears and he's flickering lights in His invisible bedroom!" I very much doubted the Lord ever wept, but I, too, wondered what caused the Heavens to roar and crackle with lights. When William was occupied outside the home, Horace's play grew more intimate. He would remove the head of a doll and replace it with me. Holding me in place, he would treat me as a puppet and provide his voice to speak for me. The speeches I gave in this arrangement were hardly fitting for the Lord Protector; my juvenile ravings about the loo and other scatological matters brought him endless laughter, and in turn offered me profuse gratification.

Time moves rapidly. This is most evident with the growth of children, and Horace was no exception. Our childish encounters waned as he matured. William and Ada

continued to dote upon the boy and sporadically entertained visitors (though phrenology was scarcely practiced,
presumably because of Ada's rational influence), but they
had recently discovered a most interesting hobby involving a new contraption intended for transportation.[2] They
spoke of it often, referring to it as a "bicycle," yet I had
occasion to witness this apparatus only when William and
Ada agreed to take me to a neighbour who had fallen ill and
wished to draw strength from my presence. The creation
consisted of two wheels, one in front of the other; the former was quite large, the latter, rather small. A steel tube ran
from the centre of the large wheel, along its circumference,
and trailed off to the rear wheel. Ada placed a foot upon a
peg over the small wheel, grabbed a handle atop the large
one, and lifted herself up to a leather saddle. Her feet rested
on two small platforms, which she rotated by exerting her
legs. This, which she did with a great deal of joy, caused
the machine to move forward, though when she struck a
devious pebble in the road she nearly fell forward over the
wheel. William placed me in his bag and mounted his own
riding machine with notable ease.

Our short journey was a testament to the marvelous
nature of this device. As with other inventions this, too,
made me ponder the impact it might have fashioned during
my time on the battlefield. Its speed, durability and inanimate nature would have rendered a cavalry unnecessary—
along with the breeding required to build a suitable one.
These wheeled units would also spare the procurement and
dressing of thousands of horses, allowing men to quietly and

stealthily ride into battle, not on a galloping creature that must eat, sleep, defecate and eventually die, thenceforth littering the battlefield with additional corpses and odours. Furthermore, the large wheel allowed the same elevated seating the horse provided. Save for the power of the Almighty, there is no greater force than the ingenuity of men.

Our visit to William's ailing friend proved futile. His fever ran high, and although I provided him with one final, meagre grin, a rotting head was simply not the remedy his body sought.

Afterlife carried on, uneventful, as the Wilkinson family went about their business, of which I had little insight. William had not followed his father's footsteps into the medical arena, but he seemed to provide for Ada and Horace suitably. I speculated that he delivered messages by way of his bicycle; surely one would pay a handsome sum to have correspondences or goods transported so speedily and without the potential scent of manure upon arrival. It would also account for his frequent absences. In the meantime, my bond with Horace grew stronger as he studied my history. For this, I was extremely grateful. I knew it would serve me well one day, but woefully, that day arrived too soon.

I had initially marvelled at the bicycle and began to prophesy equine unemployment, until tragedy struck. It was several months after my wheeled jaunt with William and Ada when my guardian was descending a well-trafficked street and the chain of his machine broke, causing him to lose control and collide with the diminutive corpse of a dormouse strewn across his lane. I heard Ada, through her tears and sniffles, describe the tragedy to an eavesdropping neighbour who offered his condolences. The jolt had caused the bicycle to turn sharply and fling William over the high handlebars directly into a telegraph pole. He lay on the ground unconscious for nary a second when unfortunate timing brought a large four-wheeled horse-drawn carriage racing perpendicular to William's path, whenceforth he was crushed by the hurried hooves. Despite the many needs that put the horse at a disadvantage when compared with the bicycle, it still bested the contraption in strength. As I learned long, long ago, the horse is a beast to be reckoned with. Perhaps the Lord had taken offense at the horseless machine that so threatened the dumb creature He had provided and permitted to be subordinate to mankind, and William was the unfortunate harbinger of this message. Surely his blasphemous friend with the pointy nose would have been a better candidate.

✻

Horace embraced his role as man of the house and my new guardian admirably. Like his grandfather, he held an interest in science. Of particular attention was a new, astonishing tool conceived by an Edinburgh fellow he referred to as Alexander Graham Bell. The invention, Horace rambled to all who would listen, converted a human voice at one end into electricity, transmitted it to another location, then converted the electricity back into a voice. It had the superb effect of yelling and being heard in an entirely different town, yet a normal vocal tone could be maintained so one could speak to another as if he were at his side. William's bicycle had seemed a miracle in mobility, but Bell had far surpassed him, for now a man needn't travel at all to deliver a message. The bicycle, presumably, would become obsolete. Many lives would be saved, yet no invention would bring back William (though a grave robber certainly could). The telegraph, too, suddenly seemed archaic and impractical, as did the poor clerk who operated it.

This "telephone" created much stir within the household, as did an exquisite portrait that Horace acquired of himself, which he set upon a mantelpiece near me. The likeness was so striking, so perfect, even Samuel Cooper's skilled brush could scarcely come near the level of realism Horace's artist achieved. It was as if he looked in the mirror and transferred the image to a small canvas. The artist, whom Horace referred to as a "photographer," had developed a new skill that involved some form of intricate apparatus. Du Puy and Cox—bless their buried, imprisoned souls—would have appreciated this enchanted device.

Human achievements without the aid of machinery also presented conversation fodder, such as the recent news of a sea captain who swam across the English Channel.[3] The feat required nearly twenty-two hours of swimming, covering thirty-nine miles. Adulation showered him from all parts of the world, according to the local chatter. I failed to understand why a man so learned in the ways of the sea would be foolish enough to tempt death instead of simply crossing in the safety of his ship. Should he have succumbed to the might of the waters and drowned, what sort of eternity would he have faced? For that matter, what did any man who died at sea experience at the furthest depths of the waters? Were there creatures feeding far below the sights of any ship? Did God's artistry extend into the wet blackness? Perhaps someday I will discover the answers for myself.

The excitement helped both Horace and Ada carry on after William's unexpected death. Another distraction soon arrived in the post, which, I noted, was not delivered upon a bicycle. Marvelous inventions and feats of endurance had their moment, but neither could overcome the allure of me for long. A letter from a professor of anatomy at Oxford, made sure of it:

> Dear Sir,
>
> I venture to address you in my capacity of Professor of Anatomy in this place upon the question of Oliver Cromwell's skull, the reason for my writing being that we have here in our Museum a skull which has often been measured and referred to as being that skull. I have, however, never so referred to it, having never been satisfied as to its authenticity. Its history so far as I know is this: When our New Museum was built and the natural history Collections of the Old Ashmolean Museum were transferred to it and put, so far as their anatomical specimens went, into my hands, I had the so-

called skull, or, more properly speaking *calvaria* of Oliver Cromwell handed over to me. Knowing that it had often been measured and referred to by craniographers and craniometricians, I had it carefully mounted on an oaken stand and covered with a glass shade, but all that I had to refer to as evidence for its authority was the accompanying extract from the Ashmolean's catalogue, which I enclose. I had heard some years ago that the real skull was in the possession of a gentleman of your name, but I never obtained your address.

I should very much value the opportunity of being allowed to see your specimen, the evidence for the authenticity of which seems so much more complete than I had any idea. And if it should meet with your approval it might be well to publish what such an examination enabled me to say about it.

I am dear sir
Yours truly,
George Rolleston
Professor of Anatomy
Oxford

Impostor! Was this Ashmolean skull one that others had referred to in years past? Perhaps we would soon meet, embalmed face to embalmed face.

"Mum, let us invite Dr. Rolleston here to Kent," Horace said, clutching the letter. "His observations and writings will add to father's and grandfather's authentica-

tion efforts, and help end the idiocy put forth by Thomas
Carlyle."

Ada agreed and they promptly sent a response to the
Oxford anatomist. I reckoned the telephone had not performed its miracles in that royalist town yet.

The doctor made no delay upon receipt of the letter and arrived a fortnight later with two fascinating items:
the Ashmolean skull that had been masquerading as me
for centuries and a copy of my death mask. It pleased me
greatly to see several of these still existed beyond that which
William had attained. Truly, I lived on in many forms.

Rolleston had neatly trimmed brown hair and wore
a dark frock coat over a burgundy vest. His brown trousers nearly reached the floor. I had taken note of this shift
in fashion with the Wilkinson men; the simplification of
clothing was an improvement, and it occurred to me that
declining a periwig was a sign of self-respect since it forced
men to care for their God-given hair, rather than ignore
and cover it with prepared locks. As I inspected the doctor,
he eagerly reciprocated. Like the phrenologist Donovan,
Rolleston spent quite some time thoroughly measuring all
angles of my head. Unlike Donovan, however, he had the
death mask to compare me against and he wasted no time
with gibberish about Amativeness and other nonsense.

"Mr. Wilkinson, this is undoubtedly Oliver Cromwell," Rolleston reported several hours later.

"I never questioned its veracity," Horace said.

"Many at the Ashmolean Museum have," Rolleston
responded. "But as I stated in my letter, I always knew the

evidence did not present itself properly. I believe the museum suspected it, too, but rather enjoyed upholding the tale for the benefit of publicity and visitors. Income at a museum is always tenuous."

"May we compare the heads?" Horace asked. "I see it has made the journey with you, and for what other purpose than to set them side by side?"

"But of course, Mr. Wilkinson! Yes, yes, you are absolutely correct."

Rolleston fetched the head from the foyer and sat it beside me. The two leaned in close to us and stared pensively.

"There are several pieces of evidence here that clearly dismiss this head as the true Cromwell," Rolleston said of the Ashmolean skull, and pointed to the hole at its summit. "Here, you can see the sharp edges splaying inward, which indicates the blow was made externally, and not from a pike being thrust upward and out from the inside of the skull. The hole, you'll note, is also off centre—not a common practice when impaling for display."

"'Tis obviously someone else," Horace said. "Besides, the head does not even appear to have ever been embalmed. There is no flesh, no trace of hair."

"Yes, you are correct. It appears macerated, but fails to demonstrate any true similarities. Its story differs greatly to the story of yours as well. The museum catalogue states that the head blew off at Westminster in 1672 and was retrieved by a Mr. John Moore, who later gave it to a Mr. Warner, an apothecary living on King Street, Westminster.

Thence it was sold for twenty broad pieces of gold to Humphrey Dove, Esquire, who was at the time the deputy paymaster to the treasurer of the chamber. Following his death in 1687, his daughter, Mrs. Mary Fishe of Westminster, removed the skull from an iron chest. It remained with her family for many years until being passed along to Mr. E. Smalterrall and, thence, to the Ashmolean Museum."

"Goodness! What a flock of lies," Horace said with a laugh of disbelief.

Rolleston then jotted down a quick notation: "No. 561, imperfect calvaria with a hole in the right parietal. Once supposed to be that of Oliver Cromwell."

He explained to Horace that the Ashmolean head would remain on exhibition and in the catalogue, but with this renewed description. As they discussed museum matters and tales of Horace's grandfather's acquisition of me, I turned my attention to my Ashmolean foe, but he addressed me before I could initiate any interrogation.

"It is good to see you again, Lord Cromwell."

I cannot be certain, but I do believe the shock forced several of my remaining hairs to stand. Was this fraud a friend? "I should like to say the same, but I know not who you are, only that many have believed you to be me," I said. "Tell me, what is your true name?"

"I am Archibald Campbell, First Marquis of Argyll," said the misunderstood head. "If your memory still serves you, you will recall I received you in Edinburgh in 1648 as a member of the Whiggamores. We fought against the Engagers of Charles the First."

The memory was faint, but his name rang familiar as I considered the many men I had encountered in life. More important, his story was agreeable with my beliefs. "Yes, but of course! Tell me, Marquis, first, what caused your head to be separated from your body, and what is this Ashmolean matter all about?"

Fortunately, Horace and Rolleston continued their discourse, allowing time, I hoped, for a comprehensive answer.

"I refused to support Charles the First, though His Majesty sought it," the Marquis said. "His despotic ecclesiastical ways were rubbish. But you know this. Despite my efforts against the king's policy, I was not pleased with his execution. All of Scotland, for that matter, was horrified."

"I am sorry it frightened you so," I said.

"I became distracted at this time, I lost control of national policies, I ambled through life during that period. Perhaps you did not know that it was I who invited Charles the Second to come to Scotland. In fact, he was to marry my daughter in 1651, but my loss of power prevented me from pursuing the nuptials. This disappoints you, I realise, but I later found my way again and served in your son's Parliament in 1659 as a member for Aberdeenshire. Afterward Richard abdicated—were you aware of this?"

"I have heard of this misfortune, yes. Please continue."

"Well, after Richard fled, Charles the Second regained the throne and had me arrested for high treason for my role in the death of his father. I nearly escaped the charges, until letters were found offering evidence that I had collaborated with your government. I was subsequently sentenced on a Friday to be beheaded the following Monday. Such hasty punishment! Terrified, I dropped to my knees and begged the bastards for a fifteen-day reprieve—time to come to terms with my final hours, and perhaps persuade them for a less drastic sentence—but Parliament would not grant it. No, they could not wait for the cruelty to begin. Mercifully, the executioner's blade was swift. His cold steel shot pain through my entire being for only a split second before the Lord reclaimed my ability to feel. Though it was painless, witnessing my own blood splatter and my body drop away from my head was mentally challenging. This is not an experience you would be familiar with, though, is it, Lord Protector? God showed you greater mercy, postponing your beheading to a posthumous date."

"Marquis, I am sorry for your loss, but please, continue," I said. "How did you become me—and I must know, have you enjoyed it?"

"My severed head was sloppily shoved onto a spike, upside down—the careless fools—and displayed on the west end of Tolbooth with all the other execution victims, where the world around me was inverted for many years.[4] Oh, how I disliked that dreadful view. It was disorienting and maddening, quite honestly. Imagine standing upon your head indefinitely! Forgive me for carrying on, perhaps another time we may share tales of impalement."

"Perhaps."

"Where were we now?" he resumed. "Ah yes, by

my account, it was the early 1670s, as the professor stated, when my head was at last removed. The flesh had slowly eroded away, partly eaten by birds and insects, and partly washed away by the rains. I was kept in a private home for many years before the owner learned your head had disappeared from Westminster. No one came forth to announce your discovery, so this fellow had the cunning notion to claim I was you. I was then sold several times before finally being donated to the Ashmolean Museum as a historical artefact. Impersonating you begat many benefits, for you were a sight to behold, you drew crowds, you were a star. I should hardly think anyone would pay a penny to see the Marquis of Argyll. So, indeed, I enjoyed being you. I had sided with you. I shared your beliefs. I welcomed you to my home. Suddenly, I felt more connected to you in death than I could have ever hoped for in life. This was a blessing, for it hath kept me on a pedestal throughout this afterlife, whereas I easily could have been discarded or reburied. I was treasured and adored by thousands upon thousands of museum visitors and became one of Oxford's most celebrated residents. It was a wonder no one had discovered that my hole was inconsistent with your impalement until Dr. Rolleston. Please know, I had no idea that you had survived your fall. If I may say, my lord, you look quite well for a dead man nearing his three hundredth birthday. Finally got rid of those warts, did you?"

I thanked the Marquis for his tale and assured him that he would still be treasured, for though the truth was now known, interest always remained in what was once thought true. Rolleston would see to it. He and Horace had just clasped hands in a sturdy shake and were now bidding each other good-bye. The doctor then collected the Marquis for his return journey.

How fortunate to have learned that this impostor was in fact an old acquaintance. Of course, had God been more mischievous and ironic, He would have revealed the Ashmolean skull—this soul spending its afterlife as me—as none other than Charles I.

XIII

SPIRITUALISM, CHARLATANS AND SHOWMEN

———

I was quite fond of Horace Wilkinson. The young man matured with wisdom favouring his soul. God was with him; Horace reciprocated as an ordained reverend, which afforded him the ability and platform to help others find their way into the one true Kingdom—that of the Almighty Lord. This provided me with renewed confidence that I remained within the Creator's good graces, for He saw to it that I lay within the possession of a proper guardian.

Horace's gift for guidance was exceptional; his personal mission from God harvested this talent and involved no usurpation and required not a single drop of bloodshed or slaughter. Words alone were his weapon against lost souls. Grieving parishioners frequently visited our home in need of aid and granted me the privilege of observing his expertise in action. Horace was a listener first, able to understand problems and soothe those in pain by offering hope in the Lord. Unlike his grandfather, he refrained from employing my services to aid in these feats of healing. Ofttimes his competence helped mourning widows, widowers and children cope with the death of a loved one. Though his methods were effective, it pained me to witness it, knowing that everything he assured them of was utterly wrong. Temporary relief of sadness would eventually be replaced with eternal misery from within their own coffins. Such is death.

Horace's love for the Lord was challenged only by a dear woman, called Hattie, whom he wooed persistently until she found him agreeable. Like Ada before her, she was eventually introduced to me and was immediately horrified. These moments had become a tradition, which I began to relish simply to witness the ways in which the human face is uniquely malleable under the power of emotion and able to contort in so many unusual ways. Time softened her soul, and with the encouragement of Ada, who had aged gracefully, Hattie grew to accept me. I, too, accepted her. She lacked Ada's natural beauty, but her healthy charisma most assuredly offset her narrow face, bulging brown eyes and bulbous proboscis. She would, someday, be the mother of my next guardian.

As Horace and Hattie's relationship grew, I detected their strong religious beliefs evolving, twisting into a new area of practice. Horace spoke of it as a recent phenomena, called Spiritualism, which spread from America and had grown considerably in England.[1] My initial impression was that he had taken after his father, who was easily susceptible to the absurdity of the phrenological fad. Spiritualism, I learned, promised the astonishing ability to communicate with the dead. Hark! Not a single living soul had heard my thoughts.

Horace began to weave his Spiritualism experiences into his grief counseling, assuring mourners that their loved ones were still with them and reachable through the science of séance. He attended many such events, one of which he described to a widow as involving several men and women seated around a table in a darkened room, led by a medium by the name of William Lawrence. Lawrence had gone into a stupor causing motley contortions and convulsions at the outset of the séance, and with his eyes nearly closed and face twisted, he addressed the assembled group regarding the erroneous ways of current religions and the enlightenment of Spiritualism. Bells rang and tambourines were beating along with his words. A blank sheet of paper lay on the table for the spirits' writing or drawing desires. Lawrence drew upon his audience for energy by requesting they sing hymns. Horace claimed mysterious marks soon appeared on the paper, accompanied by whistling and voices in hollow tones emanating from Lawrence that were not his own, but rather manifestations of spirits present in the room. It was an initial contact, he alleged, and though little was learned, it showed great promise for truth and understanding with future connections.

These tales became commonplace. Some described variations in the practice: mediums with paintbrushes furnished full portraits of the deceased and exhibited the artistry of Titian and Vermeer, though no mention was made of conversations with their particular spirits or those of other masters; healing mediums consulted spirits for prescriptions to cure a host of ailments, supposedly producing wondrous results that would have warranted the envy of Hippocrates and Galen; and tipping mediums miraculously shook and altered the positions of tables and other household furnishings (Horace reported no damages to personal property).

The excitement extended all the way to the queen—named Victoria—who by all accounts practiced Spiritualism passionately. It was said that a thirteen-year-old medium, Robert James Lees, had informed her that her deceased husband, Prince Albert, had come to him with a message shortly after his death and produced a voice that witnesses claimed was unmistakably Albert's.[2] Among the words delivered were many that were of a private nature, known only by him and Victoria; thus, she believed Lees to be authentic and invited him to lead numerous séances at her palace. During the last of these communications through Lees, Albert directed the queen to another medium, John Brown, for all forthcoming messages. Brown and Victoria grew close, and séances were held regularly to seek Albert's opinion on various leadership and policy matters (if she wished to be with him, more drastic measures could certainly be taken). Victoria, it was speculated, had begun a romance with Brown, though I did not hear whether the spirit of Albert spoke up about his posthumous cuckolding. Regardless of her private affairs, her method of decision making once again proved the ineptitude of the monarchy. Truly, the Commonwealth needed a new Cromwell.

Horace, however, surely adored the queen. "This is the dawn of a new day that shall be marked by a total and fundamental change in all things," he preached to a believer eager to help spread this new doctrine. "'Tis the beginning of an entirely new system of thought and belief upon the kingdom of earth, with a new gift from the Lord, a new religion and a new order of all living—and dead— men and women. We shall make it known and disseminate it through every land—wherever breath may flow from God's creations."

This dogma of the deceased reminded me of a preacher, John Pordage, from my living days, who claimed to speak with the departed and gathered scores of followers wishing to experience his power.[3] I recall his claims of having intercourse with spirits—these phantoms roamed in and out of his chamber, allegedly witnessed by his wife. His flock fell into trances and reported visions of Heaven and Hell, angels and devils, and omnipresent spirits of both good and bad nature. I found him a fool, denounced his otherworldly sexual proclivities, and I know personally that his necromancy never made contact with me after my death.

Witchcraft, too, felt like an equally accurate, al- beit less acceptable, name for these Spiritualist practices.

Though Pordage escaped the fate of sorcerers and witches of the era, I suspect that many of the Spiritualists whom Horace spoke of would have been burned to death two hundred years before. Yet his passion made me wonder: Had there truly been new developments in the efforts to communicate with my kind? I had, in recent years, witnessed the evolution of technology make the unimaginable possible. Would not those who scorched witches long before have done the same to the fellow who put together the telephone? Its communication abilities seemed just as magical as the effects the séance produced. Still, I was skeptical. Aside from logic and experience, my doubt was driven by the fact that none of the spirits Horace discussed wished to warn the living of the true nature of death and the error of burial. This message, I presumed, would be a top priority.

Fuelled by ignorance, Horace and Hattie were confident in the power of Spiritualism, and having used it to help so many others, they set forth on a new personal mission. It was a natural quest and one I had been anticipating; the time had come to communicate with yours truly. The veil of doubt that shrouded my soul remained, yet it was thin and left me with a sliver of hope. If I was ever to connect with the living, this was my opportunity.

✦

Placed in the middle of a table in a darkened room, I was surrounded by a shadowy audience of eight participants holding hands. I faced Horace, Hattie and a bearded medium seated next to them. Blank paper and a writing instrument lay in front of me. All eyes were closed; the medium tilted his head back as if looking up to the Heavens to seek out my soul, yet it was right here, within reach. The group began with a hymn, though none appeared to have had any vocal training:

> Safe in the arms of Jesus,
> Safe on His gentle breast;
> There by His love o'ershaded,
> Sweetly my soul shall rest.
> Hark! 'tis the voice of angels
> Borne in a song to me,
> Over the fields of glory,
> Over the jasper sea.
> Safe in the arms of Jesus,
> Safe on His gentle breast;
> There by His love o'ershaded,
> Sweetly my soul shall rest.
> Safe in the arms of Jesus,
> Safe from corroding care,
> Safe from the world's temptations;
> Sin cannot harm me there.
> Free from the blight of sorrow,
> Free from my doubts and fears;
> Only a few more trials,
> Only a few more tears!

This went on for quite some time and grew a bit repetitive, but the chant seemed to have the effect of placing the Spiritualists in a trance. Why had I not been held in the arms of Jesus or experienced His gentle breast? How would this hymn enable them to hear my thoughts?

When the psalm reached its end, the group continued to hum the tune. The medium lifted the pen, looked upward and began to speak slowly and methodically:

"O Lord in Heaven above ... Creator of all that is holy ... know that we, gathered here ... are all seekers of truth ... and wish for universal understanding. ... Lend thy hand to the spirit of your child, Oliver Cromwell. ... His embalmed head lies before us. ... Deliver his spirit to us. ... Guide his soul so that he may be present in this room. ... Let our energy raise his consciousness ... for he is among friends who wish to communicate with him."

His monotone voice was almost hypnotic; I myself was nearly lulled into a slumber until the table suddenly jolted me from my torpor by jerking upward at a slight angle. I slid a touch toward Horace. One of the women seated round the table shrieked, while the others remained calm and maintained a quiet hum. I had not yet been acquainted with these "friends," save Horace and Hattie, though the Wilkinson family historically kept good company.

"Oliver Cromwell, art thou with us? ... Art thou here, Oliver Cromwell, Lord Protector of England, Ireland and Scotland?"

Yes, you brought me here.

"We are here for thee on this night. ... Horace and Hattie Wilkinson are here, Oliver ... art thou with us?"

Yes, you can see me. Can you not hear me?

"Please manifest thyself. ... Speak, Oliver Cromwell! We await thy signal. ... We await thy wisdom."

The intensity of the medium's voice rose, perhaps with the notion that I could better hear him if he spoke louder. Thus far, my soul could offer no signal, nor could it manifest noises, writings or a body. Hope and desire had clouded my judgement.

"Please, Oliver Cromwell, we are waiting! ... By the love of God and all that is holy, we are here for thee ... seeking truth. ... Join us! ... Come through, Oliver Cromwell, so that we may reunite thee with thy head! ... 'Tis here, your one true head. ... Art thou with us, Oliver Cromwell?"

The table tipped once again, rocking me nearly to my side. Bells began to jingle like a church gone mad, and the pen, held loosely in the medium's hand, suddenly began to move over the paper, slowly, purposefully, the sound of each stroke amplified to enhance the drama. The hum of the shadowy figures grew thunderous and I could feel vibrations of the attendees' legs around the table, shaking from anticipation and nerves. These manufactured manifestations were indeed effective. The medium read aloud the letters being formed:

"Y ... E ... S ... Yes!"

This first written answer at least had the merit of being correct. He cast the paper aside and addressed me again. Gasps let loose round the room and the hum intensified.

"Providence hath delivered the spirit of Cromwell... for this we thank thee. ... Welcome, Oliver. ... Thou art welcome here. ... Wilt thou speak with us? ... Wilt thou speak with Horace and Hattie?"

Nothing would give me greater pleasure. Once again, bells jingled and the pen forcibly scratched letters onto a new sheet of paper. Voices quivered.

"Y ... E ... S ... Yes!"

Another accurate response.

"The Wilkinson family has cared for your head for many years now. ... Art thou content with this? ... Horace and Hattie want thee to be pleased."

Elation was building—bells rang with greater haste and a knocking rapped the table, which tipped with increased ferocity that caused me to skip about. The hum was unwavering. Latches on the doors sounded as if they were rising and falling. Yet despite the showmanship, the medium's questions did nothing more than create tedium within my skull.

"Is thy soul able to rest? Thy head has been separated from thy body for many years now. ... Is thy soul at peace?"

At last, an enquiry with substance. In the spirit of Spiritualism, I responded with all my ability. A simple "Y-E-S" or "N-O" could not express my feelings on the matter. I am indeed at peace in countless ways, for I know that the existence I have escaped through the generous hatred of Charles II is blessed, and experiences over the centuries have shown me wondrous things, yet I am equally tormented through my knowledge and lack of power to effect change. How can my soul ever truly be at peace knowing that every being I've cared for, save Ireton and Bradshaw, has been sentenced to a personal Hell in a buried, blackened box? Will I someday find myself there again in a smaller chest suited to my severed self? More important, where is my Maker? God, Creator of all Things, I reach out to you now as this Spiritualist has—where art Thou? I hear you and praise you in life, yet in death you are absent. Is this it? My soul is in a purgatory of feeble ignorance and futile wisdom. I wonder now, having just raised their names: Where are Ireton and Bradshaw? Have their heads been collected and treasured, or discarded and submerged in the soil? Though I am free to observe my surroundings, I am trapped and confined to them, beholden to the whims of my guardians. I seek the freedom to wander and explore, to regain the artificial limbs James Cox had provided me with, and the ability to control them. To live again.

Bells hastily jingled. The pen etched new letters into a clean piece of paper.

"N...O... *No!*"

A not entirely accurate and rather brief summation of the message I attempted to communicate. But the pen continued its swift markings.

"P ... R ... A ... I ... S ... E ... W ... I ... L ... K ... I ... N ... S ... O ... N ... *Praise Wilkinson!*"

Naturally, I very much appreciated their passion for me.

"Thy soul is not at rest. ... Oliver Cromwell, we are here for thee. ... All of us in this room ... myself ... Horace and Hattie Wilkinson ... Elizabeth and Nathan Steger ...

the Reverend William Stainton Moses and Lottie Fowler ... Dr. Edgar Monck. ... Can we help thy soul find peace?"

This is unlikely. By all means, do not attempt to reunite my head with my lost body and return me to the grave! And who were these strange persons helping Horace and Hattie? Parishioners perhaps?

"N ... O ... *No!*"

Strangely, these markings did put my soul at peace, at least momentarily.

"Oliver Cromwell ... are you with God? ... Do you reach us tonight from Heaven above?"

The humming swelled and the bells clinked closer. Something thin made contact with a flake of my flesh as the table jerked upward once more, startling me and all present. I suspected that an unseen accomplice concealed in the darkness was tugging a thread to tilt the table, and if he grew more aggressive, I feared I might roll right off and very well suffer irreparable damage. The pen continued its magical markings.

"Y ... E ... S ... *Yes!*"

Thus far, this medium, this charlatan, had put on an impressive exhibition with clever theatrics. But with this response, he gave proof that he had not heard a word I had communicated. My existence was what it was and should remain so.

"Oliver Cromwell, ... Horace and Hattie wish to know ... art thou with William Wilkinson? ... Art thou with Josiah Wilkinson?"

From my perspective, the most remarkable feat of

the evening was the endurance Horace, Hattie and the others had in their humming abilities. Would not their voices go dry soon?

"Y ... E ... S ... *Yes!* ... Wait, there is more coming! ... B ... E ... W ... E ... L ... L ... *Be well!* ... L ... O ... V ... E ... G ... O ... D ... *Love God!*"

On the contrary, Horace had buried William, and William his father. Thus, they were nowhere near me. This was an elementary fact. Yet the response caused rapid rapping upon the table and shouts of joy, shock or possibly both to break the hum. A murmur replaced it straight away. Horace and Hattie let out a sigh of relief.

"We thank thee, Oliver Cromwell," the medium continued, "for visiting with us tonight. ... You have touched us all. ... We thank thee for thy wisdom. ... We are enlightened by thy words. ... We thank thee for thy kindness. ... We are blessed by thy presence. ... May God protect thy soul and bring thee peace. ... Amen."

The medium released the pen and gathered the scattered papers, and the crowd collectively exhaled.

"Amen," they said in unison.

The show was over. 'Twas a fantastical success for all present, with the most vital exception of me. My sliver of hope had been foolish. In retrospect, how could I ignore the Lord's words in Deuteronomy 18:9–11?

> ⁹When you are come into the land which the LORD your God gives, you shall not learn to do after the abominations of those nations. ¹⁰There shall not be

found among you any one that makes his son or his
daughter to pass through the fire, or that uses divi-
nation, or an observer of times, or an enchanter, or
a witch. "Or a charmer, or a consulter with familiar
spirits, or a wizard, or a necromancer.

Spiritualism was certainly the Devil at work, dup-
ing those wishing for an early admission to the heavenly
realm.[4] Yet one does not drink from the chalice of the Devil
and the cup of the Lord. I feared Horace and Hattie had
sipped too much, their cognisance blinded by the craftiness
of demons. If this supposition were true, it would be most
distressing—for this indicated Satan had been busy at play
whilst God had not even been in the game.

I would soon discover that evidence of this was
mounting.

✳

I prayed Horace's relationship with the Lord would save
him from the clutches of the Devil. Satan's powerful grip
was reaching into the terrestrial world and, I feared, had
grabbed hold of numerous Spiritualists, delivering the connections they sought at the price of their souls. What manner of torture must a soul confined in Hell endure, and how
much more dreadful could it be than what others are experiencing thus far? I shuddered to think of the wretched
possibilities: loss of memories stripping away all sensations
of joy; enhanced consciousness of decomposition; a high-

er concentration of voracious insects; or perhaps demons simply ripped them from their caskets and dragged them deeper into the earth, where worse, unimaginable horrors await. Horace deserved no such fate; his guidance had simply become misguided.

After my séance, the Wilkinsons' confidence in Spiritualism intensified and they endeavoured to devote even more time to communicating with departed souls. The perceived success of my soul's manifestation led them to believe I was a source of power, and thus I accompanied them on missions with mediums around Kent and into London. It also enabled more opportunities to share me outside the confines of their home. Those who sought the Wilkinsons' services now believed they would be entreating the aid of the Lord *and* the Lord Protector to reach deceased loved ones. Darkened rooms filled with rappings, tippings, markings and far too many hymns offered attendees frights, chills and ultimately peace of mind. Angst aside, I admit the events were captivating.

During a trip to one these séances in the grey fog of London, in which we were to help an anguished widow contact her husband, who had, it was said, recently perished after suffering an extreme case of gout, we made a brief detour at a show that had been creating a stir around town. I sat comfortably in my box but listened intently as Horace and Hattie spoke about the exhibit, which took place in a small room off Whitechapel Road and advertised a horribly deformed young man named Joseph Merrick. The impresario, Tom Norman, had likened him to an elephant, and thus billed him as "The Elephant Man." I imagined his snout to be unusually large and perhaps dexterous, similar to that of the elongated trunk that defines the beast. I envied Hannibal, whose good fortune allowed so many of these creatures to serve him in battle.[5]

A man standing at the door demanded a penny per entry. His voice sounded weak and scrawny; I expected a portion of the proceeds collected would enable him to purchase a meal. Horace paid for himself and Hattie, and we made our entrance. Murmurs drifted through the room until finally a hush came over the crowd as Norman stepped forward to address the audience.

"Ladies and gentlemen, welcome," he began. "And thank you for stepping inside to witness the most shockingly deformed being you shall ever set eyes on. Your generous donations at the door shall go toward aiding this poor wretch. What you are about to see is the result of a most unfortunate accident, a condition rendered whilst this man still formed within his mother's womb. 'Twas during her last few months of pregnancy that she innocently walked along a narrow cobbled street and was attacked by an elephant fleeing from a travelling menagerie. The beast knocked her to the ground and frightened her so badly that the shock affected her entire system. The horrific image left in her mind transferred the impression to her unborn child, who sits behind this curtain. If there are any pregnant women present, I do ask that you leave at this time and protect your own child from such a calamitous fate. ..." Norman paused, but everyone remained still. "Ladies and gentlemen, I present to you now, Joseph Merrick—The Elephant Man!"

I heard him step aside as the curtain drew. Gasps, shouts and groans of pity immediately echoed throughout the makeshift theatre. Merrick's trunk must have been more significant than I envisioned. A woman's whimper was quickly followed by a thud. Memories of Westminster Hall flashed by. Aides rushed to assist the lady as people began to scurry out; presumably they had seen enough.

Horace, however, stepped forward. "Hello, Joseph," he said. "My name is Horace Wilkinson, and this is my wife, Hattie. We are pleased to meet to you."

"H' ... lo ..." Merrick slowly uttered back with great effort, in a soft, gentle whisper.

"This tale about your mother, do you believe it to be true?" Horace asked.

"Yyy ... esss ..." Merrick responded.

I hoped Horace and Hattie were not considering a séance with his mum. This tale perhaps gave him peace in knowing he had done nothing wrong to deserve such an ill fate.

"Well, Joseph, I know not God's reason for your suffering," said Horace, his voice brimming with sympathy. "His motives are not always evident to us. But I do know this: You are not here today, behind this curtain, to be *seen*. You are here to be *found*. You, my friend, are here to attract the attention of someone who can help you, care for you, and give you a better, more fulfilling life. With God, there is always hope."

Optimism has a way of being infectious, though did
Horace not wonder whether a hospital lobby would have
offered a more promising wealth of help?

"Would you like to see something?" Horace asked
Merrick. "An exhibit for an exhibit, if you will."

He lifted the lid of my box and drew me out slowly.
Casualties of war, beheadings, the plague, my embalmed
self—nothing in life or death had prepared me for this
sight. The majority of Merrick's body was exposed and gro-
tesquely deformed. Dark hair lay over interfluent tumours
covering his head, with the right side especially thickened
and enlarged, causing a completely asymmetrical, twisted
face. Irregular outgrowths along his forehead added to the
misshapen contour. Though his left arm and hand were
well formed, the other was massive, like a cumbersome oar.
The lumps ran down his twisted torso and legs, dominating
the right side. He sat crouched over a small brick heated
by a lamp to warm himself within the filthy room. Despite
this malformed exterior and a face that seemed incapable
of expression, an intelligent, beautiful soul beckoned from
within his eyes. Merrick was a good man who carried a fate
I would even hesitate to wish upon Charles I. If God was
to offer hope, He ought to wait no longer. Hope begets opportunity, which begets happiness and success. Yet every
crevice outlining a tumour showed that God had suspended hope. If Christ was in Merrick's heart, He was paying no
attention, for this body was Satan's foul canvas.

Horace introduced me, then eloquently shared my
glorious history—England's history, I should say—with

Merrick, who absorbed every word spoken. This was a man who had not been acclimated to the pleasures of conversation and knowledge; his was a life of stares, demands and pain. Here, Horace gave him a gift far more valuable than the monetary amount he would receive from our admission, he offered a brief education, and more important, a moment of humanity. Merrick's unblemished hand reached out and stroked my head, as if confirming I was genuine through his sense of touch.

Horace replaced me in my box, and he and Hattie tipped their hats to say a proper good-bye. Merrick's guttural sound indicated reciprocity and we made our way through the damp fog under the twilight sky to the séance. There, Horace and Hattie would act much like God in recent years—offering false hope and withholding the real thing.

XIV

SYMPATHY FOR THE DEAD

——————

The dead have never been more unfortunate. Ignorance, quite fortunately, is their salvation; if the billions of souls whose time has passed knew of the many glorious wonders that permeate the world today, they would be tormented by their inability to experience them. This was an age of invention that blurred science with sorcery and prestidigitation to enhance life considerably. It was as if God awoke from His day of rest and worked prodigiously for another six. A plethora of such new developments were revealed to me as my travels with the Wilkinsons continued.

The telephone that Horace and Hattie had spoken so fondly of became commonplace and was soon followed by a similar device that transmitted voices wirelessly—at speeds that outraced a lead ball fired from a pistol. Spiritualism had failed to establish a connection from my thoughts to the consciousness of others, but this wireless arrangement showed promise to succeed. We, the dead, desperately needed an ally. We needed someone to advance this wireless system and create a network for souls to communicate with one another, bringing light to the depths of blackness.

Oh, think what could be if every soul through time could freely speak with others! No longer would departed souls be confined to thoughts of their own existence. Was this not how men have envisioned Heaven? Infinite learnings and equally unending tales from history's most well known, accomplished, eccentric and powerful men would be readily available for all to simply listen in on. The greatest pleasures would be had in hearing their thoughts and stories: Moses describing his techniques in parting the Red Sea and how his people withstood the desert after their enslavement; Methuselah sharing his secrets of longevity; Judas reminiscing about his betrayal of Jesus and whether or not it was worth the thirty silver coins; the disciples of Christ debating with Leonardo da Vinci over the accuracy of his well-regarded painting of the Last Supper; Aristotle discussing philosophical matters with more recent thinkers (would his stutter persist in the afterlife?); Julius Caesar regretting his dismissal of Calphurnia's prophetic dream and ignoring the warning note he received whilst entering the senate house on that day of his violent murder; Thomas Aquinas reflecting on theology, having spent more than six hundred years in a box; Paracelsus discussing his methods for man to achieve immortality, yet explaining why he himself died at the age of forty-seven; Athanasius Kircher explaining the magnetic arts with meticulous specificity and then expounding on the musical merits and methods of the shrilly cat piano to that Mozart fellow and my phrenological acquaintance, Haydn; executed criminals discovering what the anatomists learned through the ravaging of their bodies; Polydamus, whose unparalleled might I oft admired, speaking of his bare-handed slaying of a lion on Mount Olympus and how his superior strength eventually failed him when the earth shook and stones crushed him to death in a cave; Maximinus, the emperor who was said to stand eight and a half feet tall, discussing his ferocious power and temper in life, and his weakness and entrapment in death; Ladislaus the Short, the fourteenth-century dwarf king of Poland, reminiscing on his military victories against those who towered over him and pointing out their follies; Charles I, should he dare speak up, whimpering about the loss of his kingdom and head; and of course, I would lecture on the tyranny of monarchs, sharing all that I have seen, and when not expounding my views, I would cherish newfound moments with family to hear of their triumphs and perils, which would surely include an explanation from Richard on his shameful abdication. Why, every man, woman and child that has perished from the land of the living could spiritually reunite and connect with ancestors. This was an exhilarating notion, but until such an idea was realised, I would be unable to share it with anyone. A conundrum, indeed; brilliance is terribly lost in the afterlife.

Wireless communications were but one fascination. Lighting, too, had been revolutionized by globular forms of glowing glass resembling the rays of the sun. Candles and gas lamps gave way to what Horace called the "electric light bulb." Days now extended into the night's territory with the greatest of ease.

Photographers had also elevated their art to a new form and created quite a spectacle through pictures that now moved, as if alive. Yet as the Wilkinsons described this miracle, I wondered whether they had simply been further fooled by a crafty Spiritualist or other mountebank. How could the inanimate suddenly be animated? This sounded like nothing more than a variation on the Frankenstein tale, and that, science had already shown, was but mere fantasy. I would need to witness this phenomenon for myself to believe it true.

As my guardians, Horace and Hattie spoke fondly of one particular moving picture sequence because of its playful story involving severed heads.[1] They did not appear mystified by the motion of the pictures, but the ability of a man to remove his head, place it upon a table where it retained its functions and expressions whilst the fellow grew another anew stymied them entirely. I, too, was intrigued by this enigma, but held greater interest in discovering how the severed heads clung to life.

However, of the many marvels I had the pleasure to observe, the most magnificent was the horseless motor car. Unlike the bicycle, this vehicle offered four large, thin wheels and required no pedalling effort to move it forth.

Instead, a loud machine had been crafted that miraculously propelled it, as if God's very own invisible finger were pushing it along at a moderate speed. Men steered it by shifting a tiller, allowing them full control of the car's motion. This would surely be a boon to the military! I envisioned bayonets lining the perimeter of the vehicle and mounted muskets shooting balls as it travelled. Armed with a fleet of motorised war cars, a battlefield could be conquered with wonderful expediency. The horse, that poor beast, had been spurned once more. It would likely find itself forced to race for the pleasure of pitiful spectators yet again.[2]

The Wilkinsons continued to preach in Kent as time ushered in the twentieth century. Their travels diminished for reasons I gladly approved of, one of which revolved around the fact that Spiritualism had begun to lose its appeal, perhaps because police had arrested several mediums proven to have misled their vulnerable patrons or because intelligent people attended séances and their intelligence prevailed. Horace spoke angrily of a case in which a medium took advantage of an elderly woman who wished to speak with her deceased husband, and persuaded her to turn over tens of thousands of pounds and rewrite her will to leave the medium everything. She sought aid from the local Vice Chancellor and hoped to regain some of her losses.

The other, more important reason, however, involved Hattie's ceasing her efforts to reach the dead so that she could create a new life. Horace Wilkinson, Jr., was born with superb vigour in a room adjacent to mine after many

long, agonising hours of labour; to judge from her screams
and moans, Hattie paid for Eve's sin dearly. It was impera-
tive that Horace Jr. maintain the good health God granted
him throughout his infancy, and extensive travelling to
conjure ghosts was not conducive to nurturing a newborn
(this boy, after all, I assumed, would one day control my
future).

Still, certain events continued to energise the Wilkinsons, particularly a visit to Buckingham Palace after the
death of Queen Victoria. There, they partook in a séance
hailed as a smashing success, complete with rappings and
messages regarding Victoria's concerns for events that
transpired in the world of the living, her hopes to inspire
her country's people as well as she could from the spirit
world and entreaties to the group to relish the reign of her
son Edward VII. I knew of no particularly bold feats or
ground-breaking policies from the king to earn such reverence—he merely shared Victoria's blood. Had there been
no man brave and cunning enough to do the Lord's bidding
and end the monarchy once again? Or was the continuation
of royalty further evidence of Almighty apathy?

News of another ghost soon after could not be ignored. Two motor-car engineers, Charles Rolls and Henry
Royce, had manufactured an exquisite vehicle and labelled
it the Silver Ghost. The name infinitely intrigued Horace
and Hattie—was this vehicle designed to aid in the manifestation of poltergeists? Could it be that one with the vision to architect something as intricate as a motor car could
also be so myopic as not to see more suitable and worth-

while applications? Not surprisingly, Rolls and Royce had heard tales of Wilkinson's possession of me and wished for a meeting in Manchester. I prayed this would lead to nothing more than a fruitless attempt at seeking spirits along the local roads; yet fear overcame me, for what if these men, who certainly had acquired wealth, wished to offer Horace and Hattie a sizeable sum of money? Would they part with me if it meant funding Horace Jr.'s rearing? So I prayed, though of late it seemed that the Lord, like the Spiritualists, had found difficulty in hearing my thoughts.

✴

It was springtime as our horse-drawn carriage made its way north. I was stowed away in my box, but it was clear that the weather had co-operated with our long journey; no rains slowed us and Horace, Hattie and the child gave no indications of discomfort throughout the nearly thirty-hour excursion. Hitherto, the elements and occasional bandits were the main obstacles along the roads, but the advent of the motor car proved a new and equally formidable threat. These horribly loud, horseless machines were growing ever more popular on the road and frightening our steeds at every passing. They were indeed shocking and the equine mind had no way in which to process the vehicles aside from obeying its natural instincts, which perceived danger. At the sight of a car, the horses came to a halt, rose upon their rear legs and neighed mightily, jerking the entire carriage. I was rattled in my casing, but thankfully Horace's diligent care ensured that the sides of the small chest were softened with padding, mitigating any potential damage to me.

Despite the occasional frights, we arrived safely in Manchester and were greeted warmly by Charles Rolls and Henry Royce. Horace wasted little time in sharing me with the two men inside their small office. I sat between the Wilkinsons and the motor-car gentlemen, atop a rugged table layered with paperwork and detailed engineering sketches, brightly illuminated by light bulbs positioned overhead. Rolls wore a dapper coat and trousers, and had neatly trimmed hair and a slight moustache. He was a young fellow whose intelligence had evidently brought him a wealth of early success. Royce, too, was young, thin and debonair with a well-groomed beard. The two men spoke passionately about their work; Royce, I learned, was the genius who had devised the engine that propelled the vehicle, whilst Rolls was the financier of the endeavour.

Their most recent creation, the Silver Ghost, we discovered had earned its title because of the sheer silence of the engine. A relief, indeed; the news offered solace for our servile horses and confidence that this was not a senseless attempt at creating a mobile Spiritualist enterprise. Horace and Hattie, on the contrary, appeared dismayed. The vehicle was visible through a long window running the length of the room behind Rolls and Royce. Truly this was a marvelous contraption, with a regal air. Two rows of grandiloquent passenger accommodations rested above slick silver sheets of steel gracefully residing around four lavish ten-spoke wheels. The long, distinguished nose of the car thrust forward like the snout of a powerful stallion. It did not appear, however, to be outfitted with a single bayonet or musket. Beyond the Silver Ghost were glimpses of the factory where labourers tinkered away; sheets of metal and complex machinery formed an industrial wonderland. 'Twas an unmistakable beacon of progress.

"Mr. Wilkinson, we view Oliver Cromwell as much more than a historical figure or an embalmed head on a shaft. We see vital traits in him. He is a symbol of strength and power," Rolls asserted.

"Independence, freedom, authority, control," Royce punctuated with a raised fist.

Aside from intelligence in the fields of engineering and business, they boasted a commendable sense of history.

"These are the attributes that define the Silver Ghost—and those who drive it," Rolls said cheerfully with a slightly elevated brow. "This is not a car for the everyman, but rather for a gentleman who appreciates the finer things and has earned the right and ability to possess them."

"Straight six-cylinder 7036cc engine," said Royce proudly, straightening his posture and adjusting his coat with a slight tug. The statement puzzled us all.

"'Tis a splendid car, to be sure, but Mr. Rolls, what need have you for the Cromwell head?" Wilkinson was bewildered by the entire meeting. "I trust curiosity is not the sole reason for our presence."

"Do not understate the power of curiosity, my

friend," Rolls retorted with widened eyes. "If not for curiosity, this marvel that sits behind us would never exist, now would it? Certainly Mr. Royce and I wished to see this most renowned of severed heads. It is indeed magnificent and perfectly peculiar. But Mr. Wilkinson, we yearned to see this head, here in the embalmed flesh, because we are in search of an emblem, a symbol to sit at the head of the vehicle. Something that represents all of the qualities of the Silver Ghost—all of the qualities the Lord Protector embodies. Imagine it: that glorious head moulded in steel, leading the way for every Rolls-Royce Motor Car, charging into the battle of daily business, granting freedom upon the open road—propped up by a thin metallic rod, reflecting the skewer that supports it now."

"An ornament for the bonnet, if you will," Royce said with a stroke of his beard.

"You want to attach this head to the cowl of the car?" Horace exclaimed in disbelief, rising slightly from his seat.

"Why, he would fall apart!" Hattie cried out. "You mustn't!"

Little Horace Jr. whimpered, and Hattie held him closer.

"Heavens, no! Pay attention, my good people," Rolls said, chortling. "We shall use the head as a model, then create a small mould to cast hundreds, nay, thousands of them to set upon each and every Rolls-Royce manufactured. A miniature Cromwell to symbolise the power and freedom these vehicles offer. We shall call it the Spirit of Supremacy!"

It would certainly be my shiniest death mask yet. The Wilkinsons demurred, and then Horace finally spoke up, albeit unintelligently. "Every Rolls-Royce, you say?"

"Oh, indeed, sir," Rolls said. "In fact, I have even considered it for our flying aircraft, once the Wright lads have it sorted out."[3]

Royce shot him a disapproving look. Had they mechanised a bird? Or had Rolls and his counterparts been re-creating Ezekiel's vision?[4] I struggled to imagine how the Silver Ghost could defy gravity and soar through the skies like the mighty eagle, but perseverance has a way of breaking new ground and leading to staggering results (with the notable exception of Spiritualism). The living, it seemed, were about to live like no others in the history of Creation. If the Lord is not to lift our souls to Heaven, men were about to take it upon themselves to make the journey.

"If God intended men to fly, Mr. Rolls, He would have made it so," Horace said, regaining his ministerial composure. "But we are bound to the earth, as the Wright brothers will soon accept."

Royce offered a hint of a nod, whilst Rolls shook his head with a negative gesture.

"I, however, am not here to preach," Horace went on. "Let us return to the matter of the ornament. How would you proceed to make such a mould? What would happen to the head?"

"Excellent question, Mr. Wilkinson!" Rolls slapped the table heartily. "Very fine enquiry. Yes, sir, indeed an important matter to discuss."

"It will be destroyed in the process of making the mould," Royce said matter-of-factly. "The machine will capture the likeness, but the pressure will crush the head during the procedure."

An uncomfortable silence filled the office.

"Yes, well, I'm afraid he's correct," Rolls said, suddenly sounding sheepish. "But we will pay you handsomely."

Horace turned to Hattie; they attempted to read each other's thoughts through their eyes. As usual, I had no say in the matter. An acceptance of the offer would of course be a most calamitous affair. What would become of me should my head be entirely pulverised? Where does the soul reside if not within the head? I had not ruminated on the possibility since the Great Fire. Perhaps I would be free to roam the earth, released from this hideous, decaying shell. Or would the destruction of the final piece of my earthly body at last launch me into God's heavenly kingdom? Though I would welcome the change, I also had to consider the notion that I might simply cease to exist and, if so, would truly be dead—dead at what promised to be the most exciting era mankind had ever known, when mechanised vehicles rolled independently along the streets and wandered the skies without the aid of feathers. This was no time to die again. Should the Wilkinsons choose to bid me farewell, one thing was certain: I would find an ending, for better or worse.

"Mr. Rolls, Mr. Royce, the embalmed head of Oliver Cromwell has been in our family for nearly a century,"

Horace said. He paused, took a deep breath and continued. "This child in our arms represents the fourth generation of Wilkinsons who will care for the head. Your plan is, without question, most exciting, but even with the financial reward you spoke of, we see no way in which we could part with the Lord Protector. Not only is the thought of losing him unbearable, but the notion that after all these years, after all he has been through—the bloody battles in life, the posthumous impalement, the assorted owners—after all that, mind you, Hattie and I would be the two people history would forever remember as responsible for Oliver Cromwell's complete demise is simply unthinkable. Gentlemen, I am afraid we must decline."

Spiritualism may have infected a portion of his brain, but Horace still had his integrity. I could hardly be prouder to be a preserved skewered head.

"Very well. Very well, Mr. and Mrs. Wilkinson," Rolls said. He and Royce stood from their seats and extended their hands to politely terminate the meeting. Horace, Hattie, Horace Jr. and I began our exit, but the Silver Ghost beckoned one last time. I imagined for a brief moment a thousand Cromwell heads commanding these motor cars and offering immorality in every driver's heart and mind. Still, I preferred eternity right here in Horace's hand.

XV

WAR AND PEACE OF MIND

———

Absence has oft been known to make the heart grow fonder. For the Wilkinsons, the very thought of absence had the same effect. After the proposal by Rolls and Royce, Horace and Hattie endeavoured to share me more frequently and ensure that Horace Jr. grew well acquainted with me. In regard to the latter, this included bedtime stories of my triumphs in the Commonwealth and extended into fabricated tales of my reign as Lord Protector continuing within our home, claiming that I—by existing beneath this roof—prevented a being known as the bogeyman from entering the boy's room at night. "Fear not the bogeyman, little Horace," they would tell the lad as he whimpered in the dark. "Cromwell watches over you. That vile monster may give you a fright, but Cromwell strikes fear into its wicked heart—he dare not enter a room watched over by the mighty Lord Protector!" I was pleased to oblige.

As for the general public, I offered the loftier service of encouraging historical and scientific discourse wherever the Wilkinsons could gather an audience round me. To aid in this venture, Horace arranged a photography session at a local studio to capture my image, which could be used to promote my actuality and as documentation for the annals of history. Ornate furniture, ostentatious drapery, assorted elaborate costumes and background props saturated the space to invigorate the images; Horace elected to keep mine simple and declined the use of such paraphernalia. The encounter with the photographic artist himself went quickly—remarkably faster than even the finest, most experienced painter could offer. He simply aimed the large, box-like contraption at me as his surrounding electric lighting brought forth illumination, and with graceful hands he shifted me into various positions, then allowed the device to capture and celebrate my every angle.

These images were put to use with haste in the year of Our Lord 1911, when the members of the Royal Archaeological Institute of Great Britain and Ireland, presided over by Sir Henry H. Howorth, K.C.I.E., D.C.I., F.R.S., F.S.A., held a meeting and discussion over my provenance at their quarters in London. Howorth was a towering, lanky gentleman with thick oval spectacles and a notable moustache that curled toward his balding head. A dark jacket and slim, straight trousers accentuated his height. His distinguished appearance, coupled with the many letters following his surname, indicated that he was a very learned and important man and that thus his opinion of me would be well respected—though I prayed the royal nature of the organisation would not have a biased agenda. In most gatherings the voice of doubt continued to squawk and squeal, and so I welcomed any opportunity to quiet such clamour.

Horace addressed the small roomful of attendees to share my history with his family. He explained the rarity of the exhibition, citing his distinct pleasure in presenting me to a group who would treat me with the reverence I deserved. My earlier history, as recorded by Josiah Wilkinson, ensued, to the delight of the assembly. Howorth spoke next and, to my relief and joy, delivered a speech defending my authenticity in response to an article published in the year of Our Lord 1905 by an obviously ignorant doctor, named Welldon, in the *Nineteenth Century Review*. Like my other recent detractor, Carlyle, this Dr. Welldon had never made my acquaintance. As Howorth began, his words of wisdom on the matter proved his countless suffixes were indeed credible. He presented a thorough background on my death, Dr. Bate's autopsy, my embalming, the exhumation, the decapitation, the impalement and an abbreviated account of the travels that led me to the Wilkinson family, before he finally arrived at the source of Welldon's reservations:

"Dr. Welldon objects altogether to the story of the Cox and Wilkinson head. He requires external evidence, or as he calls it, 'historical support,' and entirely neglects the internal evidence afforded by the head itself. He objects to it because there is a gap between 1684 and 1787 not bridged over by any evidence of identity. But the deed set out above, by which Samuel Russell sold the head to James Cox in 1787, is only the last act in the possession of the head by the Russell family. He objects, somewhat illogically, that the head was not sold by Cox when he sold his museum in 1775, though it was not till 1787, twelve years later, that Cox is alleged to have bought the head."

Facts, it seemed, were of interest only when supporting the doctor's suppositions.

"Dr. Welldon objects also that the head 'could not well have been sold by Cox privately without attracting attention,'" Howorth continued. "This seems to be pushing the demand for historical evidence to an absurd extreme. But Dr. Welldon admits that the Wilkinson head is probably the head sold to Cox in 1787. This traces it back into the possession of the Russells, and it is quite natural that they should have had it. For the Russells were an obscure family in Huntingdonshire, but they were related three times over by inter-marriage with the Cromwells, and it is most natural that the skull should come into their possession, and not into the possession of the Cromwells themselves, because the Cromwells during the eighteenth century preferred to lie low. One need not say they were ashamed of their descent from the great Protector, but they were reticent about it, and did not put it forward, but kept it as secret as they could because it created great odium and unpopularity in those times."

It had taken two hundred years, but my theory on my family's absence was finally corroborated by an adept historian. Time provides all at its own pace.

Aside from my period with Du Puy, my hereafter was indeed kept secretive in the early years, accounting for the dearth of historical support and evidence. But Howorth was not intimidated by the lack of records.

"At this point, therefore, we have to leave the external and to rely on the internal evidence, the evidence of the object itself," he said, "which in many cases is far more valuable than a mere oral or written testimony, since it is much more difficult to sophisticate and to invent.

"Those who dispute the authenticity of the head and consider it a fake have to argue that a bibulous and impoverished man like Russell, or some unknown person from whom he had it, was lucky enough to find a fresh corpse of which the head was so like Cromwell's that it has convinced some of the very best judges in our annals that it must have been that of Cromwell himself, and no one else. Surely a miraculous discovery! Who has ever seen Cromwell's double? Having found the corpse, this person, who must have known that Cromwell's body was embalmed—when the fact was only known to two or three persons in the realm—should have embalmed it in such a perfect way as was only possible in the case of a skilled embalmer, at a time when skilled embalmers could be counted on the fingers of one hand. He then would have beheaded the corpse by blows from a rude axe and having done so would have thrust a pike through it—a pike whose iron head in 1787 was decayed and oxidised, and the part outside the skull much more decayed than the part inside, and whose handle was so worm-eaten that a skilled witness pronounced it a century ago to be one hundred and fifty years old. That all these concurrent things should have been done in order to make believe that the head was genuinely that of Cromwell at a time when Cromwell's reputation had not been rescued from his detractors, and when even a scientific man of high repute like Sir Joseph Banks could speak of him as a mere villain.

"Those people who can believe all this," Howorth concluded, "can believe anything."

The audience applauded Howorth's lecture and Institute members swarmed around me to gain a better image to match his eloquent words. It was another welcomed step toward the universal acceptance of my authenticity.

※

As the century progressed, life continued to evolve in remarkable fashion. The streets grew more crowded with motor cars driven by eager businessman hurrying their way toward healthier fortunes. The aircraft Charles Rolls had spoken of became a reality, and now men could be spotted in the skies, but unlike angels, they were armed with enormous metal wings and a spinning propeller guiding their travels. The aristocratic class could not have been more pleased with their new conveniences and luxuries. The poor, however, laboured away as always, still prone to disease and misery—the latter exacerbated with the knowledge of all the wonders they could have no part of. ('Tis much easier to accept being poor when there is less to be had.) Royalty's sense of entitlement always favoured the wealthy; it did not consider the less fortunate, for whose benefit I, a humble servant of the people, had worked so diligently.

These brief observations were ascertained as Horace began to carry me through the streets of London more often, frequently to an area of Hyde Park he referred to as Speaker's Corner. Here, at the end of a long walkway beneath a canopy of shady trees and fields of greenery, a motley assortment of characters gathered to preach whatever thoughts ailed their minds. Horace spoke there of God's missions for us all, using me as a prime example.

During these occasions, I was held by my stake high above his head and waved when needed to accentuate a point. This provided me an outstanding vantage point to observe the throngs of people congregated throughout and, in particular, round Horace as he preached about our earthly existence and the purpose and importance of our individual plans, regardless of their size. As he delved into my history, he gave emphasis to my rise from obscurity and my devotion to serving the Lord, delivering change and so forth. It was all very pleasant to hear, with the exception of the common interruptions by argumentative people wishing to cast doubt upon God's existence or His role in daily life.

At times these arguments sparked lengthy, heated

debates, which I would have been interested in hearing had I been able to pay attention. This was an impossibility due to all the competing speakers shouting about multifarious topics. I oft heard quite a loquacious fuss over impending doom for the nation, though no logical reason or evidence was offered beyond interpretations of Bible verses. Other hullaballoos focused on Jesus, but not as Horace had spoken—these were overzealous proselytisers threatening anyone who would listen with an eternity in Hell should they not accept Christ. I abhorred religious intolerance and found these misguided souls to be little more than amusing park novelties. Many of those who expended energy arguing with Horace sought further thrills with these preachers, though neither side was to be convinced of the other's position.

On occasion, speakers fought in defence of animals. One such argument raged over the use of a new invention designed to prevent hens from sitting. The mechanism comprised a breastplate, which was to be secured to the fowl, along with two false legs attached to the plate that would force the bird to remain upright. Farmers must have wished to dissuade their feathered workers from a propensity toward laziness when not nurturing eggs. It was an entirely unnatural device and unfair to the hens, who were fortunate to have such vocal advocates. Sadly, I heard no voices quarrelling over the rapidly declining employment of our equine population.

Mixed in with the doomsayers, missionaries and animal activists were blessed opportunities to learn of news and concerns of the day. The death of King Edward VII was a popular topic: many regretted his passing and hailed him as a peacemaker throughout Europe; others lambasted him for enjoying far too many cigars and cigarettes each and every day, which they seemed to feel were responsible for his fatal bronchitis and heart attacks; some went on raving madly about his successor, King George V, who they believed was behind a conspiracy that led to his elder brother Albert's death years before, a grand plan to snatch the throne the moment it was vacated.

Another frequently vocalised concern surrounded the more intriguing subject of women's suffrage. There was much discussion about one of its leaders, Emily Davison, who had just been trampled to death by George V's horse during a derby. This woman, some said, was attempting to attach a symbolic scarf to the horse to bring attention to her mission. Some believed she had simply given up and committed suicide, perhaps hoping that the act would force the king to hasten his consideration of the matter. Others believed it was a desperate tactic from a woman who had been imprisoned multiple times and force-fed often, though there were no discussions around the quality or variety of foods forced upon her. The matter at hand, however, was less about her specific purpose that day, but more about her goal of attaining rights for women. In many ways, Davison was a weak female version of me in her defiance of tyranny. I applauded her spirit and efforts, for why should women not have a say in how they are to be governed? Are they not citizens of the state? Did a woman not give life to the very king who wished to suppress her gender? 'Twas a shame that Davison lacked the military skills and might to stage a proper uprising. A paucity of courageous men gathered in support of the women's cause, though I detected some who lingered simply to leer, entirely ignoring the affair. Had the women been endowed with the bravery and strength of men, they would have slaughtered these libidinous lurkers on the spot and usurped the king's attention immediately.

Other bellowing characters were rankled after the sinking of an enormous ship referred to as the Titanic. Anger arose over the state of shipbuilding and inspections, the lack of safety precautions and the reasons why the ship's careless captain ignored warnings. There were also the pompous attitudes of boasters who claimed the ship was unsinkable, and the beliefs of others that God Himself punished the passengers for this arrogance. To an extent, this latter thought was in accordance with Thomas Beard's thinking, but he would have argued that only those who made the haughty declaration would have suffered the Lord's wrath, not the innocents aboard the beastly boat. To my understanding, the Titanic was a peaceful ship not engaged in warfare, so its demise was a most unfortunate tragedy.

But more distracting than any of this vociferousness— whether deranged or intellectual—was the realisation that this corner of Hyde Park was once the site of the gallows of Tyburn.[1] Horace had unknowingly returned me to the very site of my hanging and decapitation. Had I had an opportunity to speak, I reckon I would have initially addressed the detestable actions of Charles II toward me. (Even though he saved me from eternal darkness, his motives sicken me to this day.) More important, the occasion would afford me the chance to explain how each and every body hanged in this very spot witnessed those who cheered his demise after succumbing to the ails of death; the true punishment was not execution, but burial. As I have emphasised earlier in these pages, I would highly encourage families to disinter their dead at once and provide them a more suitable home for the afterlife. Mass acceptance of my words would create an economic boon with new jobs employing thousands of able-bodied men—and willing women—to dig for mercy. Others would find fortunes in the craftsmanship of displays for the departed: coffins with glass ceilings, slim-tailored wardrobes, elaborate cabinets with windows and lovely silk-lined boxes for heads, such as mine.

The dead, however, soon became the most debated topic and the reason our regular visits to the corner eventually ceased. The Commonwealth had declared war on Germany. The cause, as I understood it, involved the defence of little Belgium, which had been invaded by the German military in defiance of a treaty. Horace continued to preach in the name of God, but matters of war grew increasingly dire as the number of dead soldiers escalated—eight countries, which, to my knowledge included France and Russia, and more than seventeen million men were engaged in the bloody conflict. Horace offered few answers to satisfy. Those who had suffered losses raised difficult questions in regard to the Almighty's lack of intervention and His acceptance of what had been termed the Great War.

As we made our way back home to Kent during these wartime sessions, we witnessed drills in the park and other open areas. Armed soldiers and recruits still in civilian clothing marched proudly and confidently through the streets, which were flanked by news articles and posters in storefront windows seeking the enlistment of "all unmarried men aged eighteen to thirty to serve the king and country in this hour of need." The subject dominated conversation wherever we went; people supported England's efforts and believed without that aid to Belgium, Germany would continue to conquer European nations and impose its military might over all. The English, to my boundless satisfaction, would not allow it.

I witnessed no military vehicles resembling the Silver Ghost, but my ingenious concept of affixing weaponry to motorised cars did indeed come to pass with machines referred to as "tanks." They appeared to be mechanised, rolling cannons—a frightful weapon. Oh, how I wished to be mounted upon the front end of one to head into battle with my countrymen. It would be as Rolls and Royce wanted, but with a greater purpose. I would be an inspiration, the Commonwealth's greatest military mind striking fear into the hearts of enemies—though it was doubtful they would ever get close enough to my decaying countenance for such fear to strike. At first I expected that these tanks, perhaps enhanced with telephones, would provide a swift victory for England, but talk of similar German battle vehicles and armoured cars indicated that other nations had discovered ways in which to automate carriages as well. Enormous bulbous German airships, called zeppelins, rained terror from the sky, too; I expected subterranean weaponry would soon surface as well. The Commonwealth needed an advantage. I amusingly imagined all remaining practicing Spiritualists entering combat by summoning spirit warriors (though no further endeavours to contact me were made). Surely such phantoms could rap and knock upon the tables of German military personnel, scattering schemes as they plotted, and thenceforth frightening them into submission without further need for bloodshed. Those who died in battle could have an immediate second chance in the newfound field of ghost warfare. Yes, Spiritualism could prove quite effective, but alas, the powers of charlatans, by definition, are limited in their reach. Horace and Hattie seemed to have realised this or had simply not considered enlisting the dead.

As the war progressed and danger increased, Horace, Hattie and Horace Jr.—the boy was, mercifully, too young to enlist—stayed close to home. On occasion I overheard details of battles and plans, including an uplifting anecdote that brightened the Wilkinson household: the First Lord of the Admiralty, Winston Churchill, proposed to name a new, formidable battleship the *Cromwell*. Unfortunately, the proposal failed to come to fruition; George V vetoed the suggestion, clearly upset by the anti-royalist moniker and ignorant of the military weight it carried. This Churchill, however, showed great promise.

The terrifying face of modern weaponry unleashed a brutal temper, causing massive casualties and bloodshed unlike any I recalled. In my day, carnage was often much more personal, with my own hand distributing fatalities one by one. Bellows of mercy and pain waned as my victims' blood dribbled to a halt and their final breaths evaporated into the air to be inhaled by the victors. Surely a measure of such combat continued to exist, but tanks and aircraft seemed to deliver the same assaults from afar.

Tales of the Great War subsided with Horace's decision to tuck me away in my box and take me to the cellar, where he felt I would be safe and survive should German forces penetrate Kent and destroy the Wilkinson home. I was grateful he wished to ensure my continued existence, yet I struggled with the notion that I, Oliver Cromwell, was cowering from battle.

Alone in the darkness, I heard occasional explosions, which sounded as if ammunition had soared to the ground from great heights. The thunderous detonations sent shockwaves through the earth, surely rattling anyone in the vicinity who had been just outside its lethal strike zone. Each impact left a deafening thud as though God had pummelled His omnipotent fist into the earth, cracking it open to free demons from their netherworld domain—for the sound was louder than the collective cries of a thousand slaughtered royalists. A chill ran through what little bone remained with me. How many innocent lives were unfairly taken to pay the price for freedom from an invading nation? How many children would never see their own futures? War was a ruthless, heartless beast. With each colossal blast, I immediately listened for footsteps and voices in the seconds that followed; save for the occasional cellar visits, those soft sounds were my only indication that the Wilkinsons remained safe.

Were these explosives indeed dropped from floating zeppelins, or had God finally made an appearance? Did fire rain from Heaven as it had upon the Egyptians? Notwithstanding the source, I wondered why England was on the receiving end. Had the Lord found greater favour with Germany? Were its people mobilised by a leader like me, someone whom God had spoken to and directed to take down the English monarchy once and for all? Horace had once mentioned that the German emperor was a deeply religious man who claimed, "We Germans fear God and nothing else in the world."[2] However, judging from the brutality of the Great War, as far as I had been able to learn, I considered the notion that these events might be leading to a more extreme outcome than regicide—this could very well have been that which had been prophesied: Armageddon and the second coming of Jesus Christ. This was to be a time when those who believed ascended to Heaven and those who rejected Christ would suffer forevermore. A thousand years of peace would follow. If this was that epic battle, if these were the end of days for mankind, it seemed quite possible that God would at last send Christ once again, and all of us writhing souls would be freed. All those who have endured the darkness, the travesty of burial, would at last see the light once again as the gates of Heaven would open and beckon each and every one of us to pass through. Families reunited, friends reacquainted and, finally, deceased

Spiritualists truly speaking with the dead.

I spent the next several years hidden away in the cellar, fearing for the safety of the Wilkinsons—particularly the boy, who was likely approaching the age of eighteen—and awaiting the return of Christ. Unable to assist my country, I was left to envision methods of warfare with this newer model army. Despite all the wondrous machinery on land and air, I imagined England's naval forces leading the primary efforts by stifling Germany's trade by sea. An impenetrable blockade would weaken the German economy and cause suffering amongst its citizens; without their ability to import rations, starvation would prove to be a vital threat, just as dangerous and deadly as encroaching tanks.

I know not how the frays were ultimately fought, but I eventually observed that the Wilkinsons survived and Jesus never materialised—Armageddon, it seemed, had been the one battle that had *not* been fought. When Horace at last retrieved me and displayed me in their living chambers once again, it was in a room filled with sunlight and the warm smiles of the family and several visitors who were discussing England's victory and the Treaty of Versailles, which had apparently ended the Great War. Their joy was balanced by their lament for what they believed to be more than ten million dead worldwide. God had granted us victory, but Heaven remained elusive.

*

The war having passed, victorious Englishmen once again

devoted their attention to less critical matters. Whilst I remained a treasured spectacle within the Wilkinson home, not unexpectedly, I soon became one of these distractions after a journalist uncovered pictures from my pre-war photographic session and published them. The images accompanied an article that described my residence within a private collection and surprisingly included a grievance over the fact that I had not been cherished as a national treasure for all the people to enjoy. Horace feared the editorial piece might spark a public outcry demanding the same notion, forcing George V to seize me from the Wilkinsons and display me—as a symbol of English military might—on a crowded shelf with royal décor, or worse, rebury me. Time proved him correct in regard to the former concern, but as for the latter, I found solace in hearing that the king had declined to confiscate me, out of the belief that a shred of doubt still hovered around my head. This was a quite acceptable and fair line of logic, but in truth, it was no different to his rejection of Churchill's attempt at naming a battleship.

Journalists, craniologists and historians bombarded Horace, Hattie and even Horace Jr.—by now a pleasant and devout adult—for opportunities to study me and provide final, undisputable proof that I, now referred to as the Wilkinson Head, was truly me. Following an article in *Cassell's Weekly*, the editor of the periodical wrote personally requesting permission to lend me to an "eminent craniologist," Arthur Keith, so that his studies might be published for the readers of a future edition. Horace responded:

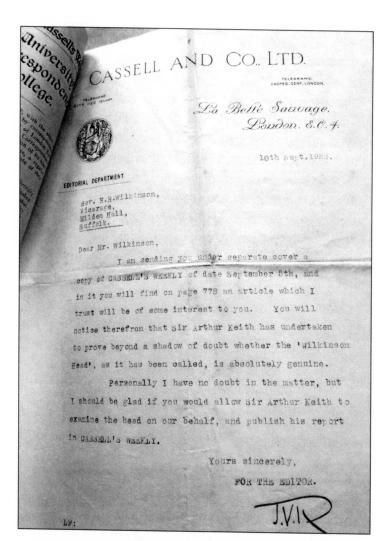

CASSELL AND CO., LTD.

TELEGRAMS:
CASPES. CENT. LONDON.

La Belle Sauvage,
London, E.C.4.

10th Sept. 1923.

EDITORIAL DEPARTMENT

Rev. H.R.Wilkinson,
Vicarage,
Milden Hall,
Suffolk.

Dear Mr. Wilkinson,

I am sending you under separate cover a
copy of CASSELL'S WEEKLY of date September 5th, and
in it you will find on page 778 an article which I
trust will be of some interest to you.   You will
notice therefrom that Sir Arthur Keith has undertaken
to prove beyond a shadow of doubt whether the 'Wilkinson
Head', as it has been called, is absolutely genuine.

Personally I have no doubt in the matter, but
I should be glad if you would allow Sir Arthur Keith to
examine the head on our behalf, and publish his report
in CASSELL'S WEEKLY.

Yours sincerely,

FOR THE EDITOR.

J.V.R

LW:

Cassell's Weekly *requested my head in 1923.*

Dear Sir,

I have read your article re Oliver Cromwell's head, in which you advocate depriving me of the relic.

I have no wish for Sir Arthur Keith's opinion, and am afraid that I cannot agree to placing the Head in any one's custody for the purpose of identification.

If you care to approach Dr. Welldon, I believe that he will assure you that the head in my possession is not that of Oliver Cromwell.

Believe me yours faithfully,

H. Wilkinson

Horace denied other requests as well, as each wished to remove me from the home for extended periods of time. The Wilkinsons had no desire to lend me to these enquiring minds, nor did Horace believe further proof of my authenticity was required. Despite his rejections, periodicals printed stories filled with conjecture, speculation and, on occasion, amusing nonsense, which Horace joyfully read aloud to Hattie, such as this anecdotal rubbish from a writer by the name of Van Zalrik:

> Some years before the late War, in Oklahoma, during a Shakespearean theatrical tour through the North American continent, I saw a mummified head, which was said to be Cromwell's. It was in company with a mummified body of Wilkes Booth, the assassin of Lincoln, though not, of course, at-

tached thereto, in the manner one so frequently sees
in Italian museums, of heads of Marcus Aurelius
fixed (by pruning the neck) on to statues of Nero
and Caracalla.

The undertaker who exhibited them declared
he had authentic documents relating to both exhibits, for seeing which latter he charged two dollars,
though it is but fair to say that, "as colleagues in
the show business" as he expressed it, we of the
Shakespeare company were admitted gratis. Unfortunately, pressure of work—the production on four
plays every week, for instance—deprived us of the
leisure necessary for the examination of the documents, the more regretted by the exhibitor as one of
our company, an Englishman, observed that he had
once seen a different-looking head of Cromwell at a
fair in a provincial town in England.

I had become an inter-continental sensation. How
many other heads of mine were being exhibited by show-
men, and what manner of documentation had they fabricated? And would anyone ever disinter William Shakespeare
so that he might at last enjoy his unwavering success?

As chatter and debate carried on with time, my good
fortune with the Wilkinsons shifted when Horace fell ill and
elected to bequeath me to Horace Jr. The young man had
followed in his father's footsteps—save the errant Spiritualist path—and become Canon Horace Wilkinson, vicar at a
nearby parish. In recent years our relationship had become

distanced, which I attributed to the Great War and my stint in the cellar, which coincided with Horace Jr.'s formative years. Though our bond was strong during his childhood, absence turned to apathy and that valued connection was weakened. Thus, unlike his father, grandfather and great-grandfather, Canon Horace elected not to treat me as a cherished centrepiece within his tranquil home and instead transferred me to a set of gleaming hatboxes—one inside the other, with unsightly green lining that fortunately was innocuous enough in the dark when the lids were firmly in place. Where headdresses once sat, now rested the head of England's greatest military hero and leader, somewhere along the eastern coast in Woodbridge, Suffolk. Considering how close my guardians had been to God, I struggled to understand why I felt closer to Hell. My new boxes were kept beneath his bed, where I myself became a bed to his slothful feline companion—until a visitor triggered Canon Horace to exhibit me, allowing the meandering cat to witness the contents of his sleeping quarters and pick up my scent. From then on, the creature found a new place to lie, leaving intermittent squeaks of the mattress springs as my only company—the frequency of which increased significantly after Canon Horace took a wife, a lass he called Norma. The fortitudinous coils and wooden frame defended me from being squashed under a collapse.

By the year of Our Lord 1934, I was to make a prolonged escape from the lonely nether region of the bed, as Canon Horace succumbed to persistent external pressures and allowed me to be taken away for a thorough examination by a eugenicist, Karl Pearson, and an anthropologist, Geoffrey Morant. I knew not the role nor the purpose of a eugenicist, but whatever his field of specialty, Pearson had allegedly achieved a great deal of eminence after founding a journal called *Biometrika* and having worked with an alleged genius named Einstein. Leaving the Wilkinson home and family was dreadfully difficult, for I had spent nearly half my afterlife so far with them.

When the gentlemen arrived to collect me, Canon Horace had already secured me within my box. There were no good-byes, no tears to moisten my lid, no sniffles brought upon by weeping, because this was not a good-bye, this was but a temporary farewell. I heard numerous expected pleasantries exchanged, but as Pearson and Morant gathered me and prepared to take their leave, Canon Horace had one final request: "I do expect you shall return Cromwell precisely as he has been handed to you within the agreed-upon three months. I am the fourth-generation owner of the Lord Protector—and I expect to bequeath him to the fifth."

His words warmed my metaphorical heart.

※

Pearson and Morant eagerly analyzed every aspect of me, though unlike Donovan, the preposterous phrenologist, their techniques and conclusions appeared rooted in logic and science. Whilst I was initially saddened to leave Canon Horace, it was admittedly a pleasure to be revered once again and freed from the iridescent hatboxes. Pearson was the elder of the two men by many years. His slow movements, greyed hair and face engulfed in wrinkles indicated he was likely a septuagenarian, though his wide eyes bulging from behind his wired spectacles still showed a youthful passion for his work. Morant looked to be half Pearson's age and perhaps served as an apprentice. He carried a portly frame but maintained an energetic disposition and was eager to please Pearson. Both wore black coats over buttoned vests and dark trousers like most every gentleman I'd witnessed in recent years. They worked in an undersized, windowless office crawling with unusual equipment, convoluted gadgetry and, along the shelving, profuse gimcrackery. I knew nothing of any of it, but assumed it served important scientific duties and generated profound knowledge. I sat upon a wooden table laden with paperwork, complex charts, several books by the Einstein prodigy and another called *The Origin of Species*, authored by Charles Darwin, stacks of *Biometrika* and other ephemera.

The two recorded copious notes daily describing my features, researching my history and comparing my visage with my likenesses in portraits and my death mask. It appeared that they had already achieved much more success in discovering my story than Cranch ever had.

Morant photographed me from every angle using a significantly smaller camera than had been used in years prior; the photographs were posted on the wall and for the first time, I could see myself in my entirety. A cincture marking the removal of my skullcap when the embalmer retrieved my brain highlighted my right profile, as did the absence of my ear. This latter mutilation was quite bothersome to see so clearly, despite the fact the atrocity had occurred nearly two hundred years before. I took solace in knowing the culprit had by now lost both his ears, along with every ounce of flesh on his body. The tip of the iron prong atop my head was corroded but remained sturdy. My left profile was similar, but featured an ear, albeit slightly distorted, a fracture toward the posterior of my skull, as well as neatly combed hair of a reddish hue on my scalp—more, perhaps, than Morant had covering his own head. A close image of my posterior offered detailed marks from the saw that had created the cincture and the sutures that reunited my skullcap and me, whilst a wider photograph displayed the crude marks from the executioner's multiple failed attempts in my beheading. My face had remained relatively unchanged over the centuries, but at last, I saw what so many others had seen. Horrific in so many ways, yet strangely handsome as well—after all, I was unquestionably a wondrous relic.

In addition to the photography, Morant and Pearson used a new machine unlike anything I had previously encountered, the Omega Electric Cabinet. With its oak cabinet and white marbled switchboard and nickel-plated fittings, it appeared to be part furniture and part laboratory. Pearson excitedly rambled on about Autoinduction, Thermo-Faradic, Sinusoidal and Phosphoric currents as he discussed making what he called a radiograph of me to better grasp my "genetics." Whatever the purpose of these

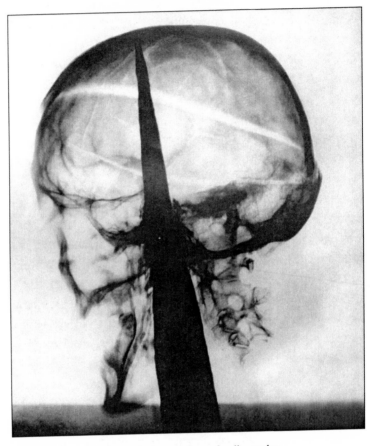

Through the wonders of radiography,
Pearson and Morant could peer inside my head.

currents, they painlessly permeated me beneath a warm lamp as Morant fiddled with the dials. Shortly afterward, the machine produced a magical image that looked like a photograph of the inside of my head. Here, I could see the entire spike invading my skull, thick toward the bottom and tapering off toward the protruding point on the exterior. It looked frighteningly painful, but I rather liked the picture. There was, however, no image or indication of my soul.

After months of study and meticulous recording of their results, Pearson and Morant invited Canon Horace to their office to share their findings before publication. At his arrival I was immediately greeted with a wide smile as he clutched me in his hands and held me up proudly, like a new father. To my surprise, that was precisely what he was—Norma now joined him and lovingly held two newborns. Cradled in one arm was a daughter, Laura, and in the other, her twin brother, Horace Norman Stanley, whom they called Norman. He, undoubtedly, would be my future Wilkinson. Norman was a plump boy and, to judge from his steady fussing, apparently hungry. Laura slept peacefully.

The scientists exchanged pleasantries with the Wilkinsons, and when Norma excused herself to calm Norman, Pearson and Morant promptly began discussing their thorough research, which corroborated Josiah Wilkinson's initial documents. Detailed observations based on historical knowledge of me in comparison with the Wilkinson Head followed—this demonstrated that the latter was indeed my head. Canon Horace remained seated as the scientists paced the room and alternated this telling of facts:

"Observation number one!" Morant began. "Cromwell had the skull-cap removed and the brain weighed. James the First's skull-cap was removed by saw and chisel."

"The Wilkinson Head has had the skull-cap removed by saw and a small piece probably by chisel," Pearson noted. "Just as James the First and Cromwell had."

"Number two!" Morant continued.

"Geoffrey, there's no need to shout, please carry on and contain your enthusiasm," Pearson commented.

"It's quite all right, I appreciate his vim and vigour," Canon Horace said with a titter.

"Number two, then," Morant said. "Cromwell's skull-cap would be stitched on again, for those death masks which show the cincture or the wrap, indicate that it must have been re-fixed."

"The Wilkinson Head shows thread holes round the border of the skull-cap," Pearson said, pointing to the photographs pinned to the wall, one by one. "The shrinkage of the flesh round the cincture indicates that the skull-cap was separated before embalmment."

"Number three"—Morant withheld his enthusiasm—"Cromwell's body was embalmed. There is some doubt as to the thoroughness of this embalmment. This could only arise from Bate's statement in the *Elenchus*, but we do not know whether this refers only to what took place immediately after the autopsy, or whether a more thorough embalmment did not follow later.[3]

"It is reasonably certain that a death mask of Cromwell was taken, ten to fourteen days after his death. It follows therefore that the account given by Bate is incorrect, grossly exaggerated, or that putrescence was checked by a later, more perfect embalmment. There is no reason to doubt that Cromwell's body went on September 20th to Somerset House, lay under the bed of state with the effigy, and was interred to Henry the Seventh's Chapel on Wednesday, October 27th."

A curious statement, indeed. The older the facts, the more fictitious they become.

"As to the effectiveness of the embalmment, we do not think much one way or the other can be deduced from Sainthill's description of the condition of the body at Tyburn," Morant said confidently.[4]

I knew nothing of Sainthill or his description, but presumed he had witnessed the proceedings following my exhumation.

"The Wilkinson Head has been embalmed," Pearson responded. "The present condition of the flesh is like tanned leather. It has been held that this head has been very badly embalmed, largely to prove that the head does not disagree with Bate's statement in the *Elenchus*.

"On the other hand, some have asserted that it has been extremely well embalmed, and to meet the evidence drawn from Bate and fearing that the genuine head would not be well embalmed, they have tried to interpret Sainthill's words 'very fresh embalmed' as indicating that Cromwell's head was actually well embalmed. On the whole it seems to us that this head must have been very thoroughly preserved, or the flesh could not have lasted at least one hundred sixty-one and very probably two hundred twenty-four years without falling to pieces. If it has lasted that time, it may well have lasted two hundred seventy-six years, even if, during some twenty-five or twenty-six of those additional years, it was exposed to the weather. We do not understand by 'well embalmed' a process which has succeeded in preserving excellently the features of the subject, but rather one which has prevented most of the facial skin and the membranes from perishing, by converting them into leather."

"There is no question, then, in your estimation, that my family's head is genuine?" Canon Horace asked.

"Please, Mr. Wilkinson, allow us to continue our analysis," Morant answered. "Number four. Cromwell's head was hewn off while his whole body was still in its cerecloths, for Sainthill tells us that owing to these it took eight blows of the axe to remove the head. There is no doubt therefore that the neck must have been badly hewn about. We know that the head was placed upon a pole on Westminster Hall. There appears to be no extant account of how the heads of traitors were attached to their supporting poles. We know that such poles were fifteen to twenty feet in length and therefore must have been of stout build. The conception that such heads were placed on pikes, which would not have the requisite length or substance seems improbable, nor are the diamond or laurel leaf sections of the pike, however suitable for piercing flesh, the best for ram-

ming through bone. If Cromwell's head had been blown
down, it might either have been thrown off its spike, or the
pole might have snapped."

"Indeed." Pearson cleared his throat. "The Wilkinson head has been attached to an oaken pole, surrounded
by an iron spike of square section tapering to a point. The
top of the oaken pole to a length of eight inches has been
broken off. The iron prong—something like the straightened prong of a pitchfork—is carried by a rudely shaped
flat inverted collar, nailed onto the top of the post. The
collar and nails are well shown in our plates reproducing
skiagrams of the head. The pole has been long in contact
with the head, for some of the worm holes pass through
the head and the pole. The spike where it has penetrated
the skull-cap has rusted away, but inside the brain-box it
has been less attacked. The iron prong and collar are rough
blacksmith's work. This prong has been so forcibly thrust
through the skull-cap that it has split it from the place of
penetration to the right border."

"Worm holes," Canon Horace said with an air of rev-
elation. "That's what those are, then. How lovely."

"Number *five*." Morant grew giddy again. "The pictures of Cromwell show generally a mass of light brown,
reddish hair. Lady Payne-Gallwey's miniatures—one certainly by Samuel Cooper—both show Cromwell with greying light brown hair. The portrait of Cromwell by Cooper
in Sidney Sussex College shows grey hair, and a portrait in
profile—a copy by Bernard Lees—in the possession of the
Duke of Portland shows Cromwell aged, and his hair very

thin. There is no doubt that he had changed considerably in appearance before he died.

"All the portraits of Cromwell show the short cut 'beardlet' below the underlip. This was the fashion of the day. Bradshaw wore the beardlet long, so that it came to a point below the chin, and Ireton's beard was of the same type."

Yes, many of us wore our beards in this style quite simply because it was a handsome look, a follicle-powered symbol of manliness that commanded respect. Morant would have done well to follow this form of grooming.

Norma now reentered the room with Norman and Laura. The boy had ceased making unintelligible noises and joined his sister in slumber at their mother's bosom. She sat beside Horace, who nodded with a smile to affirm all was going in their favour.

Pearson continued: "The hair on the Wilkinson Head is sparse, remarkably fine and of a light reddish-brown tinge. This fineness might possibly be due to the perishing of the substance of the hair, and the redness might be indicative of the diffused pigment left, after the melanotic pigment had largely perished. Again it may be that the hair was grey and the redness arises from staining by preservatives. Charles the First had grizzled black hair at the time of his execution. At his exhumation in 1813, his scalp hair was a beautiful dark brown and his beard a redder brown."

Charles I was exhumed in the year of Our Lord 1813? I knew nothing of this matter! For what reason was the traitor disinterred, and what became of him? Had his head been scrutinised as mine had been? Was it reburied after a brief tease of the world, or had it been freed to enjoy the hereafter in peace within a palace? This was a most disturbing development; if the latter concern were indeed true, why had God not allowed this news to reach me, and why had He not arranged a mission for me to once again rid England of this rubbish? Perhaps the task had been given to another—someone imbued with life and limbs.

"This was probably the combined effect of the preservatives and the one hundred sixty-five years of entombment," Pearson continued. "There was no prolonged weathering as in the case of Cromwell's head. The hair is pressed close to the head as if it had received a set from moisture, which might be from the preservatives and the binding of cere-cloth or from the drip of rain. All we can say is that the sparse hair has been pressed close to the scalp.

"The chin shows the beardlet. This, without proving it to be Cromwell's, indicates the period from which it came, if we dismiss the idea of fraud."

"But we've known the head has hair, gentlemen," Norma said. "We have cared for this personally on several occasions."

"Please, dear, allow them to continue." Canon Horace looked slightly embarrassed by her audacity. "They are simply being thorough."

"Yes, quite," said Morant, visibly perturbed. "Number six, then. Cromwell was aged fifty-nine at the time of his death. 'Before I came to him as he rode at the head of his life guard, I saw and felt a waft of death go forth against

him; and when I came to him he looked like a dead man.'
This, according to George Fox's Diary, volume one, page
four hundred forty.[5] Noble remarks of Cromwell: 'It is certain that in old age he was but a very coarse looking man,
and this for many reasons; the number and greatness of his
cares; the inclemency of the weather, which, as a soldier,
he was obliged to endure, and perhaps the loss of his teeth;
the difference of his face is very discernable in comparing
those portraits of him which were taken when he was lieutenant-general ... with those of his coins or medals struck
but a short time before his death.'[6] And again, if we turn
historical accounts, we read: 'But Cromwell wants neither
wardrobe nor armour, his face is naturally buff, and his skin
may furnish him with a rusty coat of mail; you would think
he had been christened in a lime pit, tann'd alive, and his
countenance still continues mangy. We cry out against su-
perstition, and yet worship a piece of wainscot, and idolise
an unblanch'd almond.'[7] This is no doubt exaggeratedly
satirical, but there must have been an element of truth
therein."

Pearson gestured toward a frontal-view photograph
of me that hung behind Canon Horace's head: "In the case
of the Wilkinson Head its owner retained nearly all his
teeth up to death. They have fallen out, with the exception
of an upper right third molar and a lower right third molar,
since, death.[8] But we know of no historical record of Cromwell's losing his teeth in life. It may be only a supposition
of Noble's. The nose of the head inclines to the left cheek,
but is too battered to allow us to assert anything about it.

The *present* condition of the skin of the face would almost exactly correspond to descriptions of Cromwell's face, but as the tanning of the skin is almost certainly due to the embalming, to preservatives and possibly to weather, we cannot lay any stress whatever on the correspondence. On the other hand such a skin as that which has been attributed to Cromwell might much aid in the preservation of his head. The skin of the Wilkinson Head by no means suggests that the owner had a smooth and tender skin. It appears besprinkled with pimples."

This final point was no secret.

"And finally, number seven, our *last* comparison," Morant announced.

Norma attempted to suppress a yawn as the babies remained peacefully asleep.

"Cromwell's brain weight was stated within ten years of his death to be six and a half pounds. This has been recognised by anatomists as an exceedingly improbable statement. And this is true even if all the water in the brain-box were weighed with the brain. Assuming that we may take the density of the 'water' and brain material to be about unity, and that one cubic centimeter of water equals one gramme equals fifteen point four grains, and in ignorance of what is meant by the pound, and using either apothecaries' or avoirdupois measure we have: for Cromwell's skull capacity, in accordance with apothecaries', six and a quarter by twelve ounces, thirty-six thousand grains, two thousand three hundred and two point eight cubic centimeters; and in accordance with avoirdupois, six and a quarter by sixteen ounces, forty-three thousand seven hundred fifty point five grains, two thousand eight hundred thirty-five cubic centimeters."

I have always considered myself an intelligent man, but listening to these gentlemen carry on in what were increasingly monotone soliloquies, I found myself feeling quite incompetent and ignorant of all that was being said. The specificity of each sentence, however, was commendable, and I trusted that Pearson and Morant revelled in every digit and calculation, knowing each perfectly bolstered support for my authenticity. Still, ennui had eased its way into the chamber with minimal resistance. Whilst there was little risk of waking Norman or Laura, there was a high likelihood that their parents would join them in slumber.

Morant continued his passionate analysis until the eugenicist took over. "Very good, Geoffrey. Indeed, this *is* the final comparison we've prepared for publication," Pearson said with a deep breath. The lengthy discussion was probably quite taxing for his advanced age. "The Wilkinson Head gives the following skull measurements: glabella-occipital length, one hundred ninety-two millimeters; maximum parietal breadth, one hundred fifty-one millimeters; auricular height, one hundred eleven point five millimeters."

Pearson then proved himself to be a most adept mathematician by applying his measurements to numerous formulas and comparisons, all of which led him to deduce that brain had been above average size.[10] This, of course, was evident to me without a single equation.

"On the whole, we have not succeeded in finding any characteristic of the Wilkinson Head, which directly disqualifies it from being the head of Cromwell," Pearson concluded.

Canon Horace, having listened patiently, stood and walked to the wall of photographs to look at them carefully.

"Gentlemen, I ask again, do you believe the head to be genuine?" he enquired with his back toward both Morant and Pearson.

"Why, yes, unquestionably," said Pearson. "It is a moral certainty drawn from the circumstantial evidence that the Wilkinson Head is the genuine head of Oliver Cromwell, Protector of the Commonwealth. And it shall be published as such."

XVI

DONATION

———

The initial invigoration following my triumph with Pearson and Morant rapidly subsided as Wilkinson rewarded their conclusion by returning me to the hidden hatboxes under the bed. A canon is no impresario, so I expected no grand exhibitions, but as a family heirloom I would have very much enjoyed a more prominent position within the home. Canon Horace and Norma rarely fetched me for curious observers, nor did they make concerted efforts to acclimate young Norman to his future inheritance. No sign of Laura graced my boxes, either.

In years past, afterlife in the darkness offered nary a pleasure, but technological advancements came to my aid quite swimmingly through what Canon Horace termed "radio broadcasts." The wireless communications had evolved favourably and provided entertaining sounds and stories, all coming from within a clever box covered in magical knobs. It was as if many of the little homunculi of Paracelsus resided within and performed on command. Luckily, this radio was positioned near me and was audible through the thin walls of my own box. After nearly a hundred years, the machine made one of my dreams come true, as it played countless enchanting symphonies in numerous alphabetical majors and minors from my beheaded mate Haydn. Time could not have passed more majestically.

Yet as in nature, that which is beautiful eventually comes to an end. My musical pleasures ceased abruptly with one broadcast by Prime Minister Neville Chamberlain in the year of Our Lord 1939:

> This morning the British Ambassador in Berlin handed the German Government a final Note stating that, unless we heard from them by 11 o'clock that they were prepared at once to withdraw their troops from Poland, a state of war would exist between us.
>
> I have to tell you now that no such undertaking has been received, and that consequently this country is at war with Germany.

The Germans once again. These were a feisty, belligerent people. Chamberlain continued:

> You can imagine what a bitter blow it is to me that all my long struggle to win peace has failed. Yet I

cannot believe that there is anything more or anything different that I could have done and that would have been more successful.

Up to the very last it would have been quite possible to have arranged a peaceful and honourable settlement between Germany and Poland, but Hitler would not have it.

He had evidently made up his mind to attack Poland whatever happened, and although he now says he put forward reasonable proposals which were rejected by the Poles, that is not a true statement. The proposals were never shown to the Poles, nor to us, and, although they were announced in a German broadcast on Thursday night, Hitler did not wait to hear comments on them, but ordered his troops to cross the Polish frontier. His action shows convincingly that there is no chance of expecting that this man will ever give up his practice of using force to gain his will. He can only be stopped by force.

We and France are today, in fulfillment of our obligations, going to the aid of Poland, who is so bravely resisting this wicked and unprovoked attack on her people. We have a clear conscience. We have done all that any country could do to establish peace. The situation in which no word given by Germany's ruler could be trusted and no people or country could feel themselves safe has become intolerable. And now that we have resolved to finish it, I know that you will all play your part with calmness and courage.

At such a moment as this the assurances of support that we have received from the Empire are a source of profound encouragement to us.

The Government have made plans under which it will be possible to carry on the work of the nation in the days of stress and strain that may be ahead. But these plans need your help. You may be taking your part in the fighting services or as a volunteer in one of the branches of Civil Defence. If so you will report for duty in accordance with the instructions you have received. You may be engaged in work essential to the prosecution of war for the maintenance of the life of the people—in factories, in transport, in public utility concerns, or in the supply of other necessaries of life. If so, it is of vital importance that you should carry on with your jobs.

Now may God bless you all. May He defend the right. It is the evil things that we shall be fighting against—brute force, bad faith, injustice, oppression and persecution—and against them I am certain that the right will prevail.

A loud siren followed this address. Fear immediately overwhelmed Norma, who struggled to calm herself despite Canon Horace's best efforts and reassuring words. Like Chamberlain, he explained God's role in the war. Yet as fighting escalated, the voices from the radio machine reported darker and darker tales of German evils in what had been dubbed the Second World War. Hitler, according to multiple reports, not only had invaded sovereign nations, but was murdering his own people, namely the Jewish population. These were a hard-working, shrewd people I embraced during my rule, re-admitting them into England and allowing them the freedom to worship.[1] Tales of the atrocities these people endured were absolutely horrific and ofttimes impossible to believe. For what madman fences in a people at a camp, then shoots them on a whim or offers a mass shower and inflicts gas upon them instead? On occasion, I heard stories of Jewish children being murdered, doctors performing experiments on prisoners as if they were but mere rats, and emaciated men and women finding sustenance by drinking their own urine.

Where was God amidst these monstrosities? Was He with the Jews gasping for breath and withering in the showers? If this was so, whilst the prayers of men and women went unanswered, to whom, I wondered, did the Lord cry out?

Beyond Hitler's attempt at genocide and world domination, more than thirty countries and nearly one hundred million men were reportedly fighting as the war waged. It appeared as if all of the Creator's labours would be destroyed. Mankind, the most intelligent form of life, seemed ready to eradicate itself. God had ignored Chamberlain's words. He had not blessed us all; He had not defended the right. This was not the Lord I had so fervently followed and revered, for He would reward the righteous and punish

the wicked, yet the wicked were running rampant. Hitler
was Lucifer unleashed, swinging the German flag from his
pointed tail and raising the terrors of Hell to the surface to
be spread across Europe.

As these questions and thoughts occupied my mind,
I considered my own attacks on Drogheda. At the time, I
was still angered at the savage, rebellious acts of the Irish in
1641 and sought revenge. Armed with eight thousand men
on foot and four thousand on horse for the siege, I strategi-
cally surrounded the city before offering Aston a summons
to surrender. I quite clearly explained that I had brought
the army of the Parliament of England before this place,
to reduce it to obedience and that blood might be prevented, but if surrender be refused, he would have no cause to
blame me. Aston, in control of the city in the Duke of Ormonde's absence,[2] had but two thousand men to defend his
city, yet boldly claimed that "he who could take Drogheda
could take Hell." I gave my men orders to leave the civil-
ians unharmed, yet when the battle commenced, emotions
swelled and my soldiers slaughtered not only Aston's forces, but many of the commoners as well, even burning down
churches where they sought refuge. I recall vividly one of
the friars lit afire shouting, "God damn me, God confound
me, I burn, I burn," until he was little more than ashes. As
for the defiant and cocky Aston, upon his capture we beat
him to death with his own wooden leg. Several of my men
were led to believe the limb was hollowed out and packed
with gold pieces, but when repeated blows to Aston's skull
finally broke the leg open, they discovered they had been

misled.

I then justified these actions to Parliament, saying, "I am persuaded that this is a righteous judgement of God upon these barbarous wretches, who have imbued their hands in so much innocent blood and that it will tend to prevent the effusion of blood for the future, which are satisfactory grounds for such actions, which otherwise cannot but work remorse and regret."

So many innocent lives had been lost, so many men, women and children who had no part in the 1641 rebellion. Many in Drogheda had not even supported Aston, yet we offered no quarter. Had their massacre truly been the Lord's righteous judgement? What had the Jews of Germany done to anger God? I was unaware of any rebellions, prior acts of violence, threats toward the government or deeds to inspire the wrath of Hitler and God. The Jews had done nothing more than be born.

In my youth, Thomas Beard had offered clarity: Those who sin shall be punished by the hand of the Lord. Drogheda once felt defensible under that belief, but perspectives are not always blessed with facts. Germany, and this war of the world, made little sense. I had erroneously suspected Armageddon during the first Great War, and though this offered stronger evidence of an imminent end to all things, I refused to believe that Jesus Christ could make His glorious return and reward anyone who killed those who elected to practice different religious beliefs. I shuddered at the notion that Christ should be praised for a second coming after witnessing such pointless, senseless slaughters and remaining dormant. I never supposed I, or any other man, could challenge God or understand His plans, but lying here, within my hatbox beneath the bed listening to radio broadcasts breaking through Norma's weeping, the children's fearful cries and the frequent sirens, I dared God to wake up, step forward and show His might. O Lord, millions have perished crying your name and seeking mercy! God, if you are there watching from Heaven as blood flows on earth and the souls of the dead lie trapped in graves and lumped heartlessly in mass burial pits, answer these cries. Hear them, answer them, and let there be no more.

War waged through April of the year of Our Lord 1945, when either the Almighty's somnambulism ended and omniscience returned or He grew bored of the terrestrial slaughter; finally He responded to millions of prayers and acted, though radio reports instead credited the military of the United States of America, which had shown its might and aided England and her allies. The Germans at last surrendered—having done far more damage to the world than any nation hitherto—and Hitler committed suicide. The forces of righteousness rejoiced at this news, though I, and surely others, believed suicide to be too good for this demon. His head should have been severed and buried beneath the tortured bodies of the Jews he so mercilessly annihilated; he should have been surrounded forevermore by their decomposing corpses and forced to listen to their enraged, weeping souls as worms ate away at his flesh till none remained. Thence, he would be but a miserable skull surrounded by his despicable doings; this would be Hitler's Hell.

Canon Horace and his family survived the war, safe at home in Suffolk. Norman and Laura were growing up quickly during these years, and in addition to raising them, the canon kept busy consoling countless war widows along with mothers and fathers whose sons had perished in battle. His work had never been more difficult, for invoking God to comfort others now offered less credibility. Many believed Him dead. I wondered whether any of the remaining Spiritualists had tried to reach the Lord through a séance, as did Helen Duncan, a medium who made news for being arrested under the Witchcraft Act of 1735 for falsely claiming she could contact spirits.[3] What messages would they have said God gave them? What excuses? What mysterious master plans?

✳

Over the next decade Canon Horace treated me with renewed respect, excavating me from beneath his mattress and giving me a new home within his study at the church. There, I was placed on a bookshelf next to a simple pewter chalice and a collection of tomes, presumably of a religious nature. The canon sat in a wooden chair at an oak desk supporting a telephone and a radio, which I at last had the pleasure not only to hear, but also to see. Its shape was reminiscent of and perhaps inspired by a cathedral, and its fine wood-grain face featured four knobs, one of which controlled a small dial that shifted to varying numbers as it moved. On occasion the office scenery was enhanced by troubled souls visiting Canon Horace, distressed by the war or by more recent disturbances; the latter were typically petty and due to weakened spirits. When Wilkinson took the pulpit, I faintly heard the homilies and hymns from the services, but it was his continued attention to radio broadcasts whilst whiling away time in the study that proffered entertainment once again, usually in a series of stories about Jet Morgan, a fellow who commandeered an aircraft into space and faced endless dangers en route to Mars. Weekly airings gave cause for Horace to close his door to visitors and listen intently—Jet Morgan's perils took priority over those of Horace's congregants. I confess, they were typically more compelling and imaginative.

Only on rare occasions did a member of the church discuss a matter rife with drama and intrigue; the most notable was that of a man wishing to share his concerns over an unorthodox medical procedure he had undergone some years prior. This chap explained his struggles with impotency and told of a miraculous cure he had travelled to America to receive from a doctor named Brinkley.[4] The treatment, he claimed, involved the transfer of goat glands directly into his testes, which Brinkley ensured would enhance his virility and overall energy; the doctor boasted numerous successes with thousands of patients. Brinkley's

method, the man said, required the Toggenburg breed of
Swiss goat, which allegedly offered the highest stock of goat
glands because of its excellent health and lack of persistent
odour, thus keeping the patient from smelling beastly. Despite my rearing on the farm, I knew nothing of the subtle
differences between breeds of goats, particularly in the
glandular area. Who, I wondered, had elected to be Brinkley's first willing patient?[5] This congregant, desperate and
enthusiastic at the time, was permitted to choose his own
Toggenburg goat from Brinkley's live herd and allowed the
doctor to make two incisions beneath his scrotum and in-
sert the fresh, warm glands into his system. The canon and
I listened intently, for this was an unbelievable and most
disturbing tale, which grew worse when we learned that
the results were not as he had hoped and he had since suffered bouts of fever and nausea. Yet he was more alarmed
with how the Lord would judge him, and thus he sought
the canon's help to regain mental virility—for the misdeeds
he had committed upon his being left him restless. He had,
after all, failed to honour God with his body. He rather insulted the Creator by suggesting His intricate craftsmanship of Man could be enhanced by a mere goat. The canon
had never experienced such a dilemma and could only ad-
vise the inept chap to seek repentance and gently deter him
from seeking further medical procedures in that delicate region. I recalled the many quack doctors taking advantage
of unfortunate souls during the plague years, but none had
the audacity of this goat-gland peddler. His own testicles, it
seemed, were larger than any of his patients could hope for

from even the heftiest of goats. After this particular meeting, when we were left to ourselves with the door closed, I detected a unspoken chuckle between the canon and me.

During this period within his office, as he grew older and certainly wiser—and I grew dustier—I felt our relationship had grown closer than ever.

Canon Horace's allegiance to me was confirmed when Mr. A. Rusell-Smith, secretary of the Cromwell Association, which he claimed had hundreds of chapters worldwide, enquired as to whether or not Wilkinson would be inclined to donate me. The organisation had reportedly gathered some thirty relics of mine, including the broad-brimmed hat I had worn when dissolving the Long Parliament. Yet this Cromwell collection could never be complete without, of course, me. I was quite honoured to hear that so many still respected my efforts and paid tribute to my history, and though I would very much like to meet with them and bask in their praise, I had little desire to leave my family. The canon, fortunately, refused the request, denying that he would ever donate me to a museum or the state. "I can look after it better than the state," he said. "When they had it, they stuck it on a pole."

Thenceforth, I felt secure within Horace's possession, until, as with so many of my Wilkinsons before him, he fell ill in his elder years and death claimed his body.

※

Horace Norman Stanley Wilkinson had strayed from the recent family business within the church, but took an equally noble profession as a doctor, specifically an "anaesthetist." Bequeathed to his possession, I eagerly awaited years of sitting in his medical office, startling patients and witnessing whatever manner of aid he offered. This, however, was not to be. Norman discarded the hatboxes and returned me to the original wooden box Josiah had provided, which the canon had held on to but used for storing religious baubles. There I sat, uncertain of the future for several years, hoping to be freed soon, wishing to witness new wonders of the world and curious whether Jet Morgan had safely traversed Mars. Sadly, Norman knew not what to do with me and either found me rather repulsive or pitied my enclosed existence, and so he did what his father had only years earlier said he would never do: he elected to donate me.

I had spent nearly half my afterlife so far with the Wilkinson family, but would now make a return to a place where I had spent one year of my time amongst the living. I was going back to school at Sidney Sussex College.

During my lifetime, I had lost children and grandchildren, and in my own death was taken from my beloved Elizabeth and our surviving progeny, then shamefully displayed to disgrace them all. Yet the Wilkinsons had become my new family for a far greater period of time, and so I felt even more emotional at this newfound loss. Perhaps within the walls of Sidney Sussex College I would prove more useful to students of history than I could to Norman when I was confined in a box. Though the latest queen appeared to be more of a figurehead than a ruler, and thus needed not be forcibly removed, I would be surrounded by academics properly disseminating my efforts and beliefs to inspire revolutionary confidence wherever the world might be in need of change.

It had been many years since I had last seen Laura or even heard her voice, but she at last surfaced to join us for the early-morning trip in Norman's motor car. It was a powerful vehicle, capable of high speeds, but with much less style than the one his grandfather and I had visited earlier in the century. Pale green sheets of metal did little to evoke excitement; it proved more effective at arousing motion sickness. Still, we arrived at the college hastily. There, we entered through Sidney Street and were greeted in the Porter's Lodge by the Head Master, who introduced himself as David Thomson, and several of his associates. They quietly shuffled us from the entrance through a stone archway to the south and into a newly constructed Chapel Court, opposite Hall Court (which made up the majority of the college when I attended). A blossoming lawn filled the small quad, which was surrounded by a brick walkway lined with an array of budding flowers and freshly pruned shrubbery that welcomed spring. Ivy clung to the walls of the new buildings, while a swinging bell and a crown of spires magnificently topped the soaring chapel tower at the head of the court. A clock at its centre displayed the time as seven-thirty; it was still early enough to be free of students. The school had indeed expanded mightily since my days.

The men led us around the quad's perimeter to the chapel entrance, which had replaced the sanctuary where

I once worshipped. There, in the tight quarters of the vestibule, a small pile of dirt stabbed by a garden trowel and a displaced stone slab caught my attention.

"Mr. Wilkinson, I thank you once again for contacting us," Thomson said. "We have respected your wishes for privacy, thus the expediency of our actions this morning. No media are aware of our events, and if you are ready, we are prepared to proceed with the burial."

XVII

REVELATIONS

The depths of Hell, contrary to common beliefs, have proven to be quite shallow—just a few short feet below the surface. Before lowering me into my new, dreaded grave, Wilkinson raised the lid of my box to offer Thomson and his associates a final look. Their eyes gazed into mine with fascination; through the reflections in their pupils, I captured once last glance at the monstrosity I had become. This visage had horrified so many for so long, and now, I was my own last victim. For there is no greater fright than witnessing your final moments, in life or in death. At the closing of my oak chest, it was transformed into a crude, suffocating casket. Norman lowered me into the earth and delivered a brief eulogy:

> It is with great pleasure that I stand here today, and
> I am honoured that you have all joined me in this

most unusual and remarkable occasion. Thank you, Sidney Sussex College for providing a respectable home and final burial place for Oliver Cromwell. The Wilkinson family has possessed the head of the Lord Protector of the Commonwealth for five generations, bringing joy, adventure and notoriety to my ancestors. Having proven the head authentic at long last and beyond all doubt, it is time to end the spectacle. It is time to free it from the confines of an old box tucked away on a shelf. It is time to pay respect to one of the greatest Britons to ever live. And so henceforth, this historic head shall never again be exhibited to eager curiosity seekers or scrutinised by science. On this fine spring day, the 25th of March, 1960, we bid him a final farewell and allow the Lord Protector, at last, to once again rest in peace. May God bless your soul, Oliver Cromwell.

God had, I believed, already blessed my soul, but now appeared to be damning it for eternity. The collective "Amen" that followed Wilkinson's words was accompanied by thumps of dirt, each another nail in my coffin. Every flick of the trowel severed another ray of light until none could peek through the cracks and pores; voices grew fainter with every thud.[1]

Buried again, feelings of anger and frustration soared from the tip of my iron to the bottom of my stake as I hopelessly sat, resting in anything but peace. Wilkinson was gone; the chapter closed on a rich family history and a new, far less interesting one begun. I hoped one day he would be reunited with his forefathers and would feel their collective indignation. Oh, how I would delight in attending such a meeting, not only to revel in hearing the other Wilkinsons disparage Horace Norman Stanley, but also to finally sit amongst my many caretakers on equal terms.

Wilkinson's final footsteps were soon replaced by the occasional faint sound of students scurrying about and murmuring in the antechapel. Signs of life and reminders of my absence from the world. Had they any idea who lay just beneath their feet? I oft imagined that they did, and that their conversations revolved around intricate methods to hatch me free from this wretched incarceration. What new adventures might lie ahead? What new family might treasure me, and whom might I terrify? Yes, exhumation would be my only salvation, but surely the college would go to great lengths to prevent the theft of such a celebrated occupant. Reality slowly seeped its way into my casket. There would be no escape.

After three hundred years, my afterlife was over.

This was my second death, and still the gates of Heaven remained elusive. The very spot Thomson elected to inter me—right outside the chapel—reinforced this prohibition. I lay just beyond the threshold of the Lord's terrestrial domain. Armed only with centuries' worth of memories and experiences and my cognitive powers, I sought an answer to this travesty. Where had I failed God? I served as His soldier in life and masterfully carried out His wishes. Yet as William Wilkinson's pointy-nosed friend had argued long before, it took not long for His work to be undone by the restoration of the monarchy. How was this to be reconciled? No master plan had revealed itself. If it were yet to unfold, I would never know of it, and if I were to remain ignorant of such a grand scheme, it would mean that I was but a pawn for which the Lord had no regard. It would mean God's plans are not to be revealed to those instrumental in them, but rather to satisfy His own selfish motives. Truly this was a bleak line of thought, but time allowed for every line to be thoroughly explored. Had the will of Man simply overpowered His regicidal wishes? Such a notion meant the Almighty was weak. Each explanation I conjured was counter-intuitive to logic and reason.

What if these past three centuries had not been the terrestrial Heaven I had suspected, but instead been my own personal Hell? I, the world's mightiest military leader and Lord Protector, had, after all, been able to witness the best of Man's progress but unable to contribute to or partake in any of it, and the worst of Man's evils through idiocy, charlatanism, and war—and powerless to bring order. Now, here I lay within the cold, loamy earth, entombed in blackness again, forced to wonder why. Perhaps Hell was a place not of eternal physical suffering, but merely of endless mental torture.

As time trudged along, I found but one simple explanation that accounted for it all: I was mistaken. Clarity suddenly overwhelmed me, providing a gleam of light. I had erred in life. My mission and triumphs had been misguided, for it had not been the voice of God that spoke to me.

The Lord had not, despite all my prior certainty, chosen me for a holy mission. Whatever whispers I heard or impulses I felt were not—and could not be—of divine origin. This realisation gave me much to reconsider.

A modest plaque at Sidney Sussex College in Cambridge.

NOTES

PROLOGUE

1. Many executioners refused to serve at the beheading, fearing later repercussions. The job was taken only with the agreement that the executioner could wear a mask and remain anonymous. Some believe the decapitation was the work of Richard Brandon, London's official hangman, because of the perfectly clean blow that was struck.

2. After many members were forced out of the Long Parliament by Cromwell on December 6, 1648, it was left with sixty men and became known as the Rump Parliament. Colonel Pride surrounded the House of Commons with two regiments and imprisoned forty-one members suspected of supporting Charles I. Another 160 members quit the house. This violent act was called Pride's Purge.

CHAPTER I

1. Some scholars believe Bate was involved in a conspiracy and poisoned

Cromwell. Bate went on to serve Charles II during his restoration of the monarchy.

2. Cromwell's copper plate translates to: "Here lies Oliver Protector of the Commonweath of England, Scotland and Ireland was born 25 April in the year 1599 and inaugurated 16 December 1653. Died 3 September in the year 1658."

3. In rejecting the title of king, Cromwell said, "I would not seek to set up that which Providence hath destroyed and laid in the dust, and I would not build Jericho again."

4. Mary wed Thomas Belasyse, First Earl Fauconberg, and became the Countess Fauconberg. Frances married Robert Rich, son of Lord Robert Rich, Third Earl of Warwick in late 1657, but lost him three months later after he died of consumption.

CHAPTER 2

1. John Bradshaw died on October 31, 1659, after suffering through a long sickness. On his deathbed, he proclaimed that if he had to try the king again, he would be "the first man in England to do it."

2. In May 1660, Parliament resolved to proclaim Charles II king and invited him back to restore the monarchy.

3. In October 1660, ten regicides were tried, with Thomas Harrison being first. He was found guilty of treason and sentenced to be hanged, drawn and quartered. On the scaffold, Harrison said: "Gentleman, by reason of some scoffing, that I do hear, I judge that some do think I am afraid to die ... I tell you no, but it is by reason of much blood I have

lost in the wars, and many wounds I have received in my body which caused this shaking and weakness in my nerves."

Chapter 3

1. Oliver Cromwell earned the nickname "Old Ironsides" during the Parliamentary victory at Marston Moor in 1644.

2. John Cooke served as the first Solicitor General of the English Commonwealth and was found guilty of high treason for his role in the prosecution of Charles I. He was drawn and quartered on October 16, 1660.

3. In 1605, Guy Fawkes and several English Catholic co-conspirators attempted to assassinate King James I and Members of Parliament by blowing up the House of Lords. An anonymous letter tipped off authorities and Fawkes was caught guarding thirty-six barrels of gunpowder. He and his co-conspirators were arrested and sentenced to be hanged, drawn and quartered.

Chapter 4

1. James II succeeded his brother, Charles II. Charles had no legitimate children to inherit the throne.

Chapter 6

1. Frances Cromwell was born in 1638 and died in 1720. She had one daughter, Elizabeth (1664–1733), and four sons, John (1670–1735),

Christian (d. 1669), Rich (dates unknown), and William (d. 1725) with her second husband, Sir John Russell.

2. Years after the event, this tale was retold, but the boy whom Cromwell punched was said to be a young Charles I.

CHAPTER 7

1. Will Sommers served as Henry VIII's court jester. The king enjoyed his humor, while Thomas Cromwell (Henry's chief minister and a distant relative of Oliver Cromwell's) appreciated his integrity and ability to use jokes to bring unnecessary extravagance and waste within the household to the king's attention.

2. John Hunter's Leicester Square home had a second entrance, in the rear, which led to his dissecting rooms. He used this entrance late at night when returning with fresh corpses to cut up. Hunter's actions provided the inspiration for Robert Louis Stevenson's *The Strange Case of Dr. Jekyll and Mr. Hyde*.

3. One hundred eighteen pounds would be approximately £16,000 today (just over $25,000).

CHAPTER 8

1. In the late eighteenth century, Swiss-born Pierre Jaquet-Droz was a renowned watchmaker and creator of automata (which helped sell his watches). Three of these automata, The Writer, The Draughtsman and The Artist, can still be seen functioning at the Musée d'Art et

d'Histoire in Neuchâtel, Switzerland.

2. Baron Wolfgang von Kempelen, a Hungarian nobleman, served as a counselor on mechanics to the Empress Maria Theresa of Austria. In 1769, she asked him to create an automaton after he scoffed at the work of a Frenchman entertaining at a palace party with magnetic toys. His response, which took six months to create, was a very humanlike chess player. Von Kempelen toured the world with his creation, astounding and perplexing those who witnessed it.

3. Cromwell refers to the Reign of Terror (September 5, 1793–July 28, 1794). This period of violence during the French Revolution was marked by mass executions of anyone who opposed the cause. The guillotine was responsible for 16,594 deaths during this period.

4. Cromwell refers to Louis XIV, who was executed on January 21, 1793, before the Reign of Terror began. His wife, Marie Antoinette, was beheaded later that year, on October 16. Legend states that in 1793, King Henry IV (ruled 1589–1610), like Cromwell, was exhumed and beheaded posthumously.

5. The Queen's House was purchased by George III in 1761 from Sir Charles Sheffield as a private residence for Queen Charlotte. Previously called the Buckingham House, it was built in 1705 for the Duke of Buckingham. The house would eventually be known as Buckingham Palace.

6. The Hughes brothers' offer of £230 is equivalent to just over £22,000 today (about $37,000).

CHAPTER 9

1. Cranch's advertisement ran in the *Morning Chronicle*, March 18, 1799.

2. After the execution of Charles I, Cromwell sought to eradicate all traces of the monarchy and destroyed the Crown Jewels. They were melted down and used to create coins. Only the twelfth-century Coronation Spoon survived.

CHAPTER 10

1. Sir Marmaduke Langdale was a royalist commander in the English Civil War. His cavalry of 1,500 men fought and succumbed to Cromwell's forces at the Battle of Naseby in June 1645.

2. Toward the end of King George III's life, he suffered from mental illness and blindness. It has been said the madness resulted from porphyria, a blood disease. Some have theorized the disease was brought on by a slow and steady ingestion of arsenic. In 1810, with George III unable to perform as king, his eldest son, the Prince of Wales, assumed control and ruled as Prince Regent. Upon his father's death in January 1820, he became King George IV.

3. Paracelsus lived from 1493 to 1541. The German-Swiss physician, alchemist and occultist was also known as a botanist and astrologer. In addition to trying to create life, he pioneered in toxicology and the use of chemicals in medicines.

4. Mary Shelley did not include her name with the original publication of *Frankenstein; or, the Modern Prometheus*. Critics speculated that

her husband, Percy Shelley, or her father, William Godwin, was possibly the author.

5. "I think, therefore I am." As stated in Descartes' *Discourse on the Method and Principles of Philosophy*.

6. Bilbo catchers were a simple cup and ball game, in which the two are attached by a string and the player must swing the ball and catch it in the cup. Quoits was a simple ring toss game.

Chapter 11

1. The Act issued by Henry VIII stated: "And further be it enacted by thauctoritie aforesayd, that the sayd maysters or governours of the mistery and comminaltie of barbours and surgeons of London & their successours yerely for ever after their sad discrecions at their free liberte and pleasure shal and maie have and take without cõtradiction foure persons condempned adjudged and put to deathe for feloni by the due order of the Kynges lawe of thys realme for anatomies with out any further sute or labour to be made to the kynges highnes his heyres or successors for the same. And to make incision of the same deade bodies or otherwyse to order the same after their said discrecions at their pleasure for their further and better knowlage instruction in sight learnyng & experience in the sayd scyence or facultie of Surgery."

2. William Burke and William Hare murdered sixteen people over the course of a year beginning in 1828. At their trial, Hare turned king's evidence for immunity. Burke was found guilty and hanged, and had his body dissected at the Royal College of Surgeons in Edinburgh. Dr. Knox was cleared of the charges.

3. Dr. Knox kept Mary Paterson preserved in whiskey for three months before dissecting her.

4. Cromwell speaks of Samuel Morse, who invented the telegraph in 1835 and gave his first public demonstration in 1838.

5. Cornelius Donovan served as a professional phrenologist, doctor of philosophy, and Fellow of the Ethnological Society in London from 1840 to 1870. He became a member of the Phrenology Association and founded the London School of Phrenology in 1840. His encounter with Cromwell's head was documented in the 1844 edition of the *Phrenology Journal and Magazine*.

CHAPTER 12

1. The French boy Horace refers to is Joseph Pujol, who later adopted the stage name Le Pétomane, for his fartistry act. Le Pétomane possessed remarkable control of his flatulence and performed regularly beginning in 1892 at Paris' Moulin Rouge, where he outgrossed all top performers of the time.

2. Cromwell describes the penny-farthing, which was the first machine to be called a "bicycle." The invention, however, wasn't called a "penny-farthing" until the 1890s. The name alludes to the large size of a British penny compared with the much smaller size of a farthing, which paralleled the relationship of the bicycle's wheels.

3. Captain Matthew Webb made his first attempt to swim the English Channel on August 12, 1875, but high winds and poor conditions prevented any hope of success. Two weeks later, Webb made a second at-

tempt, and despite suffering a jellyfish sting eight hours into his swim, he triumphed after twenty-one hours and forty-five minutes. On July 24, 1883, Webb attempted to extend his fame by swimming across Niagara Falls. He drowned in the whirlpool ten minutes into the stunt.

4. Tolbooth was Edinburgh's main municipal building, established in the fourteenth century. The site of political meetings and courts, it was also frequently the scene of public executions and torture. Heads and other body parts of prisoners were displayed upon numerous spikes. The Marquis of Argyll's head replaced that of James Graham, First Marquis of Montrose.

CHAPTER 13

1. The modern Spiritualism movement began in a Hydesville, New York, house in 1848, when two young sisters, Kate Fox, eleven, and Margaret, fourteen, began hearing unusual noises and "rappings" in their bedroom. They told their older sister Leah, thirty-four, that they were communicating with spirits. The phenomenon led to a career speaking with the dead in public séances. Others began claiming clairvoyant abilities as well, and Spiritualism spread rapidly. Many years later, the Fox sisters admitted they had manufactured the sounds and stories.

2. Robert James Lees channeled Prince Albert shortly after his death in 1861. Lees continued to work as medium into adulthood and transcribed several books that he alleged were dictated by spirits, including *Through the Mists*, which describes an existence within the spirit world.

3. John Pordage (1607–1681) was an Anglican priest who had a pas-

sion for alchemy, astrology and mysticism. He formed a group called the Philadelphian Society, whose members often claimed to experience religious visions. Pordage wrote the book *Theologia Mystica* and others around the topics of religion and astrology. He was charged before the Long Parliament's Committee for Plundered Ministers for a series of heresies, but acquitted in 1651.

4. The March 1, 1862 issue of *The Banner of Light*, a Spiritualist newspaper, supports Cromwell's theory that the devil was invoked by practitioners: "O thou prince of darkness and king of light, god and devil, greater and lesser good, perfect and imperfect being! We ask and demand of thee that we may know thee, for to know thee is to know more of ourselves. And if to do this it be necessary to wander in hell, yea and amen, we will wander there with the spirits of darkness." In an earlier issue, on December 21, 1861, a prayer by the Spiritualist Lizzie Doten ended with, "O, Satan, we will subdue thee with our love, and thou wilt yet kneel humbly with us at the throne of God."

5. In 218 BC, Hannibal, a Carthaginian military commander, marched an army of 38,000 men and thirty-seven war elephants over the Alps into northern Italy, where he won a series of dramatic battles.

CHAPTER 14

1. Cromwell describes Georges Méliès' 1898 film *Un homme de têtes* (*The Four Troublesome Heads*).

2. Cromwell banned horseracing during his reign over the Commonwealth. In addition to the bans on cockfighting and alehouses that Cromwell mentions earlier, dancing, theater and other forms of enter-

tainment were outlawed in accordance with his Puritan beliefs.

3. Charles Rolls died at age thirty-two in 1910, after his Wright Flyer—the first successful powered aircraft created by the Wright Brothers—lost its tail and crashed during an exhibition in England. Rolls was the first Englishmen to be killed in a flying accident.

4. Cromwell refers to Ezekiel 1-3:27, in which the prophet describes a vision of God riding in a wheeled chariot drawn by four living creatures with the "likeness of a man," four faces and four wings.

CHAPTER 15

1. Criminals who were to be executed at Tyburn were given the opportunity to address the crowd before their final breath. This was one last moment of free speech. That notion, "free speech," evolved into the concept of citizens' standing upon soapboxes of their own to speak their mind. Hence, the area became known as Speakers' Corner.

2. At a 1913 memorial service at Berlin University, Kaiser Wilhelm said that "the Prussians were a conquered folk in 1806 because they had lost faith in God and ... they won back freedom seven years later because they had regained that faith." In 1927, almost a decade after Germany's defeat in World War I, he spoke again about a lack of faith in God being responsible for its failure: "We did not obey God in all things; because we hesitated to bear the worst, because we refused in the end to face all risks in preserving faith! ... We should have fought to the very last carrot, the very last man, the very last round of ammunition. ... We should have trusted in God, not in human logic."

3. Morant consulted Dr. George Bate's account of the English rebellion, *Elenchus motuum nuperorum in Anglia, simul ac juris regis el Parliamentarii brevis narratio.* Bate was physician to Charles I before holding the same position with Cromwell.

4. Morant refers to Samuel Sainthill, a merchant who stood near the gallows at the posthumous executions and recorded his observations.

5. Morant quotes George Fox, a seventeenth-century preacher who rebelled against established religious and political leaders. He was the founder of the Religious Society of Friends, better known as the Quakers. Cromwell was sympathetic to his movement and did not believe, as did many Parliamentarians, that he intended to take up arms and overthrow the government.

6. Morant refers to Mark Noble, author of *Memoirs of the Protectoral House of Cromwell* (1787).

7. Morant quotes from Samuel Butler's "Memoirs of the Year 1649 and 1650," in *Posthumous Works* (1754).

8. Pearson and Morant note that two teeth were known to have been lost before Cromwell's death.

9. Charles I was buried in St. George's Chapel, but the precise location was disputed until renovation workers made a hole in Henry VIII's burial vault and discovered the king's coffin. It was opened for a brief examination. The flesh of the head had darkened, the nose had decayed, and the beard remained intact. The fourth cervical vertebra was split by the force of the executioner's blade. Cromwell's head would be pleased to know that Charles' head was then returned to its eternal rest in the coffin and the vault closed again. A piece of the fourth vertebra,

however, was given to Sir Henry Halford, who served as George III's physician and was involved in the king's exhumation. He displayed it at his dinner table in a handsome gold-lined box. Unlike the Wilkinsons, Halford's heirs did not cherish the relic, and it was returned to the coffin.

10. Cromwell spares the reader the full tedium of Pearson's extensive words and formulas, however, for interested parties, they continued as thus: "OH has been estimated by comparison of the male transverse type contour of the St. Bride Burial Ground (Farringdon Street) crania with the transverse contour of the Head. Using the Reconstruction Formula for the capacity of male English crania or C=.000416 x L. B. OH. + 247.86 ±44.3/√n we find the capacity of C of the Wilkinson Head to be 1592.6 cm³ ±44.3. We can safely assert that the cranial capacity of this head must have been between 1482 and 1703 cm³. There is no approach whatever to the values of the capacity indicated by 6 ¼ lbs. Indeed a capacity of 1592.6 cm³ corresponds to about 3 ½ lbs. avoirdupois, and 4 ½ lbs. in apothecaries' measure. The mean capacity of the Farringdon Street male crania being 1481.5 with a standard deviation of 130.1, we see that the owner of this head would stand about the 20th grade in 100 Englishmen or 6th in 30 cases. This is about the position the eminent chemist, Sir William Ramsay, occupied. The owner of the head had a brain well above the average, but not one of outstanding size."

CHAPTER 16

1. In 1290, during the reign of King Edward I, the Jewish people were expelled from England. Cromwell admitted them in 1656.

2. The Duke of Ormonde, James Butler, had suffered a defeat in Dublin at the Battle of Rathmines just before Cromwell arrived. He left Sir Arthur Aston, an English Catholic, in control of Drogheda in hopes its forces would prevent Cromwell from advancing farther north.

3. Helen Duncan gained prominence in 1941 when, during a séance, she claimed the battleship HMS *Barham* had been sunk, and forged a manifestation of one of the ship's dead sailors. Her séances led to arrests in 1944 and 1956, the latter just before her death. She was known as the last person to be convicted under the Witchcraft Act of 1735, which was replaced by the Fraudulent Mediums Act of 1951.

4. Dr. John Brinkley performed his goat gland operation on more than sixteen thousand patients—both men and women—in his clinic in Milford, Kansas.

5. Brinkley's first patient was a forty-six-year-old Kansas farmer named Bill Stittsworth, who complained about a declining libido. After the doctor jokingly said he needed some goat glands (on the basis of his observations of their robust mating habits), Stittsworth urged the doctor to make the transplant. The procedure was allegedly a success and Stittsworth soon after fathered a baby boy, whom he named Billy (after himself, and possibly a goat).

CHAPTER 17

1. The exact spot where Cromwell's head is buried is unknown. A plaque in a corner of the antechapel reads: "Near to this place was buried on 25 March 1960 the head of Oliver Cromwell Lord Protector of England, Scotland & Ireland, Fellow Commoner of this College 1616–7."

Timeline of Oliver Cromwell and his Embalmed Head

TRUE HISTORY

1599: Oliver Cromwell is born.

1600-1620: Cromwell grows up in Cambridgeshire. At school, he is influenced by the Puritan Dr. Thomas Beard. He attends Sidney Sussex College for a year, leaving after the death of his father.

1628-1629 and 1640-1642: Cromwell serves as a Member of Parliament. (Charles I dissolves Parliament between 1629 and 1640.)

1642: Cromwell's military career begins at the start of the English Civil War.

1649: King Charles I is executed.

1653: Cromwell becomes Lord Protector of the Commonwealth of England, Scotland and Ireland.

1658: Cromwell dies after a bout of malarial fever and kidney complaints.

His body is embalmed and then interred in a vault in Westminster Abbey.

1661: Cromwell's body is exhumed, hanged and beheaded. His head is placed on a spike atop a tower at Westminster Hall, along with the heads of Henry Ireton and John Bradshaw.

1665-66: Cromwell's head survives the Great Plague and the Great Fire of London.

1684: A storm breaks Cromwell's head free from the tower. A sentry picks up the head and takes it home. He hides it in his chimney, revealing the secret only on his deathbed. The sentry's daughter sells the head to Claudius Du Puy, who owns a museum of curiosities and places the head on display.

1710: Zacharias Conrad von Uffenbach visits the museum and writes about the head. His experience is published in London in 1710: *From the Travels of Zacharias Conrad von Uffenbach.* He believes the head is a fake.

1720s: Possession of the head is transferred from Du Puy to the Russell family. The circumstances of this exchange are unknown.

1720s-1787: The head is passed through generations of the Russell family. Details are unknown until it descends to Samuel Russell, who claims to be a distant relative. Russell is an unemployed actor who is frequently inebriated. He shows the head to friends and strangers, who pick apart pieces from it.

1787: The head is transferred to James Cox, a former museum owner and jeweler, as partial payment for debt incurred by Russell.

1799: Cox sells the head to the Hughes brothers at nearly double the amount he paid. John Cranch, a friend of the brothers, writes an advertisement and narrative for an exhibit of the head on Bond Street. Cranch has concerns about the head's authenticity, particularly after hearing about a Cromwell head on display at Butcher Row. The brothers and Cranch exhibit the head at Mead Court on Old Bond Street without much success. Samuel Russell visits the exhibit and complains about his deal with James Cox.

1813: The Hughes brothers suffer untimely deaths.

1814: A daughter of one of the Hughes brothers sells the head to her doctor, Josiah Wilkinson. Wilkinson shows the head to the eminent sculptor John Flaxman, who studies the head and believes it to be authentic. The Wilkinson family continues to offer private showings for the next century.

1845: Thomas Carlyle's *Letters and Speeches of Oliver Cromwell* was released in 1845 and renewed public interest in the Lord Protector. Its author requests a visit to the head and questions its authenticity.

1911: Horace Wilkinson presents the head to the Royal Archaeological Institution, which deems it authentic.

1934: Canon Horace Wilkinson allows a eugenicist and an anthropologist to study the Cromwell head. They prepare a 109-page document in support of its authenticity, parts of which are quoted as dialogue in this book.

1957: Dr. Horace Norman Stanley Wilkinson inherits the head.

1960: Wilkinson donates the head to Sidney Sussex College, where it is secretly buried. Its exact location at the college is not made public.

IMAGINED ANECDOTES

1680s-1700: There are no reports of the sentry speaking to Cromwell's head, or of a duel that led to his death.

1700s-1720s: Many of the items in Du Puy's collection existed as they are described, while others are imagined.

1770s: John Hunter, a famous surgeon and collector of oddities living at

Leicester during this period, owned the Charles Byrne skeleton but did not seek out Cromwell's head. Hunter was the inspiration for Robert Louis Stevenson's *The Strange Case of Dr. Jekyll and Mr. Hyde.*

1787 – 1799: James Cox was a renowned jeweler and maker of automata. However, he did not craft a mechanical body for Cromwell's head.

1828: Dr. Robert Knox never studied Cromwell's head. Knox was, however, a notorious anatomist who paid two men, William Burke and William Hare, to procure fresh corpses. Burke and Hare, looking for quick cash, went on a murder spree to acquire sixteen bodies. Their spree has been the subject of several films and short stories.

1844: An article in *The Phrenological Journal and Magazine* reported on the Cromwell head, as quoted in this book. The author, listed as Mr. C. Donovan, claimed to have seen the Cromwell head in London. The Cromwell head and the head of Joseph Haydn were never examined together, although Haydn's skull was exhumed in 1809 to be studied by phrenologists.

1870s/1880s: The rise of Spiritualism led to many séances, including many conducted by Queen Victoria, but Cromwell's head did not participate in any of them. The Elephant Man was exhibited in London, but he never encountered Cromwell's head. Professor Rolleston contacted the Wilkinson family about the Ashmolean head in 1875, but the identity of the Ashmolean head is unknown.

1907: Charles Rolls and Henry Royce did not meet with Wilkinson, nor did they consider Cromwell's head as a hood ornament.

BIBLIOGRAPHY

The following books, journals, articles and websites were instrumental in providing information, guidance and inspiration for the journey of Oliver Cromwell's head.

Altick, Richard D. *The Shows of London*. Harvard University Press: The President and Fellows of Harvard College, 1978.

Amos, Mike. "Out of His Head." *The Northern Echo*, August 12, 2009. www.thenorthernecho.co.uk/features/columnists/mikeamos/gadfly/4541830.print/. Accessed August 21, 2013.

"Another Spiritualist Prosecution." *The Blackburn Standard And NorthEast Lancashire Advertiser*, November 18, 1876.

The Archaeological Journal. London: Royal Archaeological Institute (March 1911).

Bailey, James Blake. *The Diary of a Resurrectionist*. London: Swan Sonnenschein, 1896.

Beard, Thomas. *The Theatre of God's Judgments*, 1597.

Breed, William P. *The New York Evangelist*, August 21, 1884.

Brennan, J. H. *Whisperers: The Secret History of the Spirit World*. New York: Overlook Duckworth, 2013.

Brinkley, John R., and Sydney B. Flower. *The Goat-gland Transplantation*

As Originated and Successfully Performed by J. R. Brinkley, M.D.,
of Milford, Kansas, U.S.A., in Over600 Operations Upon Men and
Women. Chicago: New Thought Book Department, 1921.

Bullock, William. *A Companion to Mr. Bullock's London Museum*
and Pantherion. London: Whittingham and Rowland, 1813.

"Canon Horace Will Not Give Up the Head of Oliver Cromwell."
Northern Times (Carnarvon, Western Australia), July 28, 1949.

Carlyle, Thomas. *Oliver Cromwell's Letters and Speeches with Elucidations,*
vol. 1. New York: Charles Scribner's Sons, 1899.

Cavendish, Richard. "The Birth of Oliver Cromwell." *History Today*
Volume: 49, No. 4. www.historytoday.com/richard-cavendish/birth-
oliver-cromwell. Accessed May 23, 2013.

Chambers, William, and Robert Chambers. *Chambers's Journal of Popular*
Literature, Science and Arts, Volume 25. (January 5, 1856.)

Cromwell, Thomas. *Oliver Cromwell and His Times,* 2nd edition.
London: Sherwood, Neely, and Jones, 1822.

Defoe, Daniel. *A Journal of the Plague Year.* New York: Modern Library, 2001.

Dickey, Colin. *Cranioklepty.* Colorado: Unbridled Books, 2009.

Donovan, C. "On the Reputed Head of Oliver Cromwell." *The*
Phrenological Journal, and Magazine of Moral Science, vol. 17, (1844).

"Edinburgh." *Kingdomes Intelligencer,* May 27–June 3, 1661.

"The Elephant Man." *Leicester Chronicle and the Leicestershire Mercury,*
December 11, 1886.

The Embalmed Head of Oliver Cromwell in the Possession of the Rev. H. R.
Wilkinson. London: Office of the Institute, 1911.

"Ex-Kaiser Says God May Call Him Back." *The New York Times,*
October 10, 1927.

"Extraordinary Action Against a Spiritualist and Table Rapper."
The Bristol Mercury, April 25, 1868.

Fitzgibbons, Jonathan. *Cromwell's Head.* Kew, Richmond, Great Britain:
The National Archives, 2008.

Fraser, Antonia. *Cromwell: The Lord Protector.* New York: Alfred A. Knopf,
1973.

Haglund, William D., and Marcella H. Sorg. *Forensic Taphonomy: The Postmortem Fate of Human Remains.* CRC Press, 1997.

A Handbook for Westminster Abbey. London: Chiswick Steam Press, ca. 1890.

Healey, Edna. *The Queen's House: A Social History of Buckingham Palace.* New York: Pegasus Books, 2012.

"The Horrors of 17th Century Witch Hunts." news.bbc.co.uk/local /cambridgeshire/hi/people_and_places/history/newsid_8998000 /8998465.stm. Accessed May 15, 2013.

How to Read Character: A Hand-Book of Physiology, Phrenology and Physiognomy, Illustrated with a Descriptive Chart. New York: Samuel R. Wells, 1876.

Howell, Michael and Peter Ford. *The Illustrated True History of the Elephant Man.* London: Allison & Busby, 1983.

Hughes, David. *The British Chronicles,* vol. 1. Great Britain: Heritage Books, 2007.

Knowles, James. *The Nineteenth Century and After,* vol. 57. London: Spottiswood, 1905.

Knyveton, John. *The Diary of a Surgeon in the Year 1751–1752.* Edited by Ernest Gray. New York: D. Appleton-Century , 1937.

Lambert, Tim. "The Salem Witch Trials 1692." www.localhistories.org/ salem.html. Accessed June 25, 2013.

M'Donald, W. *Spiritualism Identical with Ancient Sorcery, New Testament Demonology, and Modern Witchcraft; with the Testimony of God and Man Against It.* New York: Carlton & Porter, 1866.

McMains, H. F. *The Death of Oliver Cromwell.* Lexington: The University Press of Kentucky, 2000.

Milbourne, Christopher. *The Illustrated History of Magic.* New York: Thomas Y. Crowell, 1973.

Notes and Queries, ser. 10, vol. 11 (June 5, 1909).

Notes and Queries, vol. 150, no. 22 (May 29, 1926).

Pachter, Henry M. *Magic into Science: The Story of Paracelsus.* New York: Henry Schuman, 1951.

Pearson, Karl and G. M. Morant. *The Portraiture of Oliver Cromwell with*

Special Reference to the Wilkinson Head. London: University Press, Cambridge, Issued by the Biometrika Office, 1935.

Pepys, Samuel. *The Diary of Samuel Pepys.* Edited by Richard Le Gallienne. New York: Modern Library, 2003.

Pinchot, Gifford. "England in War." *Harper's Weekly,* April 17, 1915.

Roughead, William, ed. *Burke and Hare.* Edinburgh and London: William Hodge, 1921.

Rubenhold, Hallie. *Harris's List of Covent-Garden Ladies: Sex in the City in Georgian Britain.* Stroud, Gloucestershire, Great Britain: Tempus Publishing, 2005.

Shelly, Mary. *Frankenstein or The Modern Prometheus.* New York: Everyman's Library, Alfred A. Knopf, 1992.

Smyth, David. "Is That Really Oliver Cromwell's Head? Well ..." *Associated Press,* August 11, 1996.

Stone, A. P. *History of England.* Boston: Thompson, Brown, 1882.

"The Telephone—What Is It?" *The Lancaster Gazette and General Advertiser for Lancaster, Westmoreland, and Yorkshire,* November 24, 1877.

Uffenbach, Zacharias Conrad von. *London in 1710: From Travels of Zacharias Conrad von Uffenbach.* London: Faber & Faber, 1934.

Walcott, MacKenzie. *The Memorials of Westminster.* 1849.

Walford, Edward. *Old and New London, vol. 4.* London: Cassell, 1897.

Wanley, Nathan. *The Wonders of the Little World; or, A General History of Man: Displaying the Various Faculties, Capacities, Powers and Defects of the Human Body and Mind.* London: R. Wilks, 1806.

Wilson, Henry, and James Caulfield. *The Book of Wonderful Characters.* London: John Camden Hotten, 1870.

The Wonders of the Universe. J&B Williams, 1842.

Photo and Illustration Credits

Cover and chapter initial caps: Vi Luong (viluong.com)

Page 6: Cromwell's head, photo reproduction courtesy of the Sidney Sussex College Muniment Room.

Page 12: Oliver Cromwell engraving. *The History of England by Hume and Smolett.* Circa 1850. Author's collection.

Page 16: "Execution of Charles I" drawing by D. Maillard. Author's collection.

Page 21: "Cromwell Refusing the Crown of England." *History of the World, Vol. III,* 1869.

Page 134, 137, 279: Cranch's advertisement, sketch, and *Cassell's Weekly* letter, courtesy of the Sidney Sussex College Muniment Room.

Page 187: *How to Read Character: A Hand-Book of Physiology, Phrenology and Physiognomy, Illustrated with a Descriptive Chart,* 1876.

Page 286: X-ray of Cromwell's head. *Biometrika,* 1935.

Page 318: Copyright Liz Hartzman.

ACKNOWLEDGEMENTS

The memoirs of Oliver Cromwell's head have been told at long last with the help of several important people. First and foremost, my loving and lovely wife Liz, who has given me her support throughout the project—during late nights of writing and journeys through England. My agent, Katie Boyle, has offered guidance and enthusiasm since I first mentioned the idea. Her advice from start to finish has been invaluable. Anna Jardine, my amazing copy editor and a true master of the English language, made this a better book with every edit. I'm very thankful for all her time and efforts. Nicholas Rogers, archivist at Sidney Sussex College in Cambridge, provided me access to the school's Muniment Room and guided my wife and me through the grounds. The archive's numerous documents surrounding the head's history provided a wealth of information. Vi Luong's art direction and extraordinary talents turned this book cover into a phenomenal piece of art. I am so grateful he took this project on and invested as much time (and ink) as he did. Andreas Baumert gave me technical assistance whenever needed, which is greatly appreciated. Fellow writer, Shloimy Notik, championed this book since page one. And Buck Wolf, Joanna Ebenstein, Laetitia Barbier, Stephie Coplan and Dana Yee offered wonderful support in getting Cromwell's head's memoir launched properly. Going back much further, this project may not have been conceived without my eleventh grade European History AP teacher, Mr. Lawless, who led me to my first set of notes on Oliver Cromwell.

Lastly, I thank my parents, Paul and Beverly, who nurtured my interest in the unusual as a child by buying me *Guinness World Record* books and letting me watch *Ripley's Believe It Or Not!*, *That's Incredible!* and *The Elephant Man* (the latter at probably too young of an age). Travels to Cambridge and London would not have been possible without my mother making her own journey to New Rochelle to watch over our two beautiful daughters, Lela and Scarlett, during our trip.

Thank you all for everything.

ABOUT THE AUTHOR

Marc Hartzman has long held a fascination with the bizarre tales and characters that occupy history. Many of them fill the pages of his earlier works, specifically *American Sideshow: An Encyclopedia of History's Most Wondrous and Curiously Strange Performers* (Tarcher/Penguin) and *God Made Me Do It: True Stories of the Worst Advice the Lord Has Ever Given His Followers* (Sourcebooks). He is also the author of *Found on eBay: 101 Genuinely Bizarre Items From the World's Online Yard Sale* (Universe/Rizzoli) and *The Anti-Social Network Journal: A Private Place For All the Thoughts, Ideas and Plans You Don't Want To Share* (Knock Knock).

In addition, Hartzman has been a contributor to the Weird News sections of AOL and The Huffington Post. He maintains a career as an award-winning Executive Creative Director at a New York advertising agency.

He currently lives in New Rochelle, New York, with his wife, Liz, daughters Lela and Scarlett, cats Barnum and Bailey, and Patrick the bearded dragon.

CPSIA information can be obtained
at www.ICGtesting.com
Printed in the USA
FSOW01n2049060117
29354FS